NICHOL GOLDSTEIN

A Dark Omegaverse Novel Book Three

ALL'S FAIR IN HIDDEN TRUTHS

NIXCOMIX
PUBLISHING

ALL'S FAIR IN HIDDEN TRUTHS

Published by NixComix Publishing

ISBN (print): 979-8-9915029-1-7

ISBN (e-book): 979-8-9915029-0-0

An application to register this book for cataloguing has been submitted to the Library of Congress.

First Edition: October 2024

Cover design by Fiona Jayde Media

Illustrations by Nichol Goldstein

Editing by Dawn Bates International

To all the star-crossed lovers and the fated mates.

CONTENT WARNINGS

This book contains the following:

- Kidnapping
- Cults
- Violent Imagery
- Suicidal ideation
- Dubious consent
- Neurodivergence
- Pseudo-incest
- MM / MFM

Remember that your mental health matters. Take care of yourself. 

PROLOGUE

The bedroom bleeds into the hallway, piles of haphazard laundry strewn through the open-door Katelyn never bothers to close. She clutches a naked curtain rod, her grip like granite as she eases through the darkness of her apartment.

"Max!" she hisses under her breath. "You feral little bastard, I told you not to sneak in here anymore! No matter what you think, dead mice are *not* presents and I do *not* want them!"

She edges around the corner, praying to see the gold-green reflections of a stray tabby's eyes, but there's nothing save her cluttered living room, eclectic and brightly colored even in the nighttime dim.

Falling around her is a deceptive sort of stillness, but her sixth sense is telling her there's someone lurking. It screams the thought into her brain, making every hair stand on end.

Curling over like a primitive hunter, she tightens her grip on the curtain rod, clenching her teeth. She's on high alert. On edge. Ready to strike.

It doesn't matter.

Something clamps down on her mouth, firm and unshakable no matter how she twists, bucks, and bites. She flails, but her clawed hands get no purchase, raking into nothing as if trying to catch hold of a ghost.

What's happening?

Why is it happening?

Her legs kick out and meet only air as she's jerked back like a child yanked out of oncoming traffic. A rough cloth clamps over her lips and an acrid tang fills her nostrils, foreign, invasive, and all-consuming. In the span of seconds, her head lightens, and her vision darkens at the edges.

Is someone drugging her?

They are. They must be.

As her consciousness ebbs, she thinks a flitting, hummingbird thought.

She didn't even have a chance to scream.

CHAPTER 1

EIGHT HOURS EARLIER

"CAKE!" Kevin cries. Katelyn's boss launches into the box like a swimmer, his hands pointed downward as if to make the buttercream frosting part for him. Instead of going nose-deep, he latches on and holds it up like an asinine sports trophy. "We have achieved cake!"

There is a general "Huzzah" about the office kitchen, plain as a cardboard box but efficient and well-loved. Except for the instant coffee machines, that is. They stand as ongoing witnesses to every drop of office gossip but remain unused otherwise. Everything they spit out tastes like dirt. Instead of their muck, Katelyn sips her café-bought mocha latte through an earth-friendly straw wide enough for bubble tea. She watches her colleagues hustle and bustle over a sheet cake that says, "Good Luck, Katelyn!" half surprised they didn't go all-out with ice cream, cookies, and a poor schmuck with a singing telegram, paid in nickels and dimes to wail out a sappy, three minute long goodbye.

Too bad. She would have liked to see that.

"They didn't even let you cut the first piece," Niles says, tossing his slender braids over his shoulder. They're woven with a lovely teal blue that Katelyn likes. Black people can have the fanciest hair sometimes, pleats woven like artwork, though his are just simple knotless braids. Still, the color is a pop that catches the eye. She appreciates his slightly offbeat aesthetic, even if it is lowkey compared to her own. "So rude.

Shouldn't they be, like, bowing at your feet or something? Praying at the altar of sacrifice?"

"Sacrifice?" Katelyn asks.

"Yes. You're being sacrificed to the Gods of marriage."

She plops into a nearby plastic chair, taking another sweet suck of her drink and betting she's in for another rant. Niles doesn't disappoint. He gestures at the crowd before them, their faces stuffed with vanilla crumbs, and huffs.

"They don't even know why you're leaving! I overheard Pepi the other day saying what an amazing new job you must have lined up to ever leave here. We pay great! We're a decent group of people! We do creative crap with great clients! But she has no idea that you're going to go all housewife with an asshole who didn't even bother to knock you up first."

A sigh containing the words "God, I hope he never knocks me up" falls out, and an embarrassed grimace warps Katelyn's face. Niles doesn't miss a note of her tone, and she watches his expression change from general annoyance to general suspicion, his pursed lips and singular eyebrow raise saying it all.

She wants to kick herself. This isn't how a bride-to-be is supposed to sound. She's supposed to be happy about this. Ecstatic. Glowy and transcendent. So why does she feel like she's walking up the gallows?

To ignore her friend, she plucks at her paisley shirt to fluff it. No matter what anyone says, it goes well with her plaid pants and hooker-high heels. She shoves her horn-rimmed glasses up her face and tries to let the moment pass without comment. Unfortunately, that's not who Niles is.

"You smell miserable," he says. "And that's coming from me, who can barely smell anything."

"You're an Omega. No matter what, you smell things better than I do."

"You're a Beta, but your sixth sense leaps over my olfactory system any day."

"Yes. Bow before my power." She tosses her long auburn hair over her shoulder in mock preening and congratulates herself. Jokes.

Distractions. New topic. She just has to pivot away from the truth missile she just let fly.

Leaning down, Niles points his brown eyes at hers like little, stabby knives. "So why don't you want to have babies with mystery man? You against children in general? You've only gushed over every picture of my nieces and nephew."

"That's because the triplets are gorgeous beyond belief." There we go. Keep changing the subject.

"You're not wrong. Those three are like raven-haired honeypots, just waiting to catch grandmas with candy stuck to the bottom of their purses."

He flops down beside her. Still, no one has offered Katelyn a piece of cake. Bastards.

"Do you not like him or something?" Niles asks. "That's a bad sign so early in the relationship. You're supposed to hate him later, and then develop an alcohol problem."

"I what?"

"Don't get me started. In the past thirty seconds, I've planned out your entire life."

"Does it have a tragic ending?"

"Not a dry eye in the house."

"Then you're a jerk."

"One that wishes you smelled like anything but suffering."

Damn Omegas.

She immediately regrets cursing his secondary gender, though. There's enough of that going around. Katelyn snorts and leans back in her chair, crossing one arm over her chest and downing the last of her drink. The straw makes a strained, gasping sound.

"What made you fall in love with the man you'll soon be divorcing?" Niles asks, a sly smile gracing his handsome face.

Air pulls into Katelyn's lungs until her chest bulges. "It's an arranged marriage."

Damn her mouth!

Niles's eyes go round with surprise. She's cursed. Doomed. She needs to get so much better at lying or her life is about to go sideways very fast. Faster than it already is. Still, shame makes her want to scream, *"It's not my fault!"*

"My mom set it up when I was younger. I've always known, it just seemed so far away, I'd almost forgotten about it. Now I'm leaving everything I know behind for a new life I never asked for."

"Do you at least know the guy?"

That grimace returns. "Everybody knows the guy."

Katelyn is about to set herself on fire. If she lets this line of questioning continue, she's in for it. Instead, she's blessed when someone finally remembers this party is for her and brings her a piece of cake. It has a frosting balloon with a smiley face way too optimistic for Katelyn's liking. After giving her thanks, she uses the moment to switch up the conversation again, meanwhile Niles points at himself, pouting that no one bothered to bring him a slice.

"So," Katelyn says through a thick bite. "How's your partner?"

Niles gleams like a new car. "Oh, my story will absolutely not be tragic, I promise you!"

"Does he smell good?" Katelyn asks.

Her friend mock-moans and tips his head back. "So good. You know when you just *know* someone is meant for you?"

"Not everyone can follow their nose, I'm afraid."

Crap! She brought it back to herself again! This is turning into a pity party. Katelyn's mood dips deeper as she slides her fork through the yellow-centered slice, her thoughts spiraling. If only she could listen to instinct, like Alphas and Omegas can. If only she could keep her job, her favorite thing in life. If only she had the power to control her own destiny.

She's going to miss her independence. Her sense of self. Looking at Niles, she realizes she's going to miss him most of all. People like her don't get to have friends like him, no matter how much she wishes it was different.

Why does everything have to be so hard?

"Hey, don't look so sad!" Niles steals her fork and shoves a bit of cake into his mouth, speaking with his cheek full. "I promise to support you through your downward spiral."

At this, Katelyn's frown becomes a lip-tremble, and her eyes mist.

Damn, damn, double damn. She didn't want to do this here, but the thought of losing him, losing the idiot people around her, drives her loneliness home in a way she hasn't let herself feel for a long time. From here on out, what's in store for her? Nothing but zipped lips and feigned smiles.

She has not a moment before Niles shoves the cake onto the counter, snags her wrist, and drags her into an empty conference room far away from prying eyes. The heavy mahogany door shuts quietly, and the overhead lights remain off so they can stay hidden. The only thing that keeps them visible to each other is a few stray beams of ambient light trickling in from the rectangular glass pane next to the doorframe.

Niles sits her down and perches beside her. "Is he ugly?"

She scoffs a little at that. "The opposite."

"Is he poor?"

"Definitely not."

"Is he a sheik?" She pulls a face, and he shrugs. "I'm trying to think of who would have an arranged marriage these days."

It's all too common in the circle her family runs in, unfortunately. If not for that, maybe she'd have a chance to be free.

She resigns herself to the fact that Niles will know sooner or later. He'll see it on TV. Probably on online news sites and checkout counter magazines. Since this might be the last time she speaks to him, she might as well come clean.

"It's Thomas Bleaker."

The tension in the air shifts. Everything about Niles's face falls in slow motion as the weight of her words drops his full lips into a disgusted frown. "Excuse me, what? I mean…you've got to be kidding. How can you—*my friend*—be caught up with anything to do with that man?"

Her eyes sting. "I have no choice."

"There's always a choice! If we can hang out together, you have no business being beside a man like that!"

She knits her fingers, grasping at straws. "He's not as bad as the media makes him out to be."

But Niles is frothing. "No, he's probably worse! How could you do this? How could you lower yourself? How could you sell us out like we don't matter? Like we're some kind of deviants—" but he cuts himself off as Katelyn lets out a sniffle. Like a child, she brings her heels up to the seat of her chair and curls into a ball.

Pathetic.

He goes quiet, staring at his feet while she tries to reign herself in. At least the party won't mind her drying eyes. They'll just think she's going to miss this place. And she is. She really, *really* is.

After a moment, Niles takes her hands, sliding his thumbs over her knuckles. "Just don't agree with him," he says. "Help him see that people are just people."

She nods. "That's my plan."

And there it is. Finally, a good lie. She could change Thomas Bleaker the way a fish could change the tide.

She's powerless. Her fate is sealed.

She's going to be married to a monster.

If you think about it in terms of clichés, her mother has always been a "no-frills" kind of woman. A "haste makes waste" kind of woman. An "if there's time to lean, there's time to clean" kind of woman. At least, she used to be, until she got a bad case of the mom-version of Bridezilla.

This wedding has her up in knots. Each lacey thread of Katelyn's wedding dress has to be dotted with a fake crystal. Every possible breed of flower chokes Katelyn's apartment with a migraine-inducing perfume. Locked in cheap vases, they sit, inspiring a fierce, raging conflict in her mother's delicate soul. They've got peonies, but are they really setting the right tone? Should she focus on lilies? Should she trash the lilies and go with chrysanthemums? Her mother's even making Katelyn get facials of every kind—seaweed, orange peel, chocolate—anything to fix any pores she deems too large. Swedish massages and acupuncture have also become a weekly routine to relax every knot in Katelyn's stressed-out body.

It's exhausting. It's wasteful.

It's a sham.

"Now turn around, darling," her mother coos, sweetly lilting. "I think this will be perfect for your date." She holds up a cream colored something-or-other to Katelyn's chest, and Katelyn immediately hates it with a passion unbridled. A skirt comes up next, but it's not something tight to show off her butt in the way she likes. Nor is it flouncy and bohemian. It's…plain. There's no other word for it. It looks like a purchase from a catalog for overly religious teens whose only goal is to be as demure and unassuming as possible. In other words, boring, bland, and *blech*.

Her mother continues to fuss. "I'm so glad today was your last day at that horrible job."

"I loved my job."

"You loved the attention. You artsy-fartsy people are all like that. 'Look at me! Look what I did!' After a while, I feel like saying, 'Yes, Katie, I know you can draw. Now do something else.'"

Katelyn's cheeks burn with shame. Is she an attention seeker? Maybe. Maybe that's why she wears the clothes she does. Maybe she wants to stand out.

Or maybe she just thinks they're beautiful.

She doesn't know anymore.

"I love making designs for my clients and getting paid to do it. When I went to art school, you told me I'd never make a living—but I did it, Mama. Now I'll have nothing to do every day and no income."

A gleeful giggle peels from her mother's pink-lined lips. "Your soon-to-be husband definitely has you covered in that department, sweetheart."

Letting her mother strip her work clothes from her body, Katelyn muffles through her new blouse, "Mama, I don't want to do this." Like she's said over a hundred times at this point.

Her mother drags the fabric over Katelyn's head with nothing but a huff.

"I don't love him," she tries again.

"What does love have to do with anything? You think I've never sacrificed what I love for the sake of the bigger picture?" She pinches Katelyn's high cheeks before running her fingers through her wavy hair to fluff it out. "You act like I'm sending you off to the mines. This is Thomas *Bleaker*, darling. This is as high up in The Lifestyle as you can go!"

Katelyn mutters "The Lifestyle" bitterly under her breath.

Seeing Katelyn's stubborn side, her mother sobers, any hint of a smile melting from her face, leaving just a tired woman with her best years behind her. The doting picks, plucks and pats dim to a quiet caress of Katelyn's face, sweet and scolding all at once. "You realize that, without this, I have nothing, right? Your father is gone. Your brother is gone. This is my legacy to you. The Lifestyle is my family."

"I'm your family," she whispers.

"It's not good enough."

The words cut, and Katelyn's mother seems to realize it. She softens her tone. "We need to be in good standing in order for me to survive. You know I've got nothing. The Lifestyle has supported this family since you were too young to remember, and we owe it to them. And it's Thomas, darling. Out of everyone, he's the one who wants you for his own. Don't you see what a blessing that is? How lucky you are? How much he's going to change your life?"

Katelyn hugs her arms around the cotton, plain as sand blouse, not wanting her life to change. But she has to do this for her mother. That's a daughter's job, isn't it? To take care of the person who brought you into this world and loved you? A quid pro quo you inherited at birth.

"Give this a chance," her mother says, smoothing out Katelyn's clothes once more, a somber smile on her face. "I believe in you. You'll keep our family safe."

That sentence puts a boulder in Katelyn's chest. "I'll try, Mama."

She kisses Katelyn's forehead. "Thank you, baby." With that, her mother pulls back, adjusts her near-perfect camel colored pantsuit, and swipes a tear from the ever so slightly crinkled corner of one eye, a tear Katelyn can feel as clearly as if it were one of her own. "Now, finish getting ready for your date. Your wedding is less than two months away. You've got to spend as much time with him as you can. Make him like you."

Nodding is the only appropriate reaction, so Katelyn does it. Her mother whisks herself out the door with a few blown kisses trailing after her, leaving Katelyn alone in bland whites and drab beiges. But no. That's not her. Katelyn tears the clothes from her body and digs in her closet, grabbing anything that screams patterns and color, wrapping herself in a rainbow.

Let them take her future, let them take her livelihood, but she'll never let them take her personality.

Katelyn's never been sure how to feel about the sea. In the city, life is just supposed to be made of tall buildings, the required amount of trees peppered in every half block or so, and haphazardly placed parks you have no time to go to, but this city is on a crescent bay and that adds an unexpected flavor to the landscape. The ocean stares quietly up at her, the deep, undulating blue reflecting a sunlit glow along the crest of its ripples. Because the shelter of the bay cradles the water, there are no huge waves that crash, no rushes, no hisses throwing mist in the air. It's more like a lapping, placid lake. Or what Katelyn imagines one to be like, anyway.

Her hands rest on the railing as she looks over the edge of the sea walk, a concrete path that hugs the tide so you can enjoy a scenic stroll. The sun is setting, and it makes for a beautiful view, a postcard image filled with colors she'd like to wear next. Halloween oranges and electric pinks, wisps of lavender and bleached denim blues. How would she wear them? Maybe her shoes could be the electric pink. Maybe her glasses could be framed in lavender. Maybe…

"Katie!"

She looks around and spots Thomas heading her way. He doesn't rush, hands in his navy trouser pockets as he saunters over, kicking his feet out boyishly with a cocky, pleased smile on his face. God knows why, but he truly seems to like her. The feeling is not mutual.

Thomas is neither tall nor short, but he is slender. His body will never fill out like an Alpha's—and maybe that's part of the reason he hates them so much. Some childish jealousy. But Katelyn knows it goes deeper than that. It's been bred into him. Just like loyalty has been bred into her.

When he smiles, his cheeks dimple. He's your standard, run of the mill white man who tans, trying to look effortlessly debonaire. It works. He seems at ease with life, though he has no reason to deserve it.

Approaching, he holds his arms wide, just waiting for her to throw herself into them. If she was anyone else in The Lifestyle, she probably would. Still, with the best smile she can muster, she goes willingly, tucking her face into his neck. He smells overwhelmingly like coconuts, which bothers her more than it should. She must be allergic.

"Hi, Thomas. Good to see you."

He pushes her back, holding her by the arms and looking up and down, taking in her neon green zebra top and her skintight, mock snakeskin pants. His grin is wide and salacious. "Better to see you. God, I love the way you dress."

She should have worn her mother's bland outfit after all.

"Ready for dinner?" she asks, disturbing his obvious thoughts. "I've never eaten at that steakhouse before." The restaurant is about a half mile away, which might be hell on her toes in these shoes but will at least be paired with the sunset.

"I've been there a bunch of times. Let me order for you. I promise I have great taste." He tosses her a wink that she supposes is meant to be flirtatious, so she forces a smile. He wraps an arm around her back and leads her onward. "By the way, I just got the news. The college was approved."

Katelyn curses internally. "Oh? I thought they wouldn't go for it."

Thomas gets a half-lidded look on his face with a grin that seems devious. "If there can be special schools for Alphas and Omegas, why can't there be a school for people like us? Why should they get all the preferential treatment? The scholarships? The free rides?"

Probably because Betas need to make up for centuries of oppressing them and using their biology against them, but what does Katelyn know?

"The lawyers finally agreed with me," Thomas says. "Helps when you're one of them, I suppose." He waggles his finger at her. "Don't let anyone tell you that networking isn't important. It removes barriers other people can't even hope to climb. When you come out with me, you'll need to get to know everyone on the floor. Believe me, they'll want to know you."

Her stomach rolls. As if he notices, or cares, he squeezes her tighter.

"Don't be afraid of it. A woman like you will charm the world."

Not bloody likely.

"The school will be game changing. More than that, *ballot box* changing. The more Betas we have in power, the better. Not to mention, I've got another idea up my sleeve." He leans over as if to whisper the world's biggest secret. "What do you think about conversion therapy?"

Katelyn startles a little, her neck twisting towards the man whose self-confidence likely interprets her horror for insatiable curiosity.

"I'd imagine some Omegas and Alphas realize how disgusting their biology is," he says. "Hell, isn't that why they go on their suppressants in the first place? To hold back the monster inside?"

Katelyn swallows hard.

He arcs his flattened palm in the air in a slow, broad stroke, left to right. "Imagine those who want to be like Betas. Who want to renounce that instinct-driven insanity. Who want to cut their urges out of them like the filthy things they are."

Acid in her throat, Katelyn tries not to lose her footing. Does he even realize what he's saying? Because Katelyn sure as hell does. It sends needles through her skin.

He twists around, putting some distance between them so he can walk backward and watch her. "My father is against it, of course. He thinks there's no way we should let them anywhere near being accepted into Beta society but consider me more progressive." There's that smarmy wink again. Just after though, a slight wave of something passes over his face. Smile turning thin, he casts his eyes down and to the side without losing a beat of his footwork. "You don't think badly of me, do you?"

Yes. For so many things.

"Why would I?"

He brightens again. "Oh, thank God." Stopping his backward motion, he leans in toward her. "I'd hate it if my future wife couldn't get behind my vision."

He's close enough to kiss her, and for a moment, Katelyn is terrified he'll do just that.

"But does that mean you're a sympathizer?" he wonders aloud, that seductive face still plastered on, as if he's just trying to get a rise out of her.

Katelyn's honesty blurts once more. "Do you ever consider they might just be people?" Her one saving grace is that she says it in an offhand way. A "Do you suppose we might have chicken tonight?" sort of way. Her tone does her no favors though. It's her words that mattered.

Any playfulness disappears from Thomas's face, leaving it cold and pensive. Katelyn feels faint. Keeping secrets is one thing—hell, she's a genius at that—but she's never going to be able to lie to his pointed questions day by day. She's going to get herself ousted from The Lifestyle completely.

But then what happens to her mother…?

As if Thomas had heard her invoke her mother's image, he turns back around, falling in line beside her and linking his hands behind his back. "Your mother doesn't seem to think so. She hates the secondary gender as much as anyone in The Lifestyle. You should be proud of her. She's such an unwavering member, no matter what challenges life throws her way. She's committed. In fact,"—a new smile brightens his face—"I'm going to get her a role in the college. Just admissions or something clerical, but wouldn't it be nice for your mom to have something to do again? After all, she's losing her pet project."

Katelyn can't help the slight frown on her face. "Me."

Thomas loops his hand around her back again. "Of course, you. I imagine she'll really feel how empty her nest is once I whisk you away." The look he casts at her would make other women swoon. "But I'll take good care of her. She's earned it."

Teasing to cover up her faux pas, Katelyn *tsks*. "You'd think you're only marrying me for my mother."

He swoops around in front again and stops them dead in their tracks. Katelyn can hear the lapping of the gentle waves as swells rise and fall. The scent is faint, but unmistakable. Salty and singular. Nothing else smells like the ocean. It takes her by surprise when

Thomas tucks her hair behind her ear with a gentleness she wouldn't expect from someone like him.

"Don't say that," he murmurs. "You know who my father is. I had my pick. People were throwing their daughters at me. Even though you were my betrothed, I could have broken it off with you, made you need to find someone else who wasn't already paired, but I don't want to do that."

"Why?"

"Because in a world full of gray clouds, you are a stroke of color." He leans in, pressing his warm lips to her cheek. She trembles, but for all the wrong reasons. "Trust me, Katie. We're going to be so in love, we'll put everyone else to shame."

She puts a hand over his and rests it against her chest, her eyes glittering. She prays he takes it for happiness instead of the truth. No part of her wants his Lifestyle. His Beta-only agenda. *Him.*

But she resigns herself to the fact that he's kind to her. Maybe he'll stay kind. Maybe, if she's good, he might let her have a friend—probably not Niles, which breaks her heart—but someone, somewhere.

Or maybe she'll just be eccentric arm candy for a man in the public eye looking for a wife to balance out his image.

It's dark as her door slams behind her. Defeat doesn't even begin to describe the feeling sinking in her soul. Her body stinks of Thomas, that coconut-like, abhorrent scent. She prays it's a cologne she can "accidentally" toss away once they're married, but has a sinking feeling it's natural to him.

She can still see that stunning smile on his face, hear the dulcet tones of his voice, feel his hope in waves. If he was anyone else, she'd be in love. Instead, she's on the edge of a proverbial cliff, ready to toss herself off if only to escape that man and his terrible, genderist agenda.

Ripping off her high heels, she tosses them into the shadows. She doesn't bother to turn on a light. A clatter brings her from her daze as she almost upends a new pot of roses, another bouquet in a useless pile of bouquets.

She shivers suddenly, her lower belly clenching. An unexpected cold sweat blooms, threatening to stick her shirt to her skin as if she were out in the summer rain. She knows what this is.

Damn.

Tearing her clothes from her body, she clambers to her bathroom, knees weak and head pounding. She needs her medicine. The bottles are stashed in her makeup bag, and the pills tumble out like white saviors, dotting the bathroom countertop with ovals and circles. The taste is like bitter chalk, but she downs it without water, resigned to the flavor. She's taken these pills like tic-tacs half her life, after all.

Her gut churns in protest. They do this to her. Make her weak. Make her sick. But what does that matter? They are as important as air. Without these blessed concoctions, she might as well stop breathing. They save her, as much as they're probably killing her.

Maybe that's just fine.

She doesn't bother tucking her cache away, leaving the bottles on the bathroom counter like a confession she'll never make.

Stumbling to her bedroom, she tugs a tie dye T-shirt over her head and tries not to throw up. It would be counterproductive. Instead, she collapses into her soft bed and nestles into the tangle of blankets she never straightens. She'll feel better in a few hours. She just needs rest.

A wave of dizziness slips through her brain. Despite the dark room blurring and spinning, despite the acid crawling up the back of her throat, Katelyn slips into sleep.

Maybe she can do it forever.

———

The hiss of air sucking through her nose startles Katelyn from the depths of her slumber. She shoots up on her hands, head on a swivel as she peers around her room.

Something's wrong.

She eases herself up, managing to avoid the squeak of her mattress, and tiptoes to the corner. A crumpled yellow curtain lies in wait for a good washing she hasn't bothered to do yet and its lonely, bare curtain rod rests against the wall. She wraps her fingers around it, letting her knuckles creak.

There it is again. A rustle. Something that doesn't belong. Passing cars periodically grace her street, causing that iconic *whoosh*, but it's notably absent right now. It makes sense. The clock to Katelyn's right shines a digital 2:30am and even the drunkards who insist they can still drive wouldn't be out this late on a work night. But *something* is out. Katelyn can feel it.

The cold sensation travels from her spine to her skin, a crackle of static in the air. Falling around her is a deceptive sort of stillness. It dampens the beat of her heart despite its wild hammering.

The bedroom bleeds into the hallway, piles of haphazard laundry strewn through the open door Katelyn never bothers to close. She clutches the naked curtain rod, her grip like granite as she eases through the darkness of her apartment.

"Max!" she hisses under her breath. "You feral little bastard, I told you not to sneak in here anymore! No matter what you think, dead mice are *not* presents and I do *not* want them!"

She edges around the corner, praying to see the gold-green reflections of a stray tabby's eyes, but there's nothing save her cluttered living room, eclectic and brightly colored even in the nighttime dim.

Her sixth sense is telling her there's someone lurking. It screams the thought into her brain, making every hair stand on end.

Curling over like a primitive hunter, she tightens her grip on the curtain rod, clenching her teeth. She's on high alert. On edge. Ready to strike.

It doesn't matter.

Something clamps down on her mouth, firm and unshakable no matter how she twists, bucks, and bites. She flails, but her clawed hands get no purchase, raking into nothing as if trying to catch hold of a ghost.

What's happening? *Why* is it happening?

Her legs kick out and meet only air as she's jerked back like a child yanked out of oncoming traffic. A rough cloth clamps over her lips and an acrid tang fills her nostrils, foreign, invasive, and all-consuming. In the span of seconds, her head lightens, and her vision darkens at the edges.

Is someone drugging her?

They are. They must be.

As her consciousness ebbs, she thinks a flitting, hummingbird thought.

She didn't even have a chance to scream.

Katelyn's mind is like red mist. Nightmares run on heavy feet through her subconscious, dreams of despair and helplessness circling like vultures, more vivid and visceral than ever before as they spiral down to open their sharp beaks and tear into her soft spots.

Mercilessly, her vital bits are ripped through her skin as unknown birds of prey pick, peck, and pluck, showing her the glistening pieces of her own flesh. She sees them for what they are. Truths. Her secrets are now laid bare as the predators take her apart in chunks, but she can't scream. If she does, someone will hear. Then they'll ask why.

Katelyn can't lie, but she can hide—in the dark, in plain sight—but only because she's alone. Now her privacy, her moat, her armor is being stripped away.

She's going to fail. That's what these eviscerating demons are showing her. That's what drips from her bloody heart as her dreams bleed. Those red beads tell her it can't last. She's doomed. Everything will fall apart.

It's coming.

It's coming soon.

It's coming now.

In the last wisps of her nightmare, she sobs. "Mama…I'm sorry."

The caress of a breeze and the soft clatter of wooden windchimes wakes her.

Everything looks bathed in a shroud of white as she blinks back into consciousness. She battles a wave of lightheadedness as she rolls to her hands and knees, taking in the wooden paneled flooring beneath her. Its long, dark-chocolate boards draw parallel lines down a hallway that takes a sharp right. To her left, there is a pale white wall with staggered doors framed in that same dark wood. On the other side, sliding paper doors open to a center courtyard. The house seems to wrap around it, cradling it in a square nook, and a pond burbles in a pleasant arc near the corner. This is like a house in an Asian drama, coated in old world finery and craftsmanship.

Where the hell is she?

Pulling her bare legs beneath her, she almost goes straight down again but catches herself with nothing but stubborn grit.

Wherever she is, she is not safe.

Footfalls feather light, she tries the door nearest her and slowly turns the handle.

Nothing. Locked.

Sneaking to the next, she finds the same. And then the same.

She needs to find the main doorway. Pulling her T-shirt down as far as it can go, hyper-aware of her vulnerability, she looks across the courtyard where more paper sliding panels are open on all four sides. Directly in front of her, a spacious kitchen beckons with half-windows over what must be the sink. Could she squeeze out of one of them?

Coiling her muscles for a desperate run, she leans down, clenching her fists. Whoever brought her here is probably right around the corner. She can feel it. Her sixth sense never leads her astray.

In one swift plunge, she bolts across the sunlit courtyard, leaping over the small pond and letting her toes fling up the gravel. It digs into the pads of her feet, but panic disguises the pain as she rushes towards the window. Grabbing it, she strains. She fails. Patting the sill, she finds a brass lock, simple and stupid, with a series of spinning metal numbers waiting for a passcode she'll never guess.

There has to be somewhere else.

All stealth has left her as she barrels through the straight lines of the house, looking for that outer door. Her heels ram the wood as she runs. Her fists bang and rattle as she twists handles. Slowly but surely, her panic builds to a crescendo as she tries her hardest not to bawl. Where is she? Where is she? *Where Is She?*

Something snags her shoulder, and she yelps as she's pulled back. The shriek pierces even her own ears as she whips around, blocking her face and stumbling, only to land on her rear with a jarring *thump* that clacks her teeth together. Panting, her eyes lift to see a man— broad, strong, and terrifying—standing over her with redwood-colored eyes.

An Alpha.

His dark hair cascades over his shoulders, the color of his skin like cream and his five o'clock shadow rugged. His upper left arm is adorned with a stunning red and black tattoo that makes gradient patterns over a gray-toned image she can't make out. She snaps her gaze to a second man behind him—another Alpha. Blond. Big. Slightly curly hair just a shade too long. While the first one stares at her, the second one looks as far away as he can, his expression bored and placid. The first one is a complete contrast, his palms up and his face knit in concern. "Hey, calm down. It's gonna be okay. No one's gonna hurt you here."

What a ridiculous thing to say.

He reaches out fast, and despite her flinch, he catches hold of her wrists and brings her close. His grip is immovable, but not tight, though she knows a man like him could break her into pieces if he wanted to. Her stomach swoops at his strength the same way her fear strikes her with lightning.

"This is a safe place," he says, his voice deep and resonant. Some-where close to a purr.

She's going to faint. She can't be around an Alpha. All women want Alphas, so she can forgive her body's immediate reaction. One of submission. One of excitement. One that wants nothing more than to plead for both safety and roughness. She wants him to manhandle her, only to kiss the sting of his bruises away.

"You're Alphas, aren't you?" she says, and it comes out high-pitched and breathy. She doesn't know if she sounds weak or enthralled. Either is appalling.

A feral smile blooms on the first one's face. "How did you guess?"

Trying to pull her arms away, she backpedals, wanting to get distance and failing. This must be because of Thomas. Someone must have leaked the engagement. Maybe they want to cause him trouble. Maybe they want ransom.

She's in danger.

"Look," she pleads. "I have nothing against you, but if you're trying to use me to get to him, it's not going to work."

The bestial first man, beautiful and terrible, only cocks an eyebrow.

Katelyn rambles, her mouth going a mile a minute. "Think about it. This will only make his case against you worse. You can't do that to your kind. You'll set yourself back so far. This is about more than just you; you have to think of all the secondary genders. What you do reflects on all of them. Please, don't do this. You can't. If you do—"

"Hold on, little one, slow down. I don't know what my gender has to do with anything. We're just here to do a job." The dark, redwood-eyed man releases her, and she tosses herself backwards, cursing as she hits the corner of the hall, trapped in the center of the V.

The first man looms, but his expression has shifted to one of curiosity. The second one remains stoic behind him, arms crossed as if he can't be bothered. He's like a stallion, and the clench of his jaw speaks of strength. Would he bite her?

Her mouth dries. "Are you going to kill me?"

The first one chuckles darkly. "No, sweet thing. We're going to *seduce* you. Isn't that right J—"

"Don't use our names," the other says. His voice is a void. An emotionless rumble that flips something in Katelyn's tummy. He stares out at the courtyard as if she doesn't matter.

"Point taken," the first says. "But she has to call us something."

Drily, but with utter seriousness, the second one says, "Dolphin and Zebra."

What?

…What?

The first one blanches, turning around to look at his compatriot… before bursting into hysterics. Katelyn's jaw drops.

"You've got to be kidding!" The first one blatts a laugh that blooms into straight guffaws. "There was so much tension, and you just ruined it! My image consultant will have words with you about this. You're gonna be the death of me, I swear!" Tipping backward, he lets out another sharp "HA!" that makes her squeak and shrink into herself. With a swipe at his eyes, he gasps out, "Okay, okay. Which one are you?"

"Dolphin," the second one says without hesitation.

"Why?"

Monotonous: "Because they're smarter."

Katelyn has no idea what to do with these men.

The first Alpha's shoulders are shaking as he makes hissing snickers. "So, I'm a Zebra?"

"Mm. They make stupid noises."

And the first guy is off again. Katelyn startles and pushes back as he clutches his stomach with childish giggles, telling his co-kidnapper to stop, because he can't breathe. Katelyn is at a loss. What the actual hell?

The second one is unmoved. "Shorten it. Finn and Zeb."

Zeb sobers. He mutters his supposed name four times in different tones. An angry, startling "Zeb!" to a mournfully sobbed, "Zeb..." to an aghast, pearl-clutching, "Zeb!" and a low, breathy, sexually charged "...*Zeb*..." After a moment of contemplation, he nods. "Alright, I'll take it."

With a graceful gesture, he's on his haunches and leaning in, offering his hand to Katelyn as if she'd actually take it. His eyes glint in mischievous sparkles, looking like he'd worship her if given the chance. "So," he murmurs, "apparently I'm Zeb, and this is my stepbrother, Finn."

Something in her, some unwanted instinct, makes her reach out and take his hand.

Her wild imagination ignites as he presses soft, scalding lips on the skin of her knuckles, his eyes never leaving hers. "Welcome to paradise."

CHAPTER 2

STEPBROTHERS

Elijah's face is crammed so hard against the doorframe, his cheek skews upward, squinting one eye into a half-moon and dragging the corner of his mouth into an awkward grimace. It must look so stupid. He wishes he had a mirror. The show he's putting on is mostly for his stepbrother's benefit, though the man's not even looking. Instead, he's doing his best to ignore everything about their situation.

Elijah does have a purpose for his face-squashing shenanigans, though. Namely, peeking through the slim crack of the mostly closed doorway, surveying their target for seduction: one Katelyn Annamarie Jones-Masters. A froofy name…though she doesn't seem to be a froofy woman.

She *is* pretty pissed, though.

In what Elijah has designated as "her bland boudoir," she paces back and forth, bitching in muttered hisses, spewing louder curses, and snatching stuff out of the oversized canvas duffel that—*pfft*—"Finn" had put together for her last night. Mind blowingly, she's using this little respite of alone-time to dismantle the thing, crumpling piece after eccentric piece of clothing after she looks at them, scowls, and dismisses them in rapid succession.

He turns in his stepbrother's direction. James is leaning back against the wall, staring into the middle-distance like always. It makes Elijah smile. His brother can act disinterested, but James—*pfft* why did he pick the name "Finn?"—is far more considerate than Elijah has ever been. Focused, his brother had stuffed her bag with handful after handful, everything brighter than neon, ensuring he brought warm stuff, cool stuff, dressy stuff, and pajamas. More shoes than anyone has a right to. He even snagged her toiletries. Elijah would have just dragged her to this place as she was. He liked her tie-dyed T-shirt and long, bare legs.

She happens on a pair of jeans with tiger print panels sewn up the sides and tosses herself on the bed, wriggling into skin-tight fabric that shows off the curve of a perfect ass. There are worse things to do than try to seduce a Beta who looks like that. Too bad she smells like nothing, at least from this distance. He's always wanted to shove his face into the crook of a Beta's neck to see if their scent would be as strong as another Alpha or Omega if he got close enough. He'll finally get his chance. In hindsight, he should have done it when she was unconscious. Now, he'll have to finagle his way through her defenses without getting smacked.

He re-squashes his face to watch his quarry pick up a pair of glasses and slip the arms over her ears. Never mind her clothes, *these* scream fashion and flare. His own pair are simple, black wire frames that sit on his bedside table, awaiting the inevitable point in each day where his contact lenses turn to sandpaper. He could never pull off whatever she's got going for her. Who knew chicks with glasses could be so cute.

Digging in her duffel, her movement suddenly freezes. Elijah freezes too, assuming he's been caught peeping, though that doesn't seem to be the case. She doesn't even glance his way. Instead, she goes very pale, hovering as if lost in time.

Frantic now, she stops abusing her clothing and devolves into a desperate, pawing dig. Her face plunges so close to the opened zipper, she might as well be eating what's inside, devouring stripes, plaids, and prints. Finally, she unearths a bag of what looks like a litany of makeup. With it in her grasp, her expression smooths into relief, and she hugs it to her chest like a precious childhood teddy bear, one that brings nothing but comfort and good dreams. After a beat, she rips the thing open and takes out two prescription pill bottles like they're gifts from God. They must be important. Good thing James grabbed them. Elijah didn't know she needed anything. Maybe Boss Man didn't know either.

Twisting the child-proof lids, she opens her throat and downs a few tablets…one, two, four, six…completely and utterly dry.

He icks.

Looking over to James, his mouth moves in exaggerated, silent shapes. "What are those for?"

James peeks through the crack for only a moment and shrugs, which is probably all the response he'll offer at this point.

Snagging his hand, Elijah migrates them through the paper screen, across the courtyard garden, and into the kitchen. James is being…very James. If Elijah didn't know any better, he would seem like a statue, but the slight furrowing of his eyebrows—just a tic, then gone—speaks volumes. His stepbrother is *pissed.*

Squeezing his wrist in a scolding, pulsing grip, Elijah grumbles. "Listen, it's your job to try to seduce her, too."

James deigns to look at him, but no more.

"You think I'm crazy," Elijah says.

James does nothing.

"You think you're going to suck at this," he tries again.

Still nothing.

"You hate her already."

James's lower eyelid twitches and Elijah snaps his fingers. "Bingo!" He loves guessing what's on his brother's mind.

The courtyard is lit with the noontime sun, shadows perfectly placed beneath the two sculpted cherry trees and glinting off the jade pond—the same color as her eyes. He stares at the door across the way, at a loss of what to do now.

"What do you think?" he asks, not expecting an answer. "I mean, how do you even seduce someone?"

James is still staring at him, but his ice-blue eyes narrow ever-so-slightly.

"Yeah, okay, it's not like I haven't done it before." Elijah considers. "Or even that I don't do it now, but maybe I need to be more, I dunno, sensual? Dark? Mysterious?" It's him that starts pacing now, ticking off ideas on his fingers while James watches. "My voice is baritone, right? Deep? Sexy? So that's something in my favor. I'm big, above and below"—he tosses his stepbrother a smirk—"so there's that, too. But what am I supposed to say? What will get her panties in a knot?"

Asking James this question is like asking a rock, and it amuses Elijah to no end. He can't help but take a moment to tease his stepbrother, wanting to get a rise out of his familiar mountain.

He links his hands behind his back and strides in lazy circles around the man. "And once she's in a knot, I can try to use mine. Rut into her. Hot and heavy. Thick and wet. Do you think I can fit inside a Beta?" He stops in front of his brother, leaning in and intoning, "How about you?"

James's eyebrows twitch.

Yes! He got him!

"Waste of time," his brother says. "This is a distraction."

Elijah waves him away. "There's no rush."

James continues his stare.

"Okay, *you* think there's a rush, but I don't. I'm happy with the way our life is now."

With an honest grin, he grabs his brother's shoulders in what he hopes is a reassuring way, but James only lowers his eyes to the ground with a clench to his square jaw. Elijah hates that look on James's face. It's so subtle, one could take it for mild frustration or annoyance, but Elijah knows better. That face means there's a nightmare whirlwind beating the breath out of his brother. Elijah's heart aches on his behalf.

Slightly taller, but not by much, he wraps James in his arms, nudging his chin playfully into the thick muscle between his neck and shoulder and taking in his stepbrother's soothing scent. "Hey, with our charm, this won't take long. In and out, literally and figuratively. Wham and bam. You, me, either of us, both of us, it doesn't matter. And as soon as it's over, we'll move on and find you what you need."

"What we need," James corrects, but Elijah digs in his heels.

"I don't need anything." He usually bends over backward for his brother but refuses to give him this poisonous lie. He doesn't need it, he doesn't want it, the whole world's rules and opinions be damned.

James's soft exhale may as well be a stream of tears.

"It's going to be okay, Jamsie. I'll keep an open mind and try it, just like I promised. I've got you."

He always has. He always will.

Pushing away, he pats a hand on James's cheek in quick, fake smacks. Another teasing smile lights up his face as he works to get their heads back in the game. "Oh! I know why you don't like her. I bet you're jealous. You don't want anyone else taking all my attention, huh? You'd rather have me all to yourself? Is my little-wittle Jamsie-waimsie all—ow, no, hey!" he squawks as his brother tweaks his fingers backwards.

His face placid, like a pond without a ripple, James states, "I don't care what you do. I refuse to touch her."

"Saving yourself for marriage, little br—Gah! No! I said stop!"

James releases him.

Cradling his abused hand—not *that* abused, but he'll play it up for attention—Elijah sulks. "Yes, sorry, you're a pillar among men. One with so much bedroom experience, it puts other Alphas to shame. One with a knot the size of a building. One who—" He yelps, ducking to the side as James takes a swipe at him.

There's nothing better than riling up his brother.

Well, almost.

Something smells good.

This whole place smells good…for a myriad of reasons, though Katelyn is loath to admit it.

She peeks out of her doorway to look into the kitchen, wondering if she'll catch an Alpha cooking food and being domestic—a rare sight. At least, she assumes it's rare. She's never been this close to an Alpha before, never mind two. There were a few that worked in other departments around the office but, other than being large, there seemed to be nothing special about them. Not like these men. They exude power and control.

Except when that one was laughing his ass off. That was…disturbing? Endearing? Surprising?

All of the above.

Despite the delicious smells that assault her, the kitchen looks empty. The equipment and décor seem dipped in shadow compared to the bright light of the sun streaming through the garden. The courtyard that lives between the exotic rice paper screens is peaceful and idyllic. Katelyn swears she even sees a litany of sweet, fluffy bumble bees sip from the blue flowers. She thinks they're…gentians, maybe? Her mother had outlawed any flower that couldn't be bred in the white or pearl color family, but Katelyn had liked these. They reminded her of velvet curtains in kindergarten theaters back when the curriculum required you pretend to be a girl in a little red riding hood, whether you wanted to be or not.

Turning around, she flops back on the bed, wrapping her legs in lotus position. Apropos, really. In theme, as if she should be meditating out in that storybook oasis.

Why is this place so beautiful?

It doesn't matter. What matters is that she's trapped with two men she absolutely *cannot* be seen with. They're going to ruin everything. What is Thomas going to say? Her mother?

No, she can't think about her mother right now. She'd kill her. She'd hate her for the rest of her life, regardless of the fact that this was not Katelyn's fault. She can just picture the heartbroken look on her mother's face. She'd whisper, "Your father and brother are gone. All I have is you. Why did you have to betray me?"

A deep well of shame fills her.

"You're attracted to them," her imaginary mother scolds.

It doesn't matter that Katelyn doesn't mean to be. It's not something she can control.

"You let one *touch* you," the voice laments.

She did. It was instinct. She offered her hand to a man she should have run far away from.

"You'll let one of them bite you. Or both." Her mother's imaginary tone is filled with horror. Disgust. "Thomas will never forgive you. And then what am I supposed to do?" The voice turns heartbroken.

"How will I take care of myself? How am I going to survive? How could you take away my friends? My life? The Lifestyle is everything. You've ruined *everything*."

There is a sharp knock, startling Katelyn. She wipes the tears from her eyes as the door slips open to reveal the quiet one. The one without tattoos. The one for whom expressions don't seem to exist. *Finn*. Even now, he's still not looking at her, eyes pointed to the wall.

His deep voice blandly states, "Lunch."

The very thought makes Katelyn's nerves buzz. No, please and thank you, enormous Alpha man. She wants to be nowhere outside this room. Except, you know, *home*.

"Come," he states, his tone brokering no room for argument. That doesn't mean she won't argue anyway.

She holds her ground, sun-yellow fingernails digging into her thighs. "I'm not hungry right now."

"Lunch is at one. Always at one. You eat now, or you don't eat."

Stubborn bastard.

"Come out, or Zeb will drag you out."

She clenches her jaw, irritation spiking. "Oh yeah? Why don't you just do it yourself?"

"I refuse to touch you."

"Oh yeah? Why?"

"Because I hate you."

Katelyn flinches. What happens if they hate her?

He shoves his body out of the doorway and into the hall, standing to his full height before striding away. She can hear his footsteps echo, one padded step then another. Will she be punished if she doesn't follow? They said they were going to seduce her, which implies some sort of willingness on her part, but would they shift gears if she's non-compliant?

Swallowing takes real effort. What if Finn goes to get the other one? The touchy-feely one? The one she is overwhelmed by?

She's in so much trouble here.

Like a deer ready to spook, she tiptoes out of her room and falls into Finn's wake, feeling the dark wood under her feet as she walks down the hallway, taking the sharp right turn to go toward the kitchen.

As if he didn't just verbally stab her, Finn is setting food on the table. Strawberries, grapes, tomato soup, and grilled cheese. Her tummy gives a rumble of approval.

Behind her, she feels the brush of lips across the shell of her ear. "He made it especially for you."

She yelps and turns fast, plastering herself against the wall, only to find…Zeb…grinning at her.

"He looked all through your pantry and fridge, you know. He's very methodical. He figured you'd like this." Zeb waves toward the table before taking her hand in a quick grab and leading her to a seat. She barely has time to react before he's plopped her down and leaned over her back to snag a strawberry from the center plate of fruit. The hum of satisfaction he lets out runs a chill up her spine. He smells so good, she might just die. "He also hates waste," Zeb murmurs against her, "so eat up. Best to not piss him off."

Her stupid, running mouth blurts, "How could I tell? The man's face is a mask."

Looking up to see if her jab landed, Finn only sits down and eats primly. Why won't he look at her?

Because he hates her.

She doesn't know why that bothers her so much. Maybe because no one's ever said that to her before. Not even in middle school, when the bullies came out to play.

Zeb continues to lean over her shoulder, caging her as he braces one arm on the table and uses the other to load her a plate. He's… jabbering.

"Now, the question is: what to do to fill our time? There's not much here. No TV. No phones. No way out. What do you think? Shall we sing camp songs? Play board games? Hide and seek? Poker? *Strip poker?*" he says the last into her hair. At that, his free hand slides up and skirts around the curve of her shoulder and across the side of her breast.

Something in her goes electric. Shoving backwards, she puts him off balance and darts from her chair. Her feet tangle and she twists, dropping to her rump and clambering backwards until she hits the cabinet doors.

"Why would you touch me?" she cries, wrapping her arms over her chest.

His redwood eyes squint beautifully with the size of his slow smile. "Why wouldn't I touch you? We're here for a reason, aren't we?"

He drops to his haunches before crawling forward to hover in her space. Why is she always finding herself cowering before him? She quivers, wanting to throw herself on him, either to fall into his arms and see what he has in store for her or to shove him on his ass and bolt. She blames her heating cheeks on her virgin body and stays stock-still.

He lifts his hand, and his fingers graze her cheek, sliding down to lift her chin. She can't look at him. He's too enticing. Dazzling. He continues his path down the column of her throat, and she knows what he's doing. He's marking her. Rubbing his scent on her. She's read about it late at night when she'd fantasized about what it would be like to be with an Alpha. Why did she look at those things? It's not allowed.

Perversion starts at home in the dead of night, so saith The Lifestyle. They're not wrong.

No matter how she trembles under his touch, she fights it. Defiant, her eyes snap open, boring into her captor's. The muscles of his ink-adorned arm flex as he continues stroking, down her collarbone, up the crook of her neck, just under her ear. He's getting too close to something no one can ever touch. This is so dangerous.

"Get your hands off me," she says, trying her best to mean it.

Zeb's smile widens into something predatory. "So feisty." He leans in even more, near enough for his scent to take her over. "But I promise you, darling, you'll be begging me to touch you soon enough."

And, God help her, he might not be wrong.

James has no desire to see this display. The petting, Elijah's voice dropping to a register where it doesn't belong, the suggestive words he never says to strangers.

This is such an utter waste of time. James hates that they need the money. If only he could just work like normal people, but too many pitchy voices with too many pounding sentences makes his head spin. And if they try to touch him, it's all over. He has no patience when it comes to that. Only Elijah and his mother can touch him without his skin crawling. And his stepfather—barely.

He may not be making a face, but his eyes are locked on the couple before him. The Beta Distraction looks on the verge of either running or screaming. Maybe both. He doesn't care either way. He wants to be looking for their Omega—Elijah's and his. They need to become a pack. A trio. There's no other way. He could never be in a pairing that excludes his stepbrother. Only Elijah understands him. Only he sees him. Only he knows him.

James would die without him.

James would die *for* him.

He should have died a long time ago.

He flicks his eyes to the vein in his forearm and the faded scar drawn there. It's not for lack of trying. But the look of horror, fear, and desperation that had painted Elijah's face is enough to keep James on this earth. He will never cause such pain to his brother again. That's why they have to be a pack. He can't lose his brother, but their life is not normal. They shouldn't live together, talk with only each other, and be as inseparable as they are. Mom is getting worried, another thing James hates to see. He doesn't mean it. He'd fall to his knees and cry out, "I'm sorry! Please don't hate me!" but those words would never come from a cinched throat like his. He is a burden, pure and simple. Without him, Elijah would already have an Omega. Pups. A future. James is a weight, drowning Elijah so slowly, he doesn't even notice his lungs filling with water.

James looks at his scar again.

He's so tired of himself.

Getting up in one fluid motion, he collects his empty dishes and brings them to the sink while his brother and The Distraction continue their little dance of lies. Still, it's one o'clock, and one o'clock means lunch. He ladles a bowlful of soup and arranges a sandwich—cut into triangles with no crust, like Elijah likes—before setting the food on the placemat designated for The Distraction's meal.

He turns to leave but doesn't get far. Elijah is spinning him around before he knows it and sitting him back down with casual grace. Instead of cajoling The Distraction in murmurs and sweet whispers, his brother sits down beside him and pulls his lunch across the table, keeping himself in James's orbit instead of positioning himself to be closer to his target.

With a smirk and a glint in his eyes, Elijah says, "Don't be so upset." How he knows is anyone's guess. He always does, though. That's why James can never lose him.

The Beta Distraction is still on the floor, glaring at them.

He hates her even more.

"Eat," he reminds, not bothering to waste more words than he has to.

"How can I?" she shouts. "You kidnapped me, he's all over me, and you expect me to sit down and play house! I want to go home!"

James is unmoved, instead watching Elijah watch her.

His brother clucks his tongue. "Come on, sweetheart, just be a good girl. You don't want to know what he does when he's angry."

James does absolutely nothing when he's angry.

Clapping him on the back, Elijah winks again, gifting him with a ridiculous kissy face.

For Elijah, James will use his words.

He clamps a hand over his brother's mouth. "I'll sew this shut."

He feels his brother smile…and then lick the underside of his palm. With a narrowed glance, he pulls away and wipes it on his khaki pants, leaving a dark stripe of moisture. If he were another man, he would make a fuss. If he were another man, he would laugh. But Elijah is doing the laughing for both of them.

The Beta interrupts with a stomach growl that puts tigers to shame. Elijah's attention snaps to her, but James is happy enough to see her reflection in his brother's eyes.

Storming like thunder, she stomps up, snags her plate, and hustles to her bedroom, tossing a nasal grunt in their direction.

That's fine with him.

A pleased smile pulls up the corners of his brother's mouth. "Oh, I like her."

James rejects the idea.

Tapping his finger against his cheek, Elijah tries to guess his thoughts. "You think she's too dramatic."

Yes, but that's not it.

"She's too eccentric, maybe? I mean, look at her clothes."

That's not it either.

Elijah's voice drops, mimicking James near-perfectly. His face frozen in time, he says, "She's a distraction…"

James's eye twitches, and that's all the tell his brother needs. Elijah laughs, hearty and full, leaning to the side and bumping their shoulders together, an act of affection he's done since the day they met.

"It's only for a month," he reminds, stuffing the sandwich in his mouth, heedless of the scalding cheese. "And even if we can't make her open her legs, we get paid either way. More if she does spread wide, but there's no controlling that. Free will was ever the folly of the Gods." He nudges James again, his mouth full and words muffled. "Stop worrying so much. This money will get us through half a year."

James looks at his hands, feeling that familiar pang of inadequacy. All he wants to do is help, but…

"And I know we can get you a job somewhere," Elijah says. "We've just got to find the right place. Somewhere you don't have to touch people and they won't piss you off too bad. Maybe we can set you up at a gym. Do the cleaning or check in / check out sort of stuff. They expect guys like you to be the strong, silent type."

"You'd do it better than me." It comes out flat, no music in his tone, but its softness is enough to scream his vulnerability.

Bending in a groaning stretch that rests his head on James's shoulder, Elijah sighs so hard, James can feel his ribs expand and contract. "You keep that up and I'm going to do everything in my power to put a smile on that face of yours."

Impossible.

A teasing tilt of Elijah's lips means James is in for it. Using the tone he put on for the Beta Distraction, Elijah hovers just outside James's ear. "Look at you, *Finn*, so unconvinced of my power, even though you stole my middle name. Do you like me that much?"

James puts a heavy hand over his stepbrother's face again, keeping the unstoppable man at bay.

Thankfully, a chime goes off, and Elijah pulls back—no long, wet stripe licked along James's palm this time. His brother must have decided to behave himself for once. Unzippering a hidden pocket, Elijah pulls out his cell phone. The black screen is simply labeled "Boss Man," and he waggles it at James like a toy in front of a dog before looking around to make sure The Distraction is out of ear shot. Only then does he click the speaker button.

"We've got her," Elijah says to his phone without ceremony, playing with James's hair as he stares at him with a smirk. "Unharmed, of course, but she's not too keen on this."

The voice on the phone is distant and grainy. "I should hope not."

"We're starting to work our charm on her, though," Elijah says, winking at his brother. "It's only a matter of time until she lets us unlock her pretty box."

The man on the phone puffs out a breath. "You're disgusting."

Elijah only shrugs, unseen by the man who hired them. "Who's more disgusting? The man doing the job or the man who asked him to do it?"

"You're a bounty hunter. This is your daily existence."

"The sex part is new."

"Isn't that all you're good for?"

"I'll make sure that's not what she thinks. I'm a man of multiple talents. Maybe even more than you." Elijah's grin is sarcastic and mean, and James can smell his brother's scent shift into one of dominance, even as his fingers still slip through James's hair.

The man's tone hardens, but he doesn't take the bait. "There are big things at stake here. Life altering things. Just keep her quiet and under constant watch. Take shifts if you have to. I don't know how wily she might be, but we can't be too careful."

"Whatever you say, boss."

Elijah thumbs the red button on his screen without another word. As if punctuating the end of the conversation, a ringing *crash* is heard, and James whips around to see shattered trails of white ceramic on the floor across the way. They stand out like clumps of snow on a muddy mountain top, drips and drops cascading like sprinkled salt.

The Distraction apparently decided to throw her plate against a wall.

Elijah barks out laugher, tossing his phone on the table. "Oh yeah. So feisty."

James holds in a breath and counts to three before getting up and grabbing a broom. That's what he's good at. Keeping his head down and picking up the pieces.

CHAPTER 3
TRAPPED

AFTER HER SHOW OF DEFIANCE, Zeb had barged in, thrown Katelyn over his shoulder, *thwapped* her soundly on the rear, and dragged her out into the garden while his brother wordlessly cleaned up her mess. She's not entirely sure why she did it—call it momentary madness— but now that she's being harassed for her transgression, she suffers a bitter well of regret.

Felt good in the moment, though.

Zeb presently stands with his thick arms crossed, looking at Katelyn with a cocky grin that dares her to try and get past him. She wants her glare to be lava, searing him like what he's doing to her. The Alpha's scent is so strong, she can taste it, but she refuses to identify its sweetness. To give it a name is a step toward intimacy she dares not take. Finn's scent is even stronger, and somehow more enticing, like pleasure incarnate dancing through her senses until she can feel it on her skin. The fact that he hates her seems to do nothing to dissuade her body. If anything, his distance makes him more compelling.

She doesn't know what to do. She's never been a strong woman. She's only ever been weird and quirky, someone who lets her mouth get her into trouble when the truth pours out. If she does that now, she's doomed, so she meets Zeb's challenge as best she can while the omnipresent asshole Finn looks at the ground, completely ignoring her.

The bleached white garden bench digs into her back as Zeb opens his dangerous mouth. "I like those glasses. I've never seen pink frames before. Weren't they purple or something an hour ago?"

"Lavender," she says through grit teeth. "There is a spectrum of color beyond primary and secondary, you know."

"Tertiary?" he mocks. "Red-orange, green-yellow?"

"Ever have crayons? Try harder." Maybe if she irritates him enough, he'll let her hide in her room again.

"So sassy." He considers, sauntering back and forth, still blocking her path. "Rust? And Lime, maybe?"

Good enough.

"Ah-ha!" he says, snapping his fingers. "I got it right! I always get it right for him, too." He tics his chin towards his stepbrother. Finn, for his part, just walks further away to sit on the white gravel around the pond and poke at the koi fish that live there. Two, one white, one black, swirl around each other in yin-yang patterns. Zeb snickers at his brother. "*Finn*, why don't you tell her what a hellish time you had picking through which of her hundreds of pairs of glasses to bring? You must have terrible eyes, little one. Near sighted? Far sighted? Bifocals? Lazy eye? Help me out here." Each guess is punctuated by a step in her direction, and Katelyn bristles.

"Don't touch me," she warns.

"Wouldn't dream of it." Casting a shadow over her, he smiles as the sun paints a glowing halo around him, making the edges of his long, dark hair turn lightning white. The crimson on his tattoo is a stark contrast to the blackness of his outfit, a splash of color on grayscale. His lips spread into that devilish grin again. "I'll only do this."

He snags her glasses.

The bastard *snags* her *glasses*!

Katelyn is on her feet in moments, jumping as high as she can reach, but he's holding them in a straight line above his head. "Nuh-uh! Down girl!" He twists to the side and Katelyn follows, grabbing and waving uselessly on her tippy toes. "I just want to look as pretty as you!" he goads. "See the world through your eyes! See...oh my God, you can't be serious."

He's slipped the glasses on over his ears and is blinking like an owl, his grin going from teasing to elated. Katelyn's efforts halt, embarrassment burning her cheeks.

"You naughty little thing. *Finn!* All your work was for nothing!" He waves her property over his head again. "They're fake! No prescription! Just glass!"

"It's part of my aesthetic!" Katelyn cries, leaping once more only for him to lift them higher. She's hopping around like an idiot bunny, even when she knows she can't reach. He's just too tall. Too broad. Too everything. She should pull his goddamn hair.

To make matters worse, he wraps an arm around her back, pulling her flush against his chest. Heat rages through her as his warmth fuses their bodies together, making her tingle. She wants to shove her face into the hard curve of his muscle…and bite the sonofabitch.

"Well, I think it's adorable," he purrs. "Does anyone else know your devious secret?"

Cedar.

There. She's named his scent. And Finn is petrichor, the clean, soil scent after heavy rainfall. They smell like a forest to get lost in and it makes her knees turn to jelly.

Zeb slides her glasses back on her face before tracing his fingertips over her cheeks. Slowly, he slips under her chin, tipping it up and forcing her to face him, a pucker's distance away. "I think I like marking you, my little rainbow."

Then it happens. She's stupid if she thought it wouldn't. It comes on like a tornado, swirling, dipping down, and sucking her up. She's shaking. Panting. She can't help it.

With everything she has, Katelyn shoves him away.

Holding her chest and backing up, she watches Zeb's expression fall. His mouth slackens and his eyebrows knit, as if this overbearing Alpha actually cares that her body just haywired.

"I need my medicine," she chokes out.

Despite the fever suddenly clawing at her skin, she manages to fumble back to her room and slam the door. Her pills, her saviors, sit on her bedside table, ready and waiting for her. The caps take seconds to twist off, but they're seconds too long as she hears the Alpha trailing after her. A familiar bitter taste slides down her throat as she wills her body to *please stop*.

"What happened?" There is no knock, Zeb just follows her in, rambling like always. His face is the epitome of concern. "Are you sick? Usually, I can tell, but I can't smell anything about you. Is it because you're a Beta? I've never had that problem with a Beta before but… Listen, you need to tell me what's going on, okay? I'm responsible for you. I need to know if you're sick."

Alphas only care about one thing, so saith The Lifestyle. *Themselves.*

But is that true? Could he actually care about her? Or does he only care about what the police will say if he lets her fritz out?

Skin prickling into goosebumps, Katelyn's face burns. What should she say? What believable lie could she possibly give?

The one the doctor gave her.

"I'm not sick," she rasps. "I have epilepsy. So, if you don't want me to fall down and bite my tongue in half, I suggest you give me a minute."

The way he gapes, you'd think someone had just hit her with a truck. He seems on the verge of running to her rescue, but he's the cause more than the cure.

He needs to leave.

"I'll be okay," she says, easing herself onto the bed as she shakes.

He points at the pill bottles clutched in her hands. "How much do you have in there? A month's supply?"

"Why does it matter?" She hates how weak she sounds.

Raking a hand through his hair, he scowls. "Worse comes to worst, I'll see if I can get you more. What are they? Gimme."

He reaches towards the bottles, and she cringes, cradling them to her chest. If he sees, he'll know, and if he knows, this will all go to hell —worse than it already has.

"I need space," she whispers, folding in on herself.

That seems to register. Zeb hefts out a nasal sigh but lifts his hands in surrender. "Okay, okay. Just…call me if you need me."

She can't help but scoff at that. "Why would I need you?"

Zeb smiles at her again, but it's softer. Worried. Almost kind. "Maybe you'd be surprised."

Without any further teasing, he backs towards the door, never lifting his eyes off hers. Finn hovers nearby in the courtyard, still not looking, but listening. Paying attention. Why does she feel like that's a smug win on her part?

Despite her upbringing, despite the rules hammered into her head, a thought swirls up, unbidden.

Alphas want me.

With that tucked into her most secret of hearts, she watches the door close and lets her stomach roll, her sweat bead, and her shaking come on in earnest.

The pills hurt her…but it doesn't matter.

She lets herself fall into dreamless sleep.

Elijah and James trudge to their room. With practiced ease, James slips his hand into Elijah's back pocket to snag the phone hiding in his loose pants, the weight riding just under his right ass cheek. Elijah's yelp gets him nowhere, shrill though it is. James's only response is to toss himself on the bed, tap in the phone's passcode, and start up one of his sword fighting videos. The predictability is too cute.

"Two o'clock?" Elijah asks.

James doesn't need to answer, so he doesn't.

Belly diving onto the king bed next to his brother jostles the whole frame. Cheap thing. Ticking his eyebrows up, Elijah begins to bounce on his stomach, shaking the mattress in waves that test the springs, *squeak* after *squeak* after *squeak*. It sounds like they're fucking in here or something, and it sets Elijah off in giggles.

"James! James! Bounce with me! C'mon! *Mmmph!*" He finds his brother's hand over his face again, pinning down his shenanigans.

"Two o'clock," James states, turning up the volume on his video.

Elijah rolls away from his brother's palm. "Yeah, yeah."

They sit that way for a minute, in a calm, soft peace. Elijah can hear the swords clashing over each other as the instructor talks about technique, style, and the importance of pommels. He really should buy his brother a sword. A rapier or even a fucking broadsword. Whatever he wants. Hell, he'll get one for himself too, so James has someone's ass to kick. He'll put that on the list of stuff to buy when they get their money.

A wave of exhaustion pulls at his ankles, stealing his will to move. He's been up well over twenty-four hours at this point, and the last five minutes was a coronary he didn't need. "Do you think she's okay?"

James starts the next video.

"Well, I hope she's okay. She scared me. I don't want to even think about how this complicates the job. Never mind the fact that she's, you know, a person. One I'd prefer to not have die on my watch."

The next video seems to be about sparring hand-to-hand if the audio gives anything away.

"Do you think I'm doing good at it?" Elijah asks. "The flirting thing?"

The video drones, *"So, ensure your weight is distributed and your knees are bent. If you lock up, you're easy to knock down."*

Elijah puts his hands over his eyes. "Because it's so hard. I have no idea how to flirt like this."

"Then stop." His brother's answer is simple.

Elijah rolls around on the bed in response, nearly rocking himself off the edge before plowing into his stepbrother over and over again, whining, "I only know how to be ridiculous! Me trying to be a sex pot is like forcing a square block into a snake."

James looks at him askance. "…"

"I mean, you can do it, but it doesn't feel great!"

James replies with a dry, "I hate her."

Elijah grins. Rolling quickly, he rocks himself up and over his brother until he's straddling his hips. Reaching around the phone, he squashes both hands on his brother's cheeks and skews his face, first smashing the heels of his hands together and making James's mouth purse before stretching wide and putting something like a smile on his face. "She's not all that bad. Just imagine she's your Omega."

With his mouth pulled all out of place, James's words slur. "Ours."

"I don't need an Omega," Elijah reminds, sick of this conversation. "My life is perfect."

He squashes and stretches James's face a few more times, enjoying the ability to do so, while his brother pointedly ignores him in favor of his video. It makes him snicker.

"Okay. I'm going to take a shower," he says for no reason other than to say it.

They have the master bedroom with an ensuite, and he's going to enjoy every moment of it. Better than renting out rooms in group houses and off-season B&Bs. Bounty hunting pays when it pays, but it's not like he has control over how many bail-hopping fuckers run away and need to get tracked. They need something more stable. Too bad he never went to college.

The stream of water is hot enough to scald, and Elijah enjoys letting out sharp "Ah! Shit! Fuck!"s when he steps in, hoping to make James peek through the door, but knowing the man would only forsake his videos for fire and brimstone. The next thirty minutes is his alone.

When he wets his hair, it trails all the way to the bottom of his shoulder blades, which makes him happy. He wants to get it to his mid-back at the very least, but probably needs to trim the ends, which makes him pout.

Does Miss Katelyn Annamarie Jones-Masters think his mane is sexy?

Speaking of trimming, he needs to cut James's hair. It's getting longer than his brother likes and the blond curls are showing. They're grabbable now, soft and lustrous.

Elijah wonders if Miss Katelyn thinks that's sexy, too.

There has to be some way to pull her out of her shell. Get her guard down. Make her like them. Or just him. Or just James. Though, James is probably a nonstarter.

What is she into? He had to take her captive quickly, so he didn't get to do a lot of digging into her situation like he normally does. Boss Man said she doesn't work, so what does she do with her time? Who are her friends? What kind of music does she like? What hobbies does she have? Is she a dog person or a cat person? Or a crocodile person, for all he knows. Maybe some emus. Zebras and Dolphins.

He snorts, lathering his hair and trying not to get bubbles in his eyes.

What if she needs more of that medicine? She's taken two doses today, and it looks like she downs quite a few pills at one go. If she runs out, what then? He said he'd kidnap her, he didn't say he'd put her at any sort of medical risk. He'll tell that to Boss Man next time they have a little chat. Maybe she has more meds stashed at her house. He could send James back for them…provided she doesn't try to rip out his lungs and run if she gets the chance.

He'd like to see her run. He can't help it. Alphas are into that kind of shit. The chase. The hunt. The capture. He wonders if James would like it, too.

Probably not. She's not "Their Omega."

They've made no progress with her. She's shut down, gates closed and moats filled with monsters, though he supposes he'll give himself a pass. It's only day one. They *did* just kidnap her. That'll put a wrench in anyone's day.

Maybe he'll ask her more about herself. Make her feel comfortable. Maybe he can tell her about himself and make her like him more in the process. Though, there's not much safe to tell. His life is not, what he would call, "by the books." Plus, she'll probably go to the cops with all his details when this is said and done. That would cut off an income stream at the very least. Still, Boss Man said he could make any problem she causes go away. If he couldn't, Elijah never would have dared take this job. He catches criminals, not pretty ladies. Until now.

This time, Elijah knocks, but he still opens the door on his own when Miss Katelyn doesn't answer. She's sprawled on the bed alongside her rumples of fashionable—and less fashionable—clothes, but the moment he enters, she pulls into the corner, as far from him as possible.

Well, that's a little disheartening.

"Afraid of me?" he asks.

"Afraid of what you'll do to me," she counters.

"You mean, like feed you?" From behind his back, he brings a dish.

He would have liked it to be a paper plate, considering her temper, but they only have what they have. "It's a little after nine, but you never came out. I figured I'd come in."

He rests a plate of pasta at the foot of the bed, fork shoved in and half ensnared in long loops of starchy goodness. It's dotted with tomato chunks and infused with pesto, and if eyes could become stars, that's what hers do.

"I see Finn's ransack of your pantry was a good thing. At least I know you don't have a pine nut allergy."

Grumpy, but eyeing the pasta dish, she says, "I have a *you* allergy."

He presses a hand to his heart and makes a mock gasping sound.

Watching him as if he'd pounce at any minute, she grabs the side of the plate and slides it over to herself. "I'd say thank you, but instead I'll tell you to take me home."

"Alas, my boss wouldn't like that very much."

"And who would that be?" She looks bitter, like she already has the puzzle worked out in her head. If she does, she's one up on him.

"I have no idea."

One of her sculpted brows tweaks high.

Elijah shrugs, tossing his arms to the side and plunking down on the floor at the foot of the bed. "This is what I'd call a 'last minute' job. I didn't get to vet the guy, but he came highly recommended by a mutual connection, so..."

"How last minute is 'last minute?'"

"I got the call to take you around eleven o'clock last night. Address, description, vague details."

"Do you know who my fiancée is?" she asks. "He's going to lose his mind when he finds out what happened. You don't want to do this. He's...powerful."

"Concerned for me, darling?"

Her gaze drops. His acute hearing picks up the words, "For all secondary genders" before her mouth screws into a knot. Lifting her plate, she stabs in her fork and twirls, stuffing her cheeks full.

"Ask me anything you like," he tells her. "If I can answer, I will."

It seems to surprise her. Her tight posture softens and her shoulders drop as she takes him in. That's good. He needs to build some trust with the spooked, jade-eyed mare.

She considers. "Why take me?"

"Your guess is as good as mine."

She frowns and thinks for a few ticks. "Why is your brother here? He seems to want nothing to do with this."

"You're not wrong, but J–*Finn* never looks like he wants anything to do with anything. Usually I take jobs by myself, but I didn't know if you liked blonds better." He gives her his most award-winning grin. To his surprise, her lips tip up at the corners.

Falling back into seriousness, she morosely smooshes her food around. "Why are you doing this?"

"We need the money."

She scoffs. "So, you *are* ransoming me."

"No, I told you, I'm seducing you. I'm—"

"Stealing my virginity?" she cuts in. Her eyes fly wide, and she goes red from her neck to her forehead. He's guessing she didn't mean to say that.

"You're a *virgin*?"

Well, that's upsetting.

Elijah cocks his head to the side with a frown. "How old are you?"

She looks like she wants to crawl into a hole. "Twenty-eight."

He whistles. "You held on to that good and tight."

Waving her hand absently, she sulks. "It's my…religion, I guess. Staying pure until marriage."

That makes sense, he supposes. He's not sure how he feels about taking her virginity, though. "So, your fiancée never fooled around with you?"

She goes from red to purple. "He's never even kissed me."

"No boyfriends in high school? College?"

"Not allowed."

It does not compute. "Don't you have any, you know, urges?"

She groans and plops her plate back on the bed, balling her knees to her chest and tucking her face away.

So cute.

"I have urges," Elijah says. "I have them all the time. I'm usually monogamous, though, so this is new for me."

"Won't your girlfriend be upset?"

"Boyfriend," he clarifies.

Her voice is a squeak. "Is he an Omega? I heard they're very territorial."

"I wouldn't know, he's an Alpha."

That gets her attention again. "That's even more territorial."

With a teasing lift to his eyebrows, he props up his elbow on one knee. "Afraid to get chased away, little one? Afraid my Alpha will come for you?"

She shivers. After a beat and a deep breath, she says, "Just take me home. I'm sure I can pay you something. Save me and your boyfriend the heartache and let me go."

"You have seventy-five thousand dollars in cash tucked away?"

She makes a choking sound. Her face lifts again, and she goes pale. "M-my fiancée does."

"No, thank you." He has no desire to get on his mystery boss' bad side.

"You're going to ruin my life." Her voice is high and reedy, and the sound tugs at Elijah's heart. "You don't understand what will happen to me. Even if it's not my fault, being with an Alpha, being *here*…it's something I can't take back."

She looks so small, curled up like that. So frightened. The tug on Elijah's heart sharpens. "I'm here to seduce you, which means nothing happens if you don't want it to."

"Except you touching me," she says through her teeth.

"Ah, well, that's just good fun. I like to see how angry you get. I wonder how many times you'll knock yourself over when you scoot away."

She tosses down her fake glasses and presses her hands to her face, letting them drift up and embed themselves in her auburn hair. She looks on the verge of breaking down, and if she does, Elijah won't know what to do with himself.

"Listen, just take it slow. I won't hurt you. Finn won't hurt you. You're here, and I can't change that. But we can either try to enjoy our time together, or you can lock yourself in this room and go on hunger strike, which will make Finn lose his mind, so I'd prefer you obey standard mealtimes if you don't mind."

Somehow, it squeezes a huff of laughter out of her.

He'll take that as a win.

Katelyn slept like trash. She's never had to take her medicine in such huge quantities just to keep herself from—what she's coming to think of as—utterly imploding.

This morning's headache screams pain at her the same way her imaginary mother's voice weeps in lamentations. "Katie, please don't. Don't look at those disgusting Alphas today. Don't touch them. Don't speak to them."

Unfortunately, she only has so much control over the situation.

She'd snuck around like a cat burglar last night, hiding in the shadows and searching for a way to escape. Not only did she find none, but she'd rounded a corner to find Zeb watching her with his standard smug grin. He'd nonchalantly told her that she sucks at stealth and hefted her over his shoulder, putting her back to bed while she flung no less than forty curses in the Alpha's direction.

Lying there now, she peers through her very locked window to see the early morning sun stream over a long and winding driveway made of tidy blue-gray gravel. It's framed by cherry blossom trees and sculpted bushes that follow the driveway's trail toward a somewhere-road she can't see. It's picturesque. Flawless. Her view is unmarred, neither smudge nor streak separating her and the world, just a double pane of crystal-clear glass. She should break it. Turn it into a spider web of shards. But what could she possibly do it with? There are stones outside lining the path to civilization, but in here, there's only immovable furniture and perfect, puffy bedding. Not that it would matter much. Even if she had something wieldable, she'd probably shatter her bones before she'd manage to shatter glass. Her medicine makes her too weak to do damn near anything.

Scowling, she rolls over onto her back. The ceiling isn't a popcorn pattern like it is at home. It's plain and smooth, like a sheet of paper, begging to be made into a mural…though, no, that wouldn't belong in a place such as this. Even if Katelyn had buckets of paint, she would never destroy the authentic feel of this square palace. It, too, has its own aesthetic. That doesn't mean she doesn't miss the vibrancy of color splashed over walls. Her office cube was covered in postcards of her favorite paintings and magic-eye pages, the ones you had to look at with your nose to the paper to see the secret 3-D image locked inside. Her brother had taught her about those. He'd even got her a book of them on her birthday.

She misses him sometimes, even decades later. She doesn't remember much, she was six when he was twelve after all, but his warmth stayed with her.

He'd been sick, locked in his room for days while her mother refused to let anyone in or out. He was just that contagious. It had been scary, the way he cried out in pain, and she heard every whimper and moan. It still gives her nightmares. How helpless he must have felt, trapped with no one who truly understood his pain. He was so young. He must have been so scared. Felt abandoned. He suffered, and it breaks Katelyn's heart to know that he did it all alone.

Just like she's alone.

The pictures in her mind are faded and torn, his face absent, but she can still feel her brother's kindness. He was the first one who taught her how to draw. Like every other girl her age, she was obsessed with unicorns and mermaids, and her brother would sit with her for hours, showing her step by step, circle by circle, how to draw a horse. She'd kept one of their tandem attempts, even though the graphite blurred and became hazy with time. By adult standards, even her brother's rendition was terrible, but at her age, he may as well have been the artist of the century.

Melancholy, she wonders why he had to die. Both him and her father. The strong, loving, bearded man from her memory had packed her brother's things for a long stay at the hospital, but once they left, they never came back. A fated car crash took half of her family away.

At six, she'd comforted her mother as best she could. Both that night, and in the days and weeks to come. Katelyn was the mother in those long moments, giving every ounce of her love and protection to the one who needed her most. She tucked in sheets, took hands, fed and fawned. She had no time to mourn the dead males in her life; she was too busy saving the woman they left behind.

If they were still here, her mom wouldn't have to be so lonely. So afraid. Katelyn wouldn't have to be the only one to keep her smiling. She wouldn't be the only one who can save this family.

"Katie," her imaginary mother pleads, "If you go on a hunger strike, like he said, maybe they'll let you go. Or maybe it will at least show Thomas you couldn't stand being with creatures like them. If he pities you, he'll forgive you. We can keep this quiet. The Lifestyle elders will never have to know."

There is sense in those words, but then her captors would look even more like criminals, starving the woman they stole away from her deteriorating life. All Alphas would feel the backlash. She can't let that happen. If only she could lie better, she'd tell Thomas that it was Beta men who took her, though maybe anyone with a nose will be able to tell she's been marked.

Alphas and Omegas are no more than animals, so saith The Lifestyle. *Beasts who rut and leave their scent on anything they touch. Those who get too close will have their auras tainted by filth. Don't be fooled. They may look like us, but they are not us.*

Getting up, her head reels, but she stumbles to her little bedside table and takes out her daily body cream, coating herself in spackled blobs from her toes to the back of her ears and everywhere in between. It takes a good number of minutes to rub in, and it stings like a bitch, but it, like her medicine, is necessary.

Again, the ceiling calls to her with its blank canvas.

Blank…

Katelyn groans as she reaches toward her feet where the duffel bag Finn packed for her lays. The thing may as well be filled with bricks for as much stuff as he crammed in here. It even broke two pairs of her glasses. Just thinking of those makes her blush, remembering Zeb holding them above her head like a playground boy teasing a girl he likes.

Ignoring that thought, she digs for something she saw yesterday.

Tucked in the corner is a heavy, thick, tome of a book bound in sturdy black plastic made to look like leather. Its vivid white pages remind her of the ceiling above, just begging to be tagged with anything and everything that graces her mind. There must be over five hundred pages in this thing, but she's only used fifty at most.

Perusing, she reacquaints herself with cartoon doodles, lots of stick people gesture studies, some highly rendered photorealism, and practice stabs at legible graffiti until she realized that wasn't really the point. The images make her think of Zeb's tattoos. The marks on his body are geometric gradient shapes in red and black paired with inked-in dry brushstrokes, all framing a grayscale image of a clock. The style is called "Trash Polka" of all stupid things, but it's absolutely stunning. Just up her alley. For as many times as he's hefted her up, she's had ample time to stare at it, and it's something she wouldn't mind tracing with her fingers, mapping out with her touch.

Digging in the bag once more, she finds a pencil case. The thing is cracked now and more than one of her innocent mechanical pencils has snapped in half. Irritation needles her. Still, she finds one that avoided its own demise and clicks the eraser a few times, letting out the thin, dark gray point of the tip.

An empty page is daunting whether you're an illustrator or author, she supposes. Any art comes with the fear of getting it down wrong once pen is to paper, but the urge to create is stronger than her need to stay in the safe zone. But what to draw? What to capture? What to sink into?

The garden.

She doesn't want to leave the room, so she peeks out of the keyhole first. It's old fashioned, overlarge, and seemingly at odds with the rest of the style of the home—or in Katelyn's case, prison. It gives her a narrow view of the corridor, but she can't see anything interesting from this angle. Only enough to know there's no beautiful beast waiting for her outside. Feeling safe, she cracks open the door just enough to see a sliver of light tickling the dust motes and the greenery that lies beyond the rice paper screens. There are flower beds coated with the trumpet-like gentians, each petal a striking royal blue. Those would look nice on the page. She could make their stems into swooping filigrees that edge the paper like an old fairytale illustration's border.

She hunches over her paper, tongue already out of her mouth as her pencil hovers, wondering where to start…

And then Finn blocks her view.

She stifles a grunt. So much for avoiding the Alphas.

Finn's taciturn personality shines as he sprinkles a handful of what must be fish food into the koi pond. Like this, he almost looks gentle, despite his size. He's wearing a tank-top and, unlike his brother, his porcelain white skin is devoid of any markings save the thin circles of his mating glands and the muscular dips of his body as he moves. He really is quite beautiful. They both are. They're designed to be.

She wonders if she's designed to be beautiful, too.

Setting the small bag down, he presses his palms together as if in prayer and takes a deep breath. His shoulders rise and fall in a smooth motion, refined and purposeful, the light dappling shadows over his curves. Sinking his knees, he angles his arms to the side in a graceful swoop before lifting a foot and standing on one leg. He kicks his hovering toes out quickly before coiling back and dropping even lower into a squat, holding in a locked position.

Fascinated, Katelyn watches Finn move, fluid as a ballet dancer, but every transition slow and methodical. He tenses and flexes as he steps forward and back, putting himself in offensive and defensive stances as if guarding against an unseen threat. His eyes, normally so unfocused, are locked on the distance, yet still soft. There is no furrow of his brow or clench to his jaw. He is like water.

Her pencil starts to move. He never stays anywhere long enough for her to completely capture him, so she spirals out gesture after gesture in short lines and curves. The S of his backbone as it curls and arches. The lift of his biceps as a sheen of sweat begins to form. The spread of his knees as his weight firmly grounds him. He balances, sometimes on his toes, other times completely connected to the earth as his bare heels dig into the garden grass.

He is stunning.

Her stick renderings swoop like cursive, left to right, an animation flip book of pose after pose. She's wrapped up in this, barely able to waste time on a breath as her gaze flicks to him and back to paper, afraid to miss a moment of movement.

Which is why Zeb scares the hell out of her when he opens her door wide.

Another screech from her stops Finn in his tracks as she all but tosses her sketchbook in the air in surprise. The grinning fool before her uses his fingers like a comb as he stands between her and the Greek God she'd been trying to do justice to.

"Good morning. Doing something sneaky? You seem to have a habit, don't you?" He turns to look at his brother. "Did you know she was up?"

Crisis over, Finn resumes his movements. "Mm."

"And you didn't come get me?"

No answer.

"Gah!" Zeb throws his hands in the air with a grin on his face. Without warning, he drops on his haunches and snags her sketchbook off the floor without question or preamble. Why is he always taking her stuff!? Katelyn wants to shrivel to ant size and hide in the floorboard.

Again, and just as uselessly, she tries to grab her things, and again the maddening Alpha holds it just out of reach. He stands. She stands. He lifts, she jumps. He grins, she growls, which only makes his smile wider.

His free hand slides around her waist, tucking her behind him as he turns toward his brother. "Finn!" he shouts, waving her book in the air. "She's drawing you!"

She has half a mind to pinch this Alpha's mating gland and send him to the floor.

Finn looks over, but barely reacts otherwise, weaving his arms around each other like snakes before extending one palm in a blocking gesture.

Zeb twirls on her with delight. "Can I keep this? No, don't go, wait, seriously, this is really good! You got him down perfectly. It's the whole sequence. You could actually teach people the forms with stuff like this. FINN COME LOOK!"

He continues to ignore them.

Katelyn is too shocked to fight as the Alpha gleefully flips through her sketchbook. "Ohhh, rainbow, you're so good. Look at all of this!"

Her cheeks turn pink, embarrassed joy darting through her chest. Only Niles has ever looked at her sketchbook. It's like looking at someone's diary. Not every picture is beautiful, just like not every journal entry is decked out with life's best moments.

She tries to get it back again, feebly this time. "Come on. Please?"

But the sheer happiness on Zeb's face holds her at bay. "Are you kidding me? This is like a museum in my hands! Are you a professional?"

"I…I used to be a graphic designer."

"Used to be?"

And what can she say to that? *"I'm sorry, but my husband-to-be refuses to let me have a job because he wants me to focus on his Beta-only agenda. Which I don't believe in, by the way. I'm actually disgusted by it. I can't believe I'm in this despicable situation when all I want to do is go back to my life pre-Thomas, but here I am!"*

Before she has a chance to say something stupid, she's dragged close by her hips until she's staring up at his face and admiring his heavy lashes. Her body runs hot.

"You're too talented to hide this from the world," he says. "Don't let anything stop you."

He tips down and pecks a kiss on the tip of her nose. Squirming, she shoves back and knocks herself on her butt again, earning a deep bruise this time while he tears a page out of her book and waves it around. "I'm keeping this one. I'm pinning it up in my room. It's perfect."

Her blush has moved to def con one. He likes her art. A tickling bubble of happiness fizzes her nerves.

But wait…

Seduction.

Damn it, he doesn't mean any of this. This is all part of his game.

The secondary gender is full of tricks, so saith The Lifestyle.

The Lifestyle can go straight to bowls of hell, walk through its eternal flames, and fall into a chasm of spikes. Needle sharp ones, preferably.

Zeb hands the book back and turns on his heel, running to the garden. He's still waving the page in the air as he assaults his brother, slinging an arm over his neck and practically shoving the drawing in his face. Finn has no choice but to look. A slight lift pulls at the corner of his mouth as he takes the paper. For the very first time, he looks at her, and she's stunned. Somehow, a reaction from him is worth more than its weight in gold. He hates her, but he likes this, and she has a feeling he wouldn't lie.

It's only moments before Zeb bounds in again. "Can you draw him for real?" he asks, his eyes wide and the paper clutched to his chest. "In that grayscale style you have? And can you draw me as a cartoon?"

She's never had a request before. Her lips move soundlessly until her brain catches up to make real words. "T-to do him properly, I'd have to stare at him for hours!"

"He's good at holding still! You can do it at two o'clock today. That's when he watches his videos, so it's perfect."

"His videos?"

"He's obsessed with this guy online, Sensei Joe. It's where he gets most of his movements from."

"Oh. Um…okay, I guess I can do it?" It comes out as a question more than an answer. Why she just agreed, she has no idea, other than the fact that looking at Finn is like looking at a divine sculpture.

"And the cartoon of me?" Zeb runs in place. "Do you have to stare at me for a while, too?"

She shakes her head and waves her hand in a *Please No* gesture. "I think I've got you down enough to make it work without that."

He pouts. "Okay, fine. In the meantime, breakfast?"

"No, thank you."

He pouts more. "I told you about Finn and mealtime. Nine a.m. is breakfast, one o'clock is lunch."

"And when, pray tell, is dinner?"

He waggles his palm side to side. "Depends on what he's making. As long as he's cooking at six thirty, he's happy."

"And do you cook?"

"Not if you want something edible. Do you?"

She crosses her arms. "I'm not cooking for you."

His pout becomes a groan. "So cold. So cruel."

"So done with you," she says, even though she's enjoying herself for the first time in a long time. He reminds her of Niles. Still, she waves him away. "Scoot. I'll see you at two."

Cocking an eyebrow, he looks like he doubts every word coming from her mouth. After a shrewd look, though, he holds out a curled pinky finger and says, "Promise?"

Yep, definitely reminds her of Niles.

A chuckle works its way out before she stifles it. Still, that winning smile spreads on his face, as if he's won a difficult carnival prize. A Katelyn doll, ready to be kissed, hugged, and loved.

Despite the alarm bells in her head, she crooks her pinky and takes his, yanking it down as if this was a sacred vow. "I promise."

He downright *squees* and zooms back to the courtyard where his brother works his body. "She'll do it!"

That slight pull, that barely-there smile, blooms for a short moment on Finn's face before it fades again. She wonders if he was the one who wanted these pictures. If so, she has to do her very best job. She wants to impress him. Both of them. She wants Finn to make that face again and for Zeb to hold her pictures to his heart, treasuring them forever.

Can she do it? Can she be good enough for these Alpha masterpieces?

Swallowing her nerves, she closes the door and shuffles back to her bed, back to the mire of her mind and utter boredom.

She wonders what Niles is doing, wishing he was here to rescue her. Then she smiles and realizes that he would be too distracted by these Alphas and encouraging her to submit to the seduction.

Has he noticed she's missing?

No. She quit. She quit and made very clear to her one and only friend that their relationship would now be impossible.

Does he think about her, though? Do her previous clients? Her colleagues? She supposes it's only been a few days...but for her, its been a few days too long.

CHAPTER 4
ART AS LIFE

THIS IS AWKWARD. James has never been stared at in a good way, other than by Elijah. People single him out for being different. No one dares to say anything because his stepbrother would annihilate them—as he has proven on several occasions—but they've never been able to stop the disdainful and overly curious looks. At least the Beta Distraction isn't looking in a mean way. When he glances up from Elijah's phone, she's examining him with something like…awe, maybe? He can't tell. He's not good with faces.

He focuses on his video again.

In the garden, he sits on the white bench, Elijah beside him and—he can't believe he's going to bother to think her name—*Katelyn* in the grass in front of them. Her tongue pokes out as her head bobs up and down, staring at him, then diving back into her sketchbook. James pretends not to see, but she's in his peripheral vision, completely distracting him from Sensei Joe's latest kata exercise.

"I love it," Elijah says. He ruffles the picture she drew of him and shoves it in front of James's screen for a minute before pulling it away. It really is good. She'd gone above and beyond and drawn two versions. One where Elijah looks giddy and laughing, all curled up and adorable, and the other one with his eyes heavy-lidded and his smile devious and sexy. Apparently, his brother's hard work is paying off.

Sensei Joe bows to the camera and reminds James to practice and meditate on today's proverb. *"I no nake no kawazu taikai wo shirazu."* Literally: the frog in the well knows nothing of the ocean. In other words, "People who experience very little have a narrow worldview." Or: "He who stays in the valley shall never see over the hill."

Too poignant. Too applicable. He wants to skip the sentiment, but he always meditates on Sensei Joe's wisdom before bed, so that's what he'll do.

James flicks to the next video. Japanese sword fighting. That's tomorrow morning's routine. He'd like to practice Musashi, a two-sword style, but then he'd have to snap off another broomstick to match his first. He calls his oversized wooden dowel *Tamari mizu.* "Still water." Too grand a name for a stick, but he has high hopes.

"What's the word of the day?" Elijah asks him.

"Shinryaku."

"What's that mean?"

He eyes their resident artist. "Invasion."

Elijah bursts into predictable laughter and bumps James's shoulder with his own. When they have their Omega, James hopes his stepbrother treats her just as kindly. No jealousy. Maybe love. Seeing how he interacts with this…*Katelyn*…maybe it's possible. He's definitely attracted to her. Even James has to admit she's pretty. She sits there in skintight red and black plaid pants and a top that looks made for a yuppie, high and tight around her neck but loose otherwise, the shape of her breasts almost completely lost. Not that he's looking. She's just always there, mucking up his view, so he can't help but notice.

He focuses back on his video as Elijah chatters.

"What's your favorite art style?" he asks.

"All of them," she says.

"That's not fair. You have to have a favorite."

"What's yours?"

"Aw, it's almost like you care!" Elijah pauses, and James can hear the whirl of his brain ticking while wooden *bokken* slam edge against edge, two warriors practicing perfect *Kenjutsu.* Elijah perks up as if he's had an epiphany. "I guess tattoo art."

"That's not very specific. They have everything from watercolor to new school."

"Don't judge me. If it's ink on skin—well, *properly done* ink on skin —it's my favorite. I want to get a whole sleeve, but it's too damn expensive. I'd get a Japanese dragon."

James would like that very much.

"And I'd probably get straight black rings, too," he continues. "Or tribal."

She snorts. "That's so 90s."

"I told you not to judge. Classic is classic."

"You gonna get a tramp stamp, too?"

"Only if someone plans to splash cum on my back." James gives Elijah the side-eye while Katelyn chokes on her spit. "No, just think of it! I could put a bullseye with a banner that says, 'Your sperm goes here.'"

Surprisingly, Katelyn bursts out in a laugh so hard, James thinks she's going to rupture something. She takes off her leopard spotted glasses and wipes her eyes with glee.

It's hard to concentrate with all this going on around him.

"How much longer is this going to take?" he asks.

That sobers her and she slips back on her fake glasses. Why did he bother to grab so many pairs? He does like them, though. They suit her. Make her slightly quirky, slightly nerdy, and all around special.

What the hell is he thinking?

"I can stop for now. I've got the basic shape of you down. We can either do this again tomorrow, or…"

She trails off, looking into the distance. He wonders why.

"Accepting that you'll be here for a while, rainbow?" Elijah asks, a teasing lilt to his voice. He's trying to circumvent her mood with playfulness. That, at least, James understands. Elijah does it to him all the time.

Her mouth flattens as she pulls her red lips inward, biting at them with white teeth. Why is he still looking? He's going to have to start this video over again.

When she gets up to leave, he lets out an inward sigh and does just that.

Day four, and Elijah frets as their pretty captive passes up another meal. His stepbrother is about to crawl out his skin, and it's all Elijah can do to try and distract him from his impending, silent meltdown. Miss Katelyn Annamarie Jones-Masters hasn't taken any food into her room, even though James was kind enough to leave some outside the door. Lunchtime's bowl of ramen sits there like a pathetic castoff, the fat of the broth congealing into translucent clumps while the wavy yellow noodles go to mush.

At least she's been sneaking in the water. The only time Elijah's seen her this whole evening is when she ducked out to the bathroom to pee. He'd had half a mind to follow her in but figured that wouldn't do him any favors.

Digging into his food, he tries to soothe his brother's frazzled nerves with a moan of appreciation. "Oh, you saint. You used butter."

James has no response.

Shoving in another forkful, Elijah mulls over his stepbrother's state of mind as he rests his head on James's stiff shoulder. "Let me guess. You want me to regale you with a story of mealtime mayhem from a time long since passed, weaving a tale so all-consuming you forget about shoving even a morsel of food into your gorgeous mouth."

He's met with silence.

"No? Then…you want a hug warm enough to rival a microfiber blanket straight from the dryer, wrapping you up in love and fluff?"

James gives him the side eye.

"Oh! I know! You want a naked, lubed up, full body massage to loosen those knotted muscles of yours! I've got you, bro. Come on. Strip."

"…"

Elijah flutters as many eye blinks in his brother's direction as possible before giving up and guessing in earnest. "You're pissed off she's not eating."

His brother stiffens and Elijah snaps his fingers.

"Bingo. Don't worry, we can store it as leftovers. It's good! I'll snack on it at three in the morning when she sneaks out of her room again."

A tiny sigh of rushed air hisses through James's nose, missable if you're not paying attention.

"It's not the leftovers bothering you," Elijah says.

James just shoves another forkful of buttered corn in his mouth, his steak long since devoured.

"You're not actually worried about her, are you?" Elijah asks, only to have James shove him off, pushing his face away and smooshing his full cheek. Elijah's resulting grin is sly. "Ohhh, I see. Someone's starting to appreciate our resident Beta Distraction, isn't he?"

Seemingly unruffled, James looks at him with an expression still as stone, but Elijah knows better.

"It's true! You like her!" He lets out a quick laugh, turning back to dig in. "It's okay. I like her, too. When she talks to us, anyway." Chewing with his mouth open and his brain percolating, he smirks again. "I'll just make her keep talking to me. If I won you over, I can win over anyone. I'm not so bad at the dark and sexy thing, maybe, but she seems to like me when I'm just being myself, too. I make her smile, don't you think? I don't even have to try. I'm getting away with being just *me*. This might be easier than I thought, as long as I don't give up on her. Don't you give up on her either."

James puts his hand over Elijah's mouth again, earning some *mumble-bluffle-glaarb*s.

After futility nipping at his brother's hand, Elijah gets to his feet. "You're cleaning up?"

"Mm."

"Then I'm going to see my girlfriend."

James does nothing other than continue to eat. Shame. Elijah at least hoped to earn a frown. If he kissed him on the cheek, maybe he'd get one, but maybe he'd just get a slap off the back of the head.

Sneaking over to her room, Elijah slides her uneaten bowl over with his foot as he hovers outside her door. "Hey rainbow, you dying in there?"

"I'm not hungry," she says, sounding distant and muffled.

"I swear to God, you're just as stubborn as Finn. You just talk more."

As if to prove him wrong, she falls into a petulant silence, making him laugh.

"Yeah, okay, you two are definitely birds of a feather. Let's see if I can say enough for the both of us." He makes grumbling, old man noises as he eases himself down to the wooden floor, staring at the barrier between them and pretending to see her through it. In his mind, she's curled up in bed with a pout the size of a small city on her face. He'd like to pinch her bottom and make her jump. "Where to start, where to…oh! I know! Want to know about life as a bounty hunter?"

There's nothing but dead air.

At least he's familiar with one-sided conversations. "Well, I'll tell you anyway. It's not as glamorous as it is on TV. Sometimes it's downright boring. Clerical. Other times, I'm chasing people and knocking them on their ass, locking them in cuffs like a vigilante. Makes all the junk parts worthwhile. I have a little book of catch phrases I can say when I take someone down. Shit part is that I forget them all in the heat of the moment. I usually end up with something stupid like, 'I'm taking you back to the station.' Blarg! So not cool.

"How it works is: I get notice of a job, someone who skipped out of house arrest usually, or sometimes someone who missed criminal trial or escaped from minimum security prison. Then I usually growl the phrase 'The Hunt is On!' in my most sinister voice. You know, for posterity.

"I get photos and dossiers and do lots of online hunting. You'd be surprised by what people put on social media. I mean, they're not stupid enough to go out and say, 'Yo! Out of jail, bitches!' but they've usually put their favorite hangout spots in past posts. They happily stick up pictures of their girlfriends, boyfriends, best friends, too. Those people are a treasure trove of information. Then there's more research. And stakeouts. And peeking through windows. James helps me sometimes, but mostly not. I'm sure he'd kick ass in a fight, but he's actually a pacifist. Or maybe it's because he doesn't like touching people, I dunno. Either way, I usually find them. Often, they make some drunken mistake, either celebrating their victory or lamenting their lot in life, sitting on porches and silently complaining to the stars. That's when they're at their most nab-able."

Her voice leaks out. "Why don't the police catch them?"

There we go. Audible confirmation she's alive. "Meh, they're too busy. They already got credit for catching whoever in the first place, and they don't have time to redo their work. Busy with the next case and all that. They've got a budget for people like me."

"You're not the only one?"

"Oh God, no, I've got major competition, and there are only so many jobs out there. I'm thinking of branching out to more *personal* searches to help make ends meet, businesses looking for escaped embezzlers, drug dealers looking for comrades gone AWOL, but it just seems unethical."

"And this isn't?"

"Touché. But at least I don't think catching you means your death sentence."

"You can't know that. You don't even know who your boss is."

"Touché again. How about this, if I sense even a drop of danger, I'll just save you."

She scoffs. "Yeah, right."

"I will! We'll go out on the lam, just you, me, and Finn. We hop from place to place all the time anyway, so we'll be hard to pin down."

"Hop?"

"We've got no money. We couch surf or get rooms in hostels. Whatever works."

"They have those around here?"

"You'd be surprised."

"That…sounds horrible."

"Hence why I need that seventy-five grand so much." He rests his head against the door with a small *thud*. "I'm serious, though. I'd save you. You're too nice a girl to get hurt."

She sounds like she wants to throttle him suddenly. "Then don't hurt me. Let me go."

He puffs out a breath, his mind tossing scenarios back and forth and coming to an honest conclusion. "If my boss really wants you taken, even if I drop you back safe and sound, who's to say you won't be taken again? By someone else this time. Someone less scrupulous than me."

"You make yourself sound like a hero."

He grins at that. "I might just be, you never know. Stopping criminals and saving damsels."

"By kidnapping them."

"Well, the best heroes are morally gray, anyway."

She shifts on her side of the door. He wonders what she's doing over there. He wishes he could see her. Is she in pajamas? Is she tucked under the blanket? Is she giving him the stink-eye?

"Hey," he says. "What do you need right now?"

There is a long pause, one that seems to go on forever while he hangs here, waiting for her next word. It's different than waiting for James because he knows what his brother wants to say. This woman is new. She's a challenge. She's exciting.

"I want space," she says finally.

Ah, and there's the rub. "Okay, rainbow. Sweet dreams, okay?"

Unexpectedly, she replies. "You, too."

It warms him more than it should. Getting up with a quick groan, stretch, and pop to his back, he shuts the paper screen doors against the night, admiring the beauty of this place. James has perfect taste. Finding this empty home was pure luck, and their boss was more than willing to front the rental bill.

Elijah hopes Boss Man's not all bad. There must be a reason for all this.

He just wishes he knew what it was.

James wanders to the bathroom, his bladder angry at him for waiting too long. If his brother wasn't already in their ensuite, he'd use that, but apparently, he and Elijah's bodies are in sync.

The pressure below his navel makes James take longer strides than normal, wiping sleep from his eyes while simultaneously trying to keep himself half passed out. If he stays awake at night, his head starts whirling over all the things he did wrong that day, so it's better to be lulled by his brother's dreamtime breathing and follow him into oblivion. There is safety in sleep.

Fumbling in the midnight dark, he opens the main bathroom door (...why is it closed?) and squints at the mirror sconces which bleed a harsh yellow light (...why is there light?). The Beta Distraction stands, soaked to the skin with her mouth in a shocked, perfect O. Facing him, one of the burgundy red towels of this place wraps around her torso while another scrubs through her hair, leaving it wavy, long, and damp over her slim collarbones. She's showing more skin than he's ever seen on a woman, and her shape is perfect. Nipped in in the right places, flared out in others. Childbearing hips, they call them. Beta or not, she looks made for breeding.

Clean as she is, her flesh still steaming from the heat of her shower, James can smell her for the first time. Heady sandalwood soap is the first scent, but underneath, there's something sweet. Something unknown. Something he can only catch the tiniest waft of.

He wants her immediately.

Such a damn distraction.

"I'm sorry!" she blurts, hands going to her towel and cinching it tighter. "I thought everyone was asleep! It's just...it's been days, and I..."

She doesn't need to say another word. James understands the need to be clean. Sweaty, grimy clothes make him want to strip down to nothing but what God gave him, no matter where he is.

"I'm done, though!" she squeaks, rivulets of moisture trickling down her shoulders and leaving clear stripes behind. What would they taste like? Soap, or sweetness? "I'll get out of your way!"

He forces his lungs to still, not wanting to breathe her in as she blurs by. Her heels do their now-familiar stomp as James keeps his gaze firmly locked on the tiles at his feet. Only when her door closes does he allow himself to step into her humidity, but her scent remains. Her stupid, Beta, somehow perfect scent.

Turning, he flicks the light switch off—one never wastes electricity —and heads back to his own room. He'll wait for Elijah to be done, even if his bladder explodes in the meantime.

The Beta's perfume draws a line of color down the hallway, his nose making his imagination run wild.

There's no way he's sleeping tonight.

There is a brusque knock, loud and singular, making Katelyn jump out of her reverie. The now-familiar door swings open, cursing her and allowing one of her Alpha captors to catch her in the act of doodling whatever she can remember of Zeb's tattoo, the swoops and stains of it.

It's Finn. He stands, leaning against the doorframe in the early afternoon light. It casts him a bit in shadow as he delivers a flat and dispassionate "Eat"…but is Katelyn imagining things or is it in a softer tone this time?

Again, he doesn't look at her. Especially not like he did last night. Lying in bed, she couldn't stop picturing how his focus hovered on her center. What was this silent man thinking about?

"Come," he states, nodding his head toward the hallway.

She decides not to fight it. The staunch determination for her hunger strike still sits heavy in her thoughts, but the gnashing of her belly finally wins out and tells her brain to go straight to hell. It's not like she could have done this indefinitely, anyway.

You must stand strong, so saith The Lifestyle. *Weakness is what will drive you away from normalcy, giving you a list of reasons why you can trust Alphas and Omegas. But they're lies. Lies we tell ourselves when we forget that we are Betas, and Betas are best.*

Ignoring that, she asks, "Do you have coffee?" Addiction is a terrible thing.

"Yes."

"Can I have some?"

"No."

Then Zeb appears over his stepbrother's shoulder, grabbing Finn and choking him teasingly. "Yes, you sadist. Don't be so...ugh! You want it over ice, Miss Katelyn? It's already hot outside."

She salivates. "Yes, please."

Caffeine! Sweet, headache-killing caffeine!

She wants this more than food.

That sweet smile lights up Zeb's face, and he drags away his brother. For his part, Finn goes mutely, undisturbed and without fuss. Calm and collected. Cool as a sheet of marble. Katelyn, however, has a heart like a rattling tambourine as she slips out after them. Damn her grumbling belly. She shouldn't be doing this. This is their territory. No matter how much banter may pass between them, they are not friends. She is more like prey, and the haunting feeling that it might not be a bad thing makes her want to grind up her own bones for voodoo curses.

The rice paper screens to the garden have been shut as a gentle summer rain falls in the courtyard. It makes the halls narrow and dark, but in a way that's cozy instead of claustrophobic. As they make their way down the corridor, she asks, "What are these other rooms?" She's been sneaking out nightly to try and smash her way inside them after all...no matter how often she's caught in the act.

Zeb doesn't look back but juts a thumb over his shoulder at the one at the end of the hall behind them. "Our bedroom."

"You share?"

Finn deigns to answer. "Why wouldn't we?"

Zeb points again. "You know the bathroom. Across the courtyard is something like an office. Bedroom three, though it's more like a storage closet of all sorts of Chinese decorations and art."

Ooh. She wants to go into that one.

"Around the corner is the kitchen, of course. Living room. And past there is a little home gym."

That one takes her by surprise. "A place like this has a gym?"

"I know, right?" Zeb says. "I think the owner is a Beta. Alphas don't really need to gym it up, but you're welcome to as long as you don't plan to bean me in the head with a barbell. Don't know what your routine is to keep that perfect shape of yours." He does turn this time, biting his lip and ticking his eyebrows up playfully. "Aerobics? Gymnastics? Pilates? Kegels?"

She blushes again. She's just shaped like this normally. It makes sense, given her body's affliction. One of the plusses to her many minuses.

They turn the corner, Zeb jabbering. "Finn does his martial arts every day, though. I join in sometimes, but more out of boredom than any real passion. I suck at it. I'm better in a bar brawl than I am at something so technical and specific. I don't like rules, as I'm sure you've noticed by now."

He doesn't force her anywhere this time, leaving her standing in the kitchen entryway while he plunks his brother down and sits next to him, butting their shoulders together before serving himself from a center plate artfully arranged with a palette of veggies, rolled prosciutto, more cheeses than she's ever seen together, and swirled, colorful dips flecked with seasoning. There are even a few radish rosettes in the mix.

"Did you do this?" she asks, unable to look away from the masterpiece.

"Finn did." Zeb shoulders him again before grabbing his face and smooshing his cheeks. "He's a fucking artist."

Finn takes his abuse like a champ, the hovering carrot outside his lips the only sign that he had plans other than to be molested by his brother.

"But!" Zeb says, leaving Finn be and gathering more on his plate. "I wish he'd make something with cream sauce someday. Will you, darling? For me? Please?"

His brother stabs a fork into a slice of meat and nods. Pleased, Zeb wiggles happily in his chair and crunches away on celery. If Finn is stunning, Zeb is adorable. Who would have thought a large, muscular, intimidating Alpha could be so…cheerful. Childlike. Even though he flips from *that* to a sex bomb waiting to explode.

"Sit," Finn tells her.

Right. She's hovering.

Still tentative, she makes her way to the other side of the table and takes a seat. It's a shame to see the beautiful charcuterie board get slowly mutilated as the Alphas dive in. Unwilling to let everything get spoiled so quickly, she plucks up three radish rosettes and puts them on her plate, only to find Finn watching her fingers.

"They're pretty," she says. "Do you mind if I draw them later?"

Finn's eyes flick to hers, icy blue and lashed with blonde, something she'd first noticed when she was drawing him. It's exotic. Hypnotizing. Having his attention is like having an audience with a reclusive, powerful, fairy tale prince.

Mouth full, he looks down at her plate again and nods. Zeb's slow smile can't be beat as he slides his gaze back and forth between the two of them.

A lump of unnamed emotion in her throat, she tries to speak. "Coffee?"

"Oh! Right!" Zeb leaps up and goes to the gourmet countertop. Katelyn scans for a knife block but finds none. It was stupid to look. It's not like she's going to stab these Alphas to death.

No weapons to be found, she watches Zeb's strong back as he opens cabinet after cabinet to no avail. Through a mouthful of food, and without looking, Finn states, "Farthest right, middle shelf."

"Ah!" his brother chirps.

The ease between them, the closeness, Katelyn wishes she had that. Someone to share minds with, to touch without worry, to tell her secrets to. They look nothing alike, but that adds to their charm. Like the koi fish in the pond, they are yin and yang, dark and light, always swirling around each other.

If she stayed here, could she be part of their dance? Someone who belonged?

What is she thinking!? How stupid! She was supposed to have yet another painful date with Thomas last night. When she didn't show, he likely called her mother. They're probably both in a panic right now, yet here she is eating decorative crudité with one man who wants to burn her down and another who wants to eat her alive.

Absentmindedly spreading fig jam over a piece of bread and lining it with brie, she wonders where she is again. She's been obsessing over that, hour after hour in her solitude. The city would never house some-thing so beautiful, so even if she escapes this place, she's going to have a heap of trouble. She'll have to wind her way through the trees, try to find a neighbor's house, get to a phone, and call the police.

What happens after she calls the police?

That's where her mind is when Zeb plops beside her and takes hold of her wrist, guiding her food to himself so he can eat from her fingers. He moves quickly at first but slows down as he puts his mouth on her, his dark eyes slipping closed and his scent filling the air. Watching his supple lips take what she'd planned for herself makes her thighs clench and her jaw slacken.

This. This is the intimacy she wants.

He hums his approval. "Good choice, rainbow. I should have you feed me every day."

Her tummy flips and fills with butterflies. Leaning towards her, he traces her neckline, grazing the tight turtleneck she'd worn for self-defense despite the summer heat, which only seems to grow the more he touches her.

"Why are you doing that?" she asks in a way too breathless for her liking.

"To make you want me." He leans in closer. "Do you want me? Because I think I want you."

He ducks and puts his mouth just under her ear, licking a stripe that makes her cry out…then he pauses, his breath hitching.

No.

No, no, no, this can't happen. She can't let it happen.

She dives away, jamming her body against the countertop and pulling air in in jagged gasps. She clamps her hand down over the slick stripe of moisture he drew on her skin, too close to where it matters. Her body is taken over by a longing ache that centers in her lower belly, arousal tingling where it's absolutely not supposed to. She can't get wet for him. He's an Alpha, he'll smell it, so she focuses on her anger versus the feeling of him all over her. His scent drowning her. His heat welcoming her.

"You can't do that!" she yells.

He looks devilishly proud of himself. "I think you liked it."

"Like hell I did! The minute I come out, you maul me?"

"Oh, rainbow, that's not mauling. I can show you the difference. All teeth and nails and rutting into your wet heat so hard, I blow your little mind. What do you think, sweetheart? Can I make you come for me?"

Her cheeks flare. She can feel it all the way to her ears.

"Eat," Finn interrupts them. Then he levels his gaze at Zeb, holding it for far too long. "You stop."

Zeb lifts his hands in surrender. Winking at her, he leans forward and takes up another piece of bread, soft with a perfect flaky crust. He slowly spreads the fig jam over the top, dark and sweet, and lines it with brie again, replacing what he'd taken from her, his mouth against her fingertips and his breath hot against her palm. He purrs. "I can feed you too, if you want. Come on. Come to your Alpha."

She holds back a whimper.

"I said stop." Finn has said more words today than she's heard in her entire time here. If she didn't know better, it's almost like he's protecting her.

Lifting her chin in defiance, she nods toward the other side of the table. "Get away. Go sit over there."

"You gonna boss me around, Miss Katelyn?"

"If you get to bully me, I get to bully you back."

Zeb chuckles at that, and it makes her proud. She made an Alpha laugh. She made him happy.

She hates that it matters.

"Okay," he says, giving in. He lifts and circles back to the counter where the coffee brews, the small pot filling the air with something that almost disguises their scent. Despite the need for her daily dose of caffeine, Katherine regrets the loss of what makes the pair of them irresistible.

Ice clinks and clatters in the large glass he pulled down for her. He whistles all the while as if this was any other normal day and not the weirdest, most dangerous experience in her life.

They'll lull you into thinking they're just people, so saith The Lifestyle.

And maybe they are…until they aren't. Until they bite you and seduce away your young, impressionable teenagers. Until they take themselves a Beta bride, willing or not.

Making a clear statement, Finn shoves her plate closer to her chair with a heavy flick, scraping it against the wooden table. Without thought, she moves to obey. Ducking into her seat, hand still clamped on the curve of her neck, she takes a bite of what the Alpha made for her. It's like he's taking care of her, like they say in all the online forums she's absolutely not supposed to go to. Not supposed to read. Not supposed to fantasize over.

The food is delicious. Threads of sweet, tart and savory cross her tastebuds in silence while Zeb makes up her coffee, tossing out guesses she doesn't bother to answer, since they're all correct. Things like, "I bet you're a girl who likes extra cream. More than a couple sugars. Finn, do we still have hazelnut shots?"

"Mm."

"Sweet!" Zeb ducks into the fridge and digs. Katelyn tries her best not to pay attention to the hard angles of his rear wrapped in black cargo pants but fails miserably. After three flavor shots, the perfect amount, he lays her offering before her with a flourish. "As my lady requests." Leaning over the table, he runs his fingers through her hair, marking her again as he lifts her chin and lowers his voice to silk. "Go on, rainbow. Tell me to bend over backwards for you. If you want it, I'll do anything. Everything. Food, drink, talk, touch—for right now, I'm yours."

A swooping clench grabs onto her lower belly, and again she finds she can't do this. Trembling, she loads her plate as fast as she can and grabs her drink, dashing to her room and slamming the door closed with her heel. Finn's muffled voice is clipped when his words ring out, "I told you to stop."

His audible emotion makes her shiver. One is seducing her with tantalizing touches and breath-stopping licks, the other is wooing her with nothing but his existence. Knees watery, she makes her way to her nightstand and sets down her afternoon prize of long-awaited sustenance. She wants it, but she's about to give it up right quick. She takes a deep, heaving breath and opens the drawer, taking out her two pill bottles and getting what she needs, ignoring how it sours her insides and sizzles her senses.

If only she didn't have to be this way. If only she could be the perfect girl her mother wants. If only she could hate the males who have trapped her in their tangled web.

If only she wasn't an Omega.

CHAPTER 5

DREAMS

ELIJAH STANDS with his hands on his hips and sighs at his brother's tone—harsh, rare, and brain-snagging. Does that mean he owes their Beta beauty an apology? He was really into it this time. The slight hint of her scent once he got close was enough to get him half hard. Will wonders never cease.

He tugs James's hair tight, making his brother turn to face him. "Jealous, Jamsie?" James goes to wave him away, but Elijah only tugs harder, tipping his brother's head all the way back. "Tell me. Say it."

Eyes narrowed slightly, James frowns, a little pull to his lips.

"Bingo," Elijah says, soft and teasing. Quiet, so she won't hear. "I didn't take you for the jealous type."

James's voice is a low murmur. "I'm not."

"Hmm. Is that so? Then what are you?"

For that, his stepbrother has no answers, only sliding his gaze to the side. Elijah is willing to bet he doesn't even know, himself.

"I'd be good to her," Elijah whispers.

There is a thick swallow, and James's Adam's apple bobs, neck extended until his tendons draw straight lines down his throat. "She doesn't matter. You should be good to our Omega."

"What if this is practice?" James tries to pull away again, but Elijah only gets closer, daring him to put his thoughts into words. "I've never been with a woman before. I need to learn all her sensitive spots. I need her to scream for me."

Heat sings through James's eyes, a flare that makes that ice blue turn denim-dark as his pupils dilate. Oh, yes. He absolutely likes her.

"You should practice too, you know. Be ready for that Omega you dream of. Know every secret, sacred space a lady needs to be touched. Make her want you. Fall in love with you."

"With us," he says, but it comes out strained.

"We'll see, Jamsie." He presses a kiss into his brother's hair. "We'll see."

In the dark spaces within her mind, clutching her head in her hands, Katelyn is empty of everything except agony.

"But I was falling for you!" Thomas says, hands flinging into the air in frustration. "I trusted you! I was going to give you everything!"

No, he was going to take it all away. Still, regardless of whether it's a nightmare or dream, Katelyn can't find her voice when it comes to him.

"I can't marry you now!" he cries. He sounds so hurt that sympathy snares her. "I thought you were a clean girl. A nice girl. How could you lie? Don't you know how important this is?"

"I don't believe it," her mother adds through tears, wringing her hands. "We've been together all this time. How could you have possibly hidden it?"

It's the medicine. As soon as Katelyn felt the heat in her belly, she ran away. A Lifestyle doctor found her and knew exactly what she was. He saw through her like glass, and his pity was painful. Through the years, he has been her only confidante. Her co-conspirator. Her pusher and her dealer. Katelyn can't even count how much money she funneled to him once she was able, but it never mattered. His kindness mattered. Her secrets mattered.

"Keep hiding it, Katie." Thomas and her mother speak in one, over-lapping voice. It echoes in the blank void around them, a space of white light where nothing exists but the three of them, positioned in a tight triangle of blame. "Tuck it away forever. Don't let anyone see. Keep things as they are."

They are haunting, the way they look at her. Love, loathing, and loss mix while Katelyn quivers like a child, curled over and holding her belly. Her forever family and her future family stare down at her as if she were an abomination.

They are betrayed.

"But it hurts, Mama," Katelyn whimpers, clutching at herself hard enough to leave bloody nail prints in her skin.

"Oh, Katie." With low heels, her mother walks closer, the lines in her face softening as her grimace fades. "Maybe I can help you."

Thomas wisps away in a haze of smoke as her mother steps forward, slow and tentative, as if Katelyn would bite. She has the teeth to do it. She's supposed to break skin and claim her mate. A mate she will never have.

"We'll keep it a secret." Her mother clasps her hands over her breasts, fingers winding together and knuckles turning white. Despite her distance, she seems hyper real. Katelyn can see every pore, every tiny hair. Her mother's scent, soft like baby power and normally a source of comfort and home, fills her with hot shame. She is so, so sorry. It's not her fault, but she's sorry anyway. "You don't have to do this alone anymore. You can come stay with me during your heats. I'll keep you out of sight. If you can just have them in privacy, maybe you won't need to take that medicine anymore."

She's right. She could go on a regular dose. She could just be a normal Omega. Still hidden, but not hurt.

"I want that, Mama. Please help me. I can't do this anymore."

"I'm your mother, Katie. I love you. I'd do anything for you." After a long pause, she whispers, "I wish you had trusted me sooner."

Then her mother wisps away too, leaving Katelyn alone in her dream, sweating and nauseous, a tangle of pointed spikes raking through her insides and leaving open wounds behind.

"I can't hide it," she whispers, voice catching. Her tears well. Her bile rises.

Katelyn is dying.

Even in her dreams.

Another knock rouses Katelyn from her slumber. Why do they bother? They just come in anyway.

When Zeb proves her right and pokes his head in, she's woozy. Uncaring of the threat he poses, she flops her head down again and begs it not to hammer her into the ground.

"You bring on my symptoms, you know," she mutters. It's the most honesty she can give him.

"Is that why you ran away?" Concern flits over his face for a moment before he shakes his head. "Aren't you being a little dramatic?"

"Look at the evidence. Whenever you corner me, it happens."

He seems to consider this, his hand tightening on the door handle. "Maybe it's only because you're so afraid. What do you think I'm gonna do? It's not like I'm gonna mate you. Just calm down, take a breath and—"

"Let you do whatever you want to me?" She closes her eyes and curls tighter, knees to her chest. His scent dips, and she can taste his dismay in the air. She doesn't like that. She wants his undeniable cedar scent to sing.

What is wrong with her?

Alphas and Omegas are meant to be together, so saith The Lifestyle. *Betas have no place in their filthy circles. If they must exist, let them exit in their own bubble, far, far away.*

Shoving her face in her pillow, she grumbles, "I was supposed to have a date, you know. My fiancée was going to take me out last night. A stupid summer carnival."

"Didn't know one was around."

"It comes every year. It's the kind where the rides shake so badly, it's like their bolts are going to rattle out of their sockets and send everyone crashing to the ground. I get chills whenever I ride one of those things. Do you get those nightmare flashes where the ferris wheel just rolls off its track and starts crushing everyone on the fairground? It's all screams, but you're locked inside that little metal box, so you can't do anything but ride the circle."

"Sounds pleasant," he says with a grimace. "Does your fiancée know that you don't seem too keen on the idea?"

"I didn't tell him," she admits. Damn her. She's running her mouth again. "I'm trying so hard to be what he wants. You're going to ruin it all."

"Seems like you have problems with or without me."

He has no idea.

There is a long silence. Then a heavy sigh. Then a deep grunt and an exasperated, throaty groan. "I can't believe I'm going to say this. Ugh! Okay. Damnit. Fine. Listen, we take a pay cut if I can't get you in bed, but we still get a good chunk of money just for holding you here."

"So?"

"Why don't I just take the pay cut?"

She lifts her head. Zeb's eyes are locked on the ceiling as if it wronged him. His black hair cascades beautifully over his shoulders, reflecting the overhead light and, behind him, the hallway glows. Looking out her window, she realizes the sun has set. How long has she been out for? Crickets chirp in the garden, symphonic and eerie as the closed courtyard screen pins them in this space between. The rain has stopped but her heartache hasn't. He's so enthralling, she wants to dive into him, but she couldn't get up now if she tried.

"You'd do that for me?" she asks.

A sigh gusts through his nose. "I'll stop touching you." His lips pull into a lopsided smirk. "Though I can't promise to stop flirting. It seems to come by instinct."

She knows something about instinct. "What if this keeps happening? What if I can't stop?"

There is a long pause. He bites his bottom lip, the pink flesh disappearing so long that Katelyn wants to draw it out again. Maybe with a kiss.

"Then I let you go. I make sure no one else can take you until we can get that oblivious fiancée of yours to keep you close. Keep you safe. I told you, if there was danger, I'd save you." Determination flashes in his eyes. "I meant it."

"But then you get nothing."

He lowers his gaze. "I know."

She snuffles, swiping at new tears. He seems withdrawn, like he's calculating the impact she'll have on his life in tangible, weighted dollars and cents.

Or maybe he's just concerned for her.

Maybe he's thinking about what happens now. What tomorrow looks like, and the day after.

Maybe he'd really protect her.

"We saved you dinner." He shrugs. "We seem to be doing that a lot lately. If you're worried about your health, I'm sure starving yourself isn't going to make it any better."

Fair. "What are you feeding me tonight?"

"Finn made chicken with cream sauce."

"Like you asked for?"

His familiar grin returns. "Finn will do anything for me."

Would he do anything for her, too? If she stayed? If she sat between them at dinner and rested her head on his shoulder like Zeb does…

It warms her, but not with the sexiness of it. More the sweetness. They'd let her be an Omega. They'd help her stop this pain. Maybe they'd even love her.

She flicks her eyes to the radish rosettes that sit, withering on her uneaten plate from this morning. She's been…ungrateful, maybe.

"Thank you for worrying about me," she says. "I promise I'll eat."

His grin softens. It looks almost shy. "Then thank you, too."

His scent blooms into happiness. Pride. It croons in a way that calls to her whole body.

She can't help it. Her treacherous, Omega mind whimpers the dangerous word, *Alpha.*

And also, *Mine.*

James watches Elijah strut into the room with a devilish smile, as if he just snatched the world's most bejeweled crown from the king's sorry head and got away with not even a backwards glance.

"Guess who's eating?" he says.

The Distraction. Good.

"She's also feeling a bit better." Elijah closes their bedroom door and links his hands behind his back, kicking his feet out in slow sweeps as he saunters closer. "But I promised I wouldn't rub all over her anymore."

That's counterintuitive, considering.

James sits up on their wide, king size bed and stares at his step-brother, face locked in neutral even as his mind twirls.

Elijah chuckles. "I know what you're thinking."

That this new frame of mind is a complete 360 from his brother's monologue about making this woman scream for him and whatnot. Even James has considered what that would look like. Feel like. It's… intriguing. That haunting whiff of her scent tickles his memory. He wants more of it. He wants it closer and all around him. He wants to be able to identify it. Taste it on his tongue.

Distraction, indeed.

"I can still seduce her without all the touchy-feely, though," Elijah says with a sage nod.

"How?"

He taps his mouth twice. "This."

Elijah's sweet talking *has* earned them most of their successes in life. Still.

"What if it doesn't work?" James asks.

"There's where things get tricky." Elijah runs his hands through his dark hair and twists it into a knot on the crown of his head, looping it in the tie he keeps circled around his wrist. "She's worried about her fiancée, which I admit is messy, but I dunno, something about the way she talked about their relationship seems off to me. She rattles my protective bone somehow." He huffs. "I need…I dunno…her *desire* for us to outweigh her fear of whatever risks there are. If it never does… well, I told her we'd take the pay cut."

If James could blanche any whiter, he would.

"I maaay have also said we'd let her go if she keeps"—Elijah waves his hand aimlessly—"tweaking. I'm not willing to sell my soul over this."

That streak of nobility is one of the reasons James loves him so much. He runs a thumb over the scar on his inner wrist. "Then what happens to us?"

"Mom and Dad?"

No. Absolutely not. Staying with them is like slow death. Mom sees how close he and Elijah are, and she hates it. She's always trying to force them apart. If she had her way, James would stay her "poor baby" and live with her forever, like he's some kind of broken invalid. He's not. There's more to him than a cinched throat and a blank face. Elijah tries every day to make him believe that.

"You hate the idea." His brother sighs and jumps onto the bed next to him, crossing his socked feet at the ankles and tucking his hands behind his head. His elbow rests on James's lower back as he sits, the point of contact a soothing balm, and it softens the coiling knot in James's chest.

"I hate it, too," Elijah continues. "It won't be forever, though. Just for a little while. I can get another job pretty quick, and then we can go back to Felicia's."

The boarding house. James doesn't mind that place. He earns part of their keep by cooking and cleaning, and no one bothers him too much. There are enough people there to choke an elephant, though, and some of them are nosy. At least they don't know that he and Elijah are brothers. *Step*brothers. A key difference Elijah points out ad nauseam whenever James starts to feel the sting of his mother's concern.

He touches his scar again, and Elijah sees it. He swoops down and twines their fingers together with a half-smile.

"Right now, though, we're here. We've still got a shot. I never said I'd stop trying, so don't give up on me so quickly."

James nods, rubbing the soft space between Elijah's thumb and forefinger while his eyes drift around the room. The walls have dark wood stripes that line the white paint in well-spaced parallels, making them mirror the skeletons of the paper screens. The bedspread is black with slender stalks of bamboo stitched in white covering its surface. Cherry blossoms hang nonsensically from their offshoots. A fantasy image, and a little too on the nose, but he supposes whoever owns this house isn't interested in historical accuracy. Or maybe the right style of bedding is too hard to come by. With an unlimited budget, James would make this place as authentic as possible, but the way things are, he'll have to accept it as it is. Just like the rest of this situation.

"What was it?" Elijah muses. "*Anzuru yori umu ga yasashii?*"

Meaning: an attempt is sometimes easier than expected; fear is the greater danger. "You remembered?"

"I listen! When you talk, my every pore opens up to soak it in! Don't doubt my obsession or whatever. Listen to Sensei Joe. He's one smart dude."

He is. James would like to meet him one day. He'd pay for an audience with his master if given the chance. Another thing he'd do with an unlimited budget.

"Will you try for her, too?" Elijah asks.

"No." Because it's the truth. James can't lie. He can't fake it. He either feels something or he doesn't, and even though the consequences are severe, he can't change that. A mild attraction doesn't mean he's willing to fall all over her. Fawn. Cough up words he doesn't have. "Only for our Omega."

Elijah laughs. "You stubborn ass."

He's not wrong.

———

Katelyn blinks open and immediately throws an arm over her face to block out the morning sun. What day is it? How long has she been here? It must be close to a week at this point.

Rough grunts echo from outside her room, rhythmic and patterned. One harsh sound, then three seconds pass. Another sharp exhale, then three more steady beats. Finn must be doing exercises again, but he hadn't made any noise before. What's different now? Curiosity wiggles around in her mind. Whatever it is, she wants to see.

Stifling a groan, she slides her legs over the edge of the bed, creaking into a sitting position. Scrubbing her eyes, a stretch pops her back in four separate places, which makes her head reel. She breathes through it, pretending she's filling a balloon and letting it empty again. Vertigo spins her in circles and her stomach threatens to release last night's dinner when she stands, but she manages to sneak over to peep through her door.

The paper screens are open, and the courtyard is bright. Morning shadows paint the grass in a darker shade where the roof overhangs the ground. Metallic chain downspouts chime in a low breeze as Finn wields some kind of stick, moving through more formations. Different this time. Tough and gruff. Warrior formations. If she's thought him graceful before, he's aggressive now, each sharp swipe of his weapon looking like it would break an arm if it were to make contact. Every time he halts a stroke in midair—something that must take extreme strength—he lets out a gust from deep in his gut, masculine and threatening. It's enough to make a girl's knees go weak.

Alpha, her inner self sighs.

She still needs to finish drawing him. She needs to—

Her door flies open again, making her stumble back as Zeb sticks his stupid face in, a toothbrush hanging from his mouth and white foam bubbling idiotically at the corners. "Stih bwein sneakwy?"

Her brows knit, not understanding his toothpaste-talk. …Still… being…sneaky, maybe?

She's not going to be distracted by his cute man-bun. Or his naked chest. Or the smooth expanse of skin that leads down to a trail of dark hair just under his navel, disappearing into low-hanging pajama bottoms. Not even the jut of his hips and the muscular ridge that draws a line down his body can catch her attention. Nope. Absolutely not. She doesn't care at all.

Her eyes rocket to his and stay there. "I'm allowed to look out of my own room. Or the room you keep me in. Or… oh, hell, you know what I mean."

His eyebrows tick up as he smirks, the handle of his toothbrush bobbing with the motion. "Whahevah, wainbow."

He turns away and she pokes her head out after him, watching him stride back into his room down the hall. She can't hear him spit but is willing to bet that's what he's doing. She has the distinctive urge to follow him and peek through those old-fashioned keyholes. Thank God the mint overwrote his cedar smell. She's not ready for that today. She remembers his tongue on her, but that's dangerous territory. Thinking about that is like drowning herself in quicksand.

Another grunt pulls her attention. Finn has taken no notice of her, or if he has, he doesn't let it show, as focused and uncaring as always.

Her hidden, stifled, Omega ego finds that unacceptable.

She turns back and slathers herself with her morning cream—that viscous, evil, oh so necessary scent blocker—gritting her teeth through the sting. Next, she slides on a skin-tight crop top with triangles of electric blue and hot pink intersecting in pleasing ways. The neckline is still high, covering her mating glands, kept scentless and smooth as glass. She barely notices them in the mirror, but still hides them at all costs. Their thin skin can be easy to recognize, especially if she blushes. They get as pink as the apples of her cheeks sometimes.

High waisted pants, taut on her butt but flaring into bell bottoms comes next, and secretary-style glasses frame her eyes. She won't do makeup. The bag Finn packed her has some, but that's a step too far. She's already going to go to hell for this, as it is.

Modesty is a defense against the immoral thoughts of others, so saith The Lifestyle. Not that she's ever subscribed to that one.

Throwing her wavy hair into a high, messy knot, she shoves a pencil in to keep it wound tight. She doesn't have a mirror, but she can catch a ghost of her reflection in her bolted, padlocked window. Good enough.

Snagging her sketchbook, she steps outside with her head held high, as if she belongs here and isn't a prisoner. Finn still doesn't look at her when she steps into the garden, toes curling in the grass, nor does he give her a second of his attention when she hovers by the bench, perpendicular to him.

Indignancy sets her awash in heat.

Look at me, her brain pulses.

Sticking out her chin, she stands in front of him, far enough so he doesn't beat her with what looks like a broomstick, but close enough where he can't help but see her. He pauses, but the way he scans her body from bottom to top says that she won the battle he didn't even know they were fighting.

Taking a page from his book, she wordlessly folds her legs and plops on the ground, feeling the cool dew seep through her clothes. It doesn't matter. She lets her book fall open in her lap, her thumb already wedged into the place where Finn's likeness lies half rendered in mechanical pencil. Her glaring eyes dare him to tell her to stop.

She stares for just a moment too long before beginning her work. He, too, lingers for a few beats before he picks back up his routine, ensuring his steps and thrusts come nowhere near her. It's hard to capture him in motion, but the angles of his jawline in the morning sun are clear, and his glass eyes are haunting. She uses her thin eraser to draw white lines for his lashes through the deepening gray of her drawing, which is the coup de grâce, making him truly recognizable. Yes. This is the man who captivates her.

The other one pops into view behind him, still shirtless and mouth-watering. He leans onto the sturdy wood of the doorway with his arms crossed and a familiar smile blooming. She wants to invite him to sit beside her, which is moronic, so she clenches her teeth and keeps to her work, feeling the breeze pass through her hair as Finn swings his pretend-blade hard enough to make swooping sounds.

Tense as she is, this feels like home. A dream home. One where she can exist and find peace.

How strange life can be.

Taking a breath, she moves down the line of Finn's neck to the divots of his collarbone and the curve of his pectoral, just barely hidden by his tank top.

"Will you finish that today?" he asks, gracing her with words as his arm arcs to the side and his torso twists to follow.

"I think so." Which is a pity, really.

"Then you can just draw another one," Zeb calls from where he watches her. "And another. Until we have a gallery of your love for us."

She snorts. "Vain."

"And presumptuous," he agrees, "but I want it on record you didn't deny my claim."

Finn pivots, swinging a swipe in his brother's direction. There is another pause, and a dry, "Don't you own clothes?"

"Meh." Zeb shrugs. "It's gonna be hot today. Surprised our lady friend can wear so much, herself. You're gonna fry in that. We don't seem to have air conditioning."

Still focused on her drawing, she grimaces. She doesn't know what her sweat smells like but has no doubt her pheromones will make their way into it somehow. "Then I'll throw myself in the koi pool."

"Pond," Finn corrects. "And you can't."

"Yeah. You'll piss off Charlie and Wanda."

She cocks an eyebrow, sketching out Finn's broad shoulder. "Who?"

"The fish."

Oh.

"Finn, did you feed them this morning?"

"Mm."

"Well, let Miss Katelyn do it tomorrow. She has to make friends with our temporary pets."

His silence must be agreement. Oddly enough, that sounds peaceful and…nice. Domestic. Like doing laundry together or making meals. She'd kill for some scrambled eggs and bacon.

Her stomach growls a vicious gurgle that reverberates in the otherwise Zen atmosphere.

…Crap.

Her cheeks burn.

Wait! No! She's not ashamed. It's normal. It's totally a human thing to have happen when sitting in front of her Alpha kidnappers and trying not to drool all over them, right? It's normal after days of starving herself, right?!?

Finn's motions halt in mid stroke before he takes a frozen stance. Casting a cool glance over his shoulder, says, "It's not nine, yet."

Oh yeah, that tic of his. Breakfast is at nine o'clock every day.

All she can see is his white lashes, the neutrality of his expression, and his back flexing his shoulder blades. "…I'll make an exception."

Zeb doubletakes, uncrossing his arms. His face looks comical for its surprise, jaw slack and eyes wide. His brother hands him his implement of destruction before turning the corner and heading to their room, already pulling his damp shirt from his body.

Holy God Damn. If Zeb is fit, Finn is a deity.

"Not gonna lie, rainbow. This is a really big fucking deal."

Still watching where the Alpha disappeared, swooning over his scent as it hangs in the air, she promises, "I'll eat."

Elijah's mouth still hangs open, even ten minutes later. He can count on one hand the number of times James has compromised for him.

Strike that. He can count it on two fingers.

The first time was when he didn't know any better and tried to make himself something before school. James had gaped at him—which may as well have been a nuclear reaction. Boom. The second time was when they were first living on their own and Elijah went into an unexpected rut. He was going to tear the world apart if he couldn't get some fucking food in his fucking mouth. James had never moved quicker and cooked him a veritable banquet off-schedule. Other than that? No dice.

Both James and Miss Katelyn Anamarie Jones-Masters have locked themselves in their respective bathrooms to do their morning necessaries, so Elijah brings out the ingredients for their lady's request. Bacon and eggs is the breakfast of champions. He won't touch a single pan, though. He doesn't want to do anything to set off his brother. He's already going to be out of his comfort zone as is.

It's adorable.

He idly spins an egg on the countertop, whirling it and whistling to himself. There was a time when he used to eat raw eggs, but it was only to freak out his father. The old man would get the icks so bad he'd retch, and Elijah would laugh so hard he choked. Part of him misses those early days, back when family life was easy, but those were before he met James, and he'd put a rift in any relationship to have that man in his life.

Oops. Egg off the counter. Elijah groans as the damn thing splats on the floor, spitting its gooey whites in his direction.

"Goddamn sonofabitch," he mutters, fumbling for a paper towel to clean up his mess.

Katelyn peeks her head around the corner and catches him grumbling in mid-wipe, egg still smashed on the tile, but his toes now free from slime. Wonder of wonders, she giggles. He's surprised at how much the sound tickles him, and he chuckles back, shrugging. "This is why I'm not allowed in the kitchen."

"Clearly," she says through a dry smile. He can smell the scent of her toothpaste, but not the scent of her, which is disappointing. It makes him want to get up close and personal again, but a promise is a promise.

She surprises him by ripping off some paper towel herself and leaning over to help pick up what he haphazardly ruined. A little smirk lifts her cheeks. "I can cook if you want me to."

"Thought you already vetoed that."

She shrugs. "I can change my mind."

"No," James says, standing above them with his arms crossed. Elijah hadn't even noticed him come in. "Go sit."

Wiping up the last of the mess, Katelyn ignores him. "Where is the trash?"

Elijah nods his head in the general direction. "In the cabinet next to the sink."

To her credit, she doesn't look at his bare chest when he shows it off this time, fixated behind him on where her next mission objective lies. James is already in the pantry, taking out the cleaner and a rag to ensure no egg-spilled salmonella is left unsprayed and un-disinfected. Elijah grins, watching his every move, which is why he catches his stepbrother ogling Katelyn as she bends over to throw away the wad of yolk and shell.

He snaps his fingers quietly, catching his stepbrother's attention. "You think she has a nice ass," he mouths silently.

James's lips flatten into a straight line.

Bingo.

Pretending to ignore him, James hunkers down to spritz the cleaner, and Elijah sputters a laugh. Fine then. He turns to face the lady of the moment. "Miss Katelyn, would you like coffee again this morning?"

Her ass is still on display as she leans over to wash her hands. Tendrils of auburn hair trace over her covered neck and he finds he wants to nuzzle in again. "Are you trying to get on my good side?"

Ah, how he likes it when she talks. "Aren't I always?"

"I said sit," James states, bent over to pull out pans now.

Elijah's happy enough to comply, grabbing plates and scooting over towards the table, but it seems Miss Katelyn isn't in an obedient mood. She turns around, leaning her back against the sink, and stares at his brother, arms coiling over each other as her jaw ticks to the side.

It's a challenge.

Well, this is entertaining.

"You may have kidnapped me, but that doesn't mean you can control me."

James doesn't seem to agree. "Move," he says—for no reason, really. He doesn't need anything from where she is, he just wants her out of his space.

Silence is all he receives, and now their rainbow doesn't even bother to look at him. The two spend a moment avoiding each other's gaze, eyes at the ceiling, floor, and anywhere in between. She's giving his brother a taste of his own medicine.

This will not go well…

Getting bold, James reaches out and grabs her hips before stepping her sideways, moving her down the L shape of the counter, and—oh—Miss Katelyn *thwaps* his hand with a sharp snap! James glares. Elijah wants popcorn.

"You're not supposed to touch me," she says.

"He's not supposed to touch you." James ticks his chin in Elijah's direction.

"I thought you two were a package deal."

Elijah snorts. *Kid, you have no idea.*

Another stomach grumble rings out, and she lifts her hands in surrender. "Alright!" She removes herself to the ass end of the counter nearest to the dining room set and leans again. "Please, make your exception for me, *Alpha*."

James's ears...turn pink. Pink! What the absolute fuck?! No one other than Elijah has ever pulled such a response from his stoic stepbrother! He wants to tease James so bad, holding it in is literally painful, and his shoulders shake with barely contained laugher.

His brother is stalk-still for a moment, jaw tight like his insides are screaming—but screaming what? Good things? Bad things? Sexy things? Ahhhh, the tension!

At her next belly grumble, James turns and gets to work. Two overlarge pans are set on the gas stove with the familiar *tic-tic-tic* of the igniter and blue flame *whoomph*ing to life. He even digs in the upper cabinets and starts up the coffee pot.

Eggs crack, liquid gurgles, and scents and sizzles take over the room as their trio remains silent.

Katelyn is still pressed against the counter, watching James like he's a blockbuster movie. "My fiancée will be worried if I don't eat," she says, trying to cover up whatever is going on in that pretty head. "But I should take it in my room."

"I told you I won't bite," Elijah says. "Unless you ask me to. Then I absolutely will. But I can promise not to leave marks...unless you like marks, in which case I'm sure I could suck some hickeys into that silky skin."

She shivers, and he's willing to bet it's in a good way. "Is this you flirting?"

"I said I would."

"Dirty talk isn't flirting."

He grins. "It's my kind of flirting. You should ask my boyfriend. He'll tell you I have a filthy mouth when the mood hits me."

James drops something with a clatter, and Elijah's grin widens.

Food and drink are set on the table while he stares at their lovely captive. She's avoiding his eyes with a sour expression that says she'd like to set him on fire. It's cute.

James takes his seat, ripping into a slice of bacon with his teeth.

"Eat," he says with his mouth full, still bossing her. He should learn his lesson. Or maybe he just wants her to call him "Alpha" again.

She decides not to engage, instead eyeing the food. She turns her head side to side, reviewing each red place mat like she's debating where to sit. He and James are on opposite sides of the table, so no matter where she goes, she has to suffer through one of them.

"The devil or the master," Elijah says. "Pick your poison, sweetheart."

She chooses to stand, grabbing her coffee and taking a swig, hissing and panting to cool off her tongue before picking up her plate and shoveling food in her mouth with a satisfied groan. It's low, breathy and perfect.

James's ears go pink again. If Elijah could jump on him and smoosh his face, he would.

They finish their food in relative silence as his two compatriots try their hardest to pretend the other isn't there. Even Elijah is getting the cold shoulder, though she deigns to flick her eyes in his direction when he blatantly stares at her, careful to chew with his mouth closed for once. He imagines seeing scrambled eggs swimming in his mouth isn't conducive to sexual tension, but he's sure to lick his fingertips with broad stripes every time he finishes a piece of crispy bacon. She notices it without fail.

Eventually, her plate cleared, she gives them a wide berth and travels to the sink to rinse her dish.

Uh-oh.

James's shoulders tense a fraction, and his chair scrapes across the floor with a high-pitched shriek as he puts himself directly behind her. "Sit. Or leave."

She goes rigid. "I need to do something. Do you know how bored I am?"

"Let me," his brother says this time, a rare thing. It's not often he does something more akin to *asking* than *executing*. Elijah sees this gift for what it is, even if she doesn't.

The water from the faucet doesn't stop as she fumbles around, looking for a sponge despite the obvious dishwasher tucked in next to her. Who needs to wash by hand in a place this swanky?

James crowds behind her, his chest close enough to rest against her back. "Let. Me." he states again, no inflection, but the staccato thuds of his words say what his tone can't. Elijah's interest gives way to wariness. This can go sideways very fast.

He takes a deep breath through his nose, ready to intervene.

Katelyn can feel the heat of Finn as he stands behind her, pinning her to the spot. She can't let them treat her like this. If she has to spend God-knows-how-long here, she can't just sit in her room and draw. She can't avoid them all day every day, sneaking to the bathroom or spying through keyholes. She has to keep her Omega in check, yes. Ensure her secret stays safe, yes. But come on! She may still be weak, but she can't allow this masculine micromanagement to continue. Spinning around, she grits her teeth. "Back off."

Finn doesn't look at her. He doesn't have to. She knows exactly what he's feeling from his smell. His scent is one of absolute dominance, and she would like nothing better than to lunge forward to breathe him in, but she will not obey that Omega instinct. Alphas like control, but she refuses to let him have it. Her life is filled with obedience. Anything anyone wants of her is done immediately and without question—her mother, her soon to be curse of a husband—but here, with these men, she refuses to let it happen.

Even so, she can't keep it together; her body is betraying her. She thrums with his nearness, her skin tingling with the need for his touch. She's never wanted anyone like this, and she's going to drown if she lets herself.

She can't.

She won't.

"You bring on my symptoms," she tells this blond brother, sticking to her half-truth. "You want me on the floor?"

There's no change to Finn's expression, but Katelyn can smell it on him. Arrogance and disbelief.

"I think you're faking it."

Her face goes hot. How dare he? Zeb stands up as if to stop them, but she won't wait for her faux knight in shining armor to subdue her this time.

"You know nothing about it," she grits out, knees wobbling now.

"I think you're just trying to get your own way," Finn murmurs, staring somewhere around her breast line as her breath starts to pick up. "I think you're trying to play on our sympathies." He leans so close, she can feel his breath. "I think you're a brat."

Her thread of patience snaps. "Oh yeah? Well, I think you can fuck off!" She denies the urge to slap her hands over her mouth. It's running on its own again. Still, letting the anger out feels good. Cathartic. She's never said words like this, and they fly out like venom. She wants to hurt them, if only to push them away, these beautiful, dangerous Alphas. "I think you can fall off a cliff! I think you can take this job and shove it up your ass! I think you and your brother can go get mauled by a fucking tiger!"

Zeb's eyes go wider with every word and his easy smile dips into a crestfallen look she wishes didn't bother her so much.

She tosses words like javelins. "I don't care if you need money! I don't care about *you*! I don't want to be here, and I don't care if—"

There is a jarring ring, interrupting her rant, and Zeb jumps like he's been zapped. Swooping to his full height, he pulls a phone from a hidden pocket—one Katelyn will take good note of. When he looks at the screen, he shakes his head with a sigh and a resigned smirk on his face. "It's my boss."

The minute the phone goes to his ear, Katelyn shoves Finn away and screams. "HELP! LET ME OUT OF HERE! YOU DON'T KNOW WHAT YOU'RE DOING AND I NEED TO LEAVE! I'LL PAY YOU MONEY, JUST LET ME GO! PLEASE!"

Her blathering continues as her tears start to fall. She loses track of the words cascading from her mouth, only registering that they're endless as she begs and pleads for mercy.

Blocking one ear with his fingertip, Zeb's normally sunshine face becomes nothing but a self-deprecating grimace as he talks into the phone. "I told you she wasn't really into it. If she keeps screaming like this, she's gonna pop a lung. You want her to pop a lung?"

After listening for a brief moment, he advances toward her, and she outright climbs the counter, scaling it in a single jump before scrambling to stand on the high marble top. What the hell she thinks that's going to do is anyone's guess, but when she stands tall, heads over him, Zeb's playful grin returns in full force.

He holds out the phone. "Boss man wants to talk to you."

Her stomach sinks. Maybe this was a bad idea. What is she in for now? Her hand trembles as she reaches out, taking the device and willing herself to hang up and dial 911. But where is that going to get her? They'd stop her the minute she touched the dial pad. In the end, morbid curiosity makes her lift the phone to her ear.

"If…" she starts, her voice hoarse and ragged. "If you kill me, my fiancée will come for you."

There is a pause in which Katelyn wonders if she's doomed herself, until a warm chuckle fills her ears from the other side of the line.

She knows that voice.

"Hello, Katie," it intones. "You know, I think that's the first time I've ever heard you call me your fiancée."

Her train of thought glitches into static, ringing her ears and whitening out her mind.

It makes no sense. It does not compute. How could this possibly be?

It's Thomas.

CHAPTER 6
BETRAYAL

ICICLES FIND their way into her bloodstream, traveling from the center of her body to the ends of every extremity. It's like snow has fallen on her bare skin, lowering her body temperature and frosting over her veins with deadly white flakes. Her ears ring with a dreadful whine, as if she's been near an explosion, but there's nothing around her but breathless silence.

"How could you?" squeezes from her raw throat.

His voice is deep with a heavy sigh, like he's disappointed in her. "After what you said the other day, I looked into who you were close to and found that Omega friend of yours. You, my soon to be wife, friends with a…" His sigh returns. "Do I have to have to set up spies to watch you for bad behavior? You know how people are. Almost anything could give The Lifestyle a scandal. The media would have a heyday. Never mind the elders, you know my father is…not forgiving. Even if I wanted to protect you, I couldn't."

He says it like he's concerned for her. Caring and loving.

The only one he loves is himself.

"Katie, I don't want to lose you, but I can't let a full-on sympathizer into my life. You know my plans. They're going to rock The Lifestyle to its core as it is. I can't have Omegas who give into their disgusting desires in my wife's circle. I need them to reject it. I need them to be clean. To want to be like us. Please understand."

She cuts in before any other placating words have a chance to tumble from his terrible mouth. "Why am I here?"

He takes a deep breath. "Consider it a test. What better way to see where your loyalties lie than to have you live with two feral Alphas? Will you be loyal to The Lifestyle, or will you be a traitor to all we hold dear? All *your mother* holds dear."

The final comment backhands her. Her gut drops as sorrowful images of her tearful mother fill her, begging her to comply. Begging her to be a good girl. "Does she know you're doing this?" If she did, there would be no end to it.

"Of course not, Katie. I'm not a monster."

Yes, he is.

The words teeter on the edge of her tongue, threatening to fall out of her mouth and ruin everything. That can't happen. She needs to play on his sympathies. If she's going to do it, she's going to do it right here, right now. She needs to beg and plead.

She needs to tell lies.

She scours her brain. What does he want to hear? What would make her seem like a victim? Someone to save.

It hits her. She bites her lips and summons every pathetic bone in her body. "What if they hurt me?" Her eyes cinch tight, knowing her next words might be damning to the men in this room, but redeeming to the man over the phone. "I'm afraid."

"Oh, Katie…" He sounds heartbroken for her. She wants him dead. "Put me on speaker, honey."

With trembling hands, she reaches the phone out and presses the button with the megaphone.

"What's up, boss man?" Zeb says, a lift to one eyebrow and a frown on his face. He could only hear one side of the conversation, but his wary eyes are locked on Katelyn. Even Finn has his brows furrowed as he faces the window. An actual expression.

Thomas's voice is dark and grainy. "If you touch her against her will, if you harm a hair on her head, the deal is off."

It's Finn that speaks up, deep and taciturn, but clear. "How can I seduce her if I can't touch her?"

Katelyn's stomach flutters. Does that mean he wants to?

Thomas chuckles, malicious. "That's your problem." His voice softens, directing his words back to Katelyn. "See, honey? It will be okay. Just don't give in. Resist. Keep the faith, stay strong, and you can come out on the other side with every ounce of my trust."

The terrible thing is that she needs it to survive. For her mother to have everything she wants and deserves.

"How long am I going to be here?" How long does she have to withstand her Omega instincts and hide what she is while their auras wrap around her, their bodies a sinful temptation and their scents a gift from heaven. Zeb's smile alone is a siren's song and Finn's distance a baited lure.

"A month," Thomas says. "If you keep this up, stay pure and come out on the other side a good girl, I'll make all your dreams come true. You can even work again, how's that? At the college. We need people with your talent."

"I...you'll let me have a job?" she chokes out. Zeb's expression changes. Instead of staring at her with caution, he narrows his eyes in confusion. Finn's brows knit harder.

"Of course, but it would be with Lifestyle people keeping you on the straight and narrow. Keeping you mine. I'd do anything for you, Katie, can't you see that? If I say it, you know you can believe it."

The same way she believes in fairy tales.

Through bared teeth, she grinds out, "You owe me an apology." A ridiculous thing to say.

"Don't worry, sweetheart. I'll spend the rest of my life making it up to you."

And Thomas drops the call.

Elijah very much didn't like how that went. Every word of it set his teeth on edge. What the fuck have they gotten themselves into?

"Who is he?" he asks.

"My...fiancée," she says.

His whole face crinkles in disgust. She can't be serious. What the actual fuck?

"Tell me his name."

Katelyn at least has the wherewithal to look ashamed. "Thomas Bleaker."

The words douse him in cold water. His jaw drops and a sick sense of horror thuds in the barrel of his chest, ruining his lungs. "I'm working for *Thomas Bleaker*? That fucking Beta purist?"

Even standing on the counter, his phone clutched in her hands, she becomes impossibly small, shrinking in on herself. No wonder she's always running away from them at every turn. She's in that fucking Lifestyle cult. Betrayal sings through him, as if she mattered. As if he's known her for longer than just this short while.

How could he have actually wanted her?

How stupid is he?!

James presses his palms on the table, his mouth in a firm line. "Is that what you are? A purist?"

She rushes down from the countertop, her hands in front of her. She looks frantic, moisture welling in those jade eyes. "I'm not! I never asked for this! My mother is making me because—" and her trap snaps shut. Meek, she wraps herself in her arms, and a single tear drops to the floor. His foolish heart goes out to her, and he wants to scream at himself for it.

"Because why?" he asks, instead.

She is silent.

"How can you love someone like that?" he spits, vibrating with anger.

The Beta princess' lip trembles, and it's like someone reached into him and clenched his heart. Why does this hurt?

His voice breaks. "Are you really afraid of us?"

She lowers her head. "Who wouldn't be afraid of two men who kidnapped you?"

"Men?" he presses. "Not *disgusting Alphas*?"

Rushing him, she shoves his phone back into his hands with a choked sob. "I didn't say that! I would never! You're just people!"

She swipes at her eyes, tears falling in earnest, and before his buzzing instinct has a chance to stop her, she flees from the room.

Rain begins to fall outside. Only then does he realize the sky has gone dark and gray. A rumble of distant thunder almost covers her door slamming, ricocheting off its frame in a hard *thwack* that makes him flinch. He looks at James at a complete loss. Can they really do this? Can they keep this job, knowing that this is what they're doing? Helping that vicious man mind-fuck the woman he's supposed to love? A woman who doesn't seem to want him…

Before Elijah can say a word, his brother shoves himself off the table, an uncharacteristic twist to his lips. Without a sound, he rushes away, similarly locking himself in their room—a safe place. A haven.

Elijah needs his haven, too.

James stalks in their shared bedroom, his feet pounding the floor. Why does he care? Why does it matter? She's a distraction. She always has been and always will be. He wasn't lying when he said she was a brat, always causing a scene and making a bad situation worse.

But the way she looks at him…as if he's something beautiful. Something to be discovered. Admired. She's always eyeing him at a distance, unable to stay away.

He scours his hands through his hair. The door opens, and Elijah follows, locking them in and watching him with distress on his face. Is it James making him so worried, or the woman who rejects them at every turn?

"We don't need this," James insists. "Send her away."

"We need the money."

"I don't care about the money!" James hears the growl in his voice and Elijah's eyes widen.

…But they can't go back to mom and dad. If they do, they won't be able to…

James lands his rear on the floor, wrapping his arms around himself. He hates when things like this happen. Things aren't going in the way he expected, and it's like the walls are closing in. That phone call. That *man*. Her reaction. The consequences. James wants to scream and act out, but he's not a kid anymore. It's not allowed. He knows better.

It's his fault they're in this situation in the first place. He's ruining everything. His brother doesn't need him. He's holding him back. Always has been. He doesn't belong here, in this world, with this person. He is "other." He stands out for all the wrong reasons and does nothing but make trouble. He shouldn't be alive anymore, but he's too afraid to do anything about it.

Some strong Alpha. How laughable, if James ever laughed.

Elijah is on his knees in moments, cupping his hands around James's face. The touch is too rough, breaking him out of his spiral. "Eyes on me, Jamsie."

James doesn't like looking at people. Their faces shift too much and it's disorienting. He doesn't know what they want from him. He doesn't know what to do for them. They're only going to get mad at him. But Elijah—with his warm brown eyes bouncing from one of James's to the other—his brother is the only one he could watch for hours. He knows exactly what Elijah means. What he wants. He knows him as if they were soulmates.

And that's because they are.

"I know what you're thinking," Elijah says, his thumbs caressing the crests of his cheeks. "But you're wrong. I need you. Stay with me. Nothing else matters, right? Just you and me against the world. I told you we'll always be together. I meant it when we were fifteen, and I mean it now. I'll mean it for the rest of my life."

Elijah leans in, and their lips touch. It's not a gentle brush or a tease, it's a promise. Those large hands wind their way into James's hair as he moves closer, hovering above him and tilting his head backward, forcing his jaw slack. James's lips part, and Elijah cants his head to the slide, anchoring their mouths together and sweeping his tongue in, making a soft noise as James responds. James's tongue moves in waves as he tastes his stepbrother, salty from breakfast with a hint of sweetness. Maple. Elijah's scent amps up, that cedar deepening, nestling James in a forest where dappled light shines through the shadows of the trees. It's not right, not by a long shot, but this is all James has ever wanted for himself. It's selfish, but this is love. And his love is never ending.

***

Elijah worships him. His heart aches for him. Ever since he first met James, he's been all he needed. He's fascinating. When he looks at him, he never wants to look anywhere else. James is his. It doesn't matter if their parents realize how deep this goes. If they reject them, he'll deal with it. They don't need anyone who would dare separate them. The world can burn, so long as he can have this.

James is scalding beneath him as his pale hands reach around to grab Elijah's ass, pulling him tighter. His mouth is like silk as he continues their dance, pulling back to nip Elijah's lip before diving in again. Elijah clenches his fingers into fists, keeping a firm hold on James's hair, keeping him right where he is. Right where Elijah wants him. He slides his knee closer to put pressure on his stepbrother's hardening length, pulling a soft breath from the man he'd die for.

God, he's needy. His body thrums with it. It's been days, and the constant stress of trying to make a stranger want him has left Elijah cold. Why would a woman want any part of this? How could she ever fit? She'd have to be their mate. She'd have to smell like perfection. Like their pretty trapped Beta, only to the umpteenth degree. She's enticing, but they can't have her. If anything has been made obvious, it's that.

James's hands slide up the curve of Elijah's back, his nails skimming the flesh beneath the fabric of his shirt as it lifts. They dig in, and the sweet sting only skyrockets Elijah's lust to the depths of space where he floats, helpless and breathless. He prays for the day when James will put his teeth on his mating gland. Even if it's mingled with an Omega's bite, making them a pack, wearing that mark will be the trophy he's begged for since their first, fumbling ruts.

He bends over, plunging into James's neck and suckling over that soft spot, making James purr. This is the only time his brother is filled with expressions. Ecstasy. Desperation. Bliss. Elijah will do anything for those lovely faces. He'll burn down mountains. He'll sully himself beyond belief. He'll give up all morals.

Dragging his teeth over James's mating gland, he earns himself a hiss of pleasure, and it sends a pulse straight down to his groin. He's hardening more with every stroke of his tongue, and his jeans are getting uncomfortable, stifling where he longs to be free.

"Top or bottom, Jamsie?" he says, feathering kisses over his brother's forehead.

"Equal," he murmurs softly.

"Perfect."

James's fingers fumble with Elijah's buttons, and even the shadow of his hand over Elijah's erection makes him let out a quiet, throaty groan.

"That's right, Jamsie," he whispers. "Touch me."

Katelyn sits, sick of herself and her situation. Thomas…that bastard! How could he? Who would do something like this? He's a sociopath. One she is being forced to marry.

Mama don't make me, she pleads, knowing it's useless.

If she told Thomas to go to hell, she could get another job to support her mother, she knows it. If they lived together, she'd have to confess about her body, but maybe her mother would be like she was in her dreams. Maybe she'll forgive her. Hide her.

If only.

But even if she took care of her mother financially, that's not enough. All her mother's friends would abandon her in an instant for snubbing the Bleakers. The Founders. The lynchpins with their ever-strengthening tower of cards. She wants it to implode, folding in on itself and taking its dogma with it. How can she live this life?

She hurt the Alphas. *Her* Alphas. They may not be hers in bites, but they are in her fantasies.

Look at what this screwed up situation has wrought. Zeb was angry and Finn looked crushed. Of all the things to finally make him feel, it was that. Katelyn's life is an epic tragedy played out on a stage for one, but no one bought tickets to watch her crash and burn.

What will they do now, the three of them locked together in this house? She wants Zeb to get his money. If she cares about their wellbeing, it's the least she can do. But she has to keep her distance. There's a balance they need to strike. An agreement. She'd sign with blood on parchment, if only she could get them to meet her terms.

Maybe she needs to explain her situation fully. Of all the people in this world, she wants them to understand how she doesn't want this. She wants to let all her words fall out, complain and lament and have someone tell her they don't hate her for what she's doing.

Why does she want their respect so much?

More than that, she just wants *them.*

Instinct, her heart whispers. *You know what they could be for you.*

They want her. In some way or form, both of them do, and the knowledge is like molten gold in her belly, melting away her resistance. There's no time for that, though. She needs to go to them and put a stop to whatever they're thinking. She's not a purist. She might be self-loathing, but she'd never extend that vitriol and acidic hate to someone else. If she'd been born to another family, maybe it could all be different, but her mother is her anchor, and she'll give her up for no one.

She slips from her room, the paper screens open to the rain. The roof shelters the hallway from any drizzle that might slick up the hard wood, but only because not a single tickle of breeze blows. She scans the courtyard and hallways, finding no one, and knows they must be in their room, probably livid at the situation. She has to tread carefully. She doesn't want to fight. If they were to try to overpower her, she has no idea what she'd do. Would she fight or give in? Maybe both. First one, then the other.

Their bedroom is an ominous threat as Katelyn stands outside. Hand held out, her knuckles are aimed at their door, inches away from knocking and facing her fate. Then…she hears a sound. A breathy gasp that stops her in her tracks, locking her in place.

Her face goes redder than roses. Whatever that was, it was not a sound of pain. Or exasperation. It was the sound of secret videos she's not supposed to watch and dirty dreams that wake her up well past midnight.

Heat pools in her belly. Their scents ebb from beneath the door, strong and all-encompassing.

She needs to walk away from whatever this is, fast and far, but another sound catches her heart on a hook. A sighed name she's never heard them say before.

James.

Her body moves on its own. Dipping down, she silently rests on her knees, peering into a familiar keyhole. She's spied out of her own, why can't she spy into another?

It's…Oh, God.

She covers her mouth to stifle a cry. Bare skin is the first thing she sees. Zeb's tattoo is on display as he rests, naked on his hands and knees. Finn is reversed beneath him, hands slipped around the small of Zeb's back and holding him with a grip that leaves white marks on his skin.

Their hips roll, thrusting softly, sweetly…

…into each other's mouths.

She soaks in the scene like drifting in the world's most erotic bubble bath, the steam seeping into her every muscle. Zeb's dark hair is swept over his shoulder, his fist working over Finn's length as he swallows the glistening tip, wet from spit. It trails over his knuckles as he sucks in earnest, causing Finn to pant through his nose. Finn doesn't use his hand. Instead, his jaw is wide as he sucks down his… shit…his *brother*. *Step*brother. What is she looking at? And why can't she stop?

Zeb releases to gasp, his forehead resting on Finn's meaty thigh, the muscles loose as they spread wide. Finn pulls and pushes Zeb's hips, arms flexing as he takes him in and out of his mouth in slow motion, his throat working as his cheeks hollow. His brows are knit and his cheeks are pink, his eyes squeezed tight as he does what he can, letting Zeb's hips rock, slipping him in and out of his mouth.

Her heart is on overtime and a shot of desire zings between her legs. She can't look away. How could she ever? They're perfect. She wants to be with them. She wants to run her hands over them. She wants to take over.

She wants to get in the middle.

Alphas.

Their scent is everywhere as they grind against each other. She salivates. Their names—their fake names—hover on the tip of her tongue.

She wants to know their real ones.

Which one is James?

Slick gathers before she has a chance to pull her mind from the moment. Her wetness is more than a trickle. More than a Beta woman could ever make. More than can be caught in her absorbent underwear. She's flooding. Her clit aches for attention, something she only touches at her most desperate, and the pressure of her tight pants is enough to make her bite her lip. She needs to walk away, but Zeb rallies and takes his brother down again. Finn shivers and lets out a guttural sound, inhaling sharply though his nose.

Then his eyes widen.

Releasing his brother, he snaps his head towards her, as if he can see her crouched and spying through the closed door.

Did he hear her?

His nostrils flare and his eyes narrow.

Oh God. No.

He *smells* her.

Finn's eyes are laser focused on where she is with a preternatural power. He can't see her, but he knows she's there. He pushes his brother off and begins to rise, eyes still locked forward and breathing in as deep as he can go.

Shit. He's going to come for her.

Katelyn pushes off her heels…and runs.

CHAPTER 7
MINE

Peaches. It smells like peaches.

James rolls Elijah off, and his brother curses absently, but James is too enthralled to take it in. The sudden scent is all he can think about. Mouthwatering, it latches onto his brain and won't let go, pulling his insides like a rope wrapped around his middle.

"Do you smell it?" he asks, hearing the rare strain in his voice.

Elijah is red lipped and confused. "What?"

James slings on clothes, trying not to stumble through his boxers. Decent enough, he starts tossing a shirt and jeans to Elijah, whose eyes are narrowing as he comes down.

"We were kind of in the middle of something…"

But James is out the door.

This was the scent of the Beta Distraction after she'd stepped from the shower, so muted at the time, but now singing a symphony that echoes in his lungs. Hopping behind him, Elijah tries to get his foot in his pants as James narrows in on that scent. It's like he can see it. It draws that same line of bright color from their room to hers—but how can that be?

James is thrumming, his heart on fire.

Mine.

Elijah stands behind his brother, James's bare back flexed in stone. Elijah's erection has more than faded, dread slowly sinking in instead. Something is wrong. James's senses are more acute than his, always have been, so he trusts him innately. What could James have possibly smelled?

Is it her? Did she see?

James dashes away, and Elijah is helpless, throwing on clothes and following blindly. He runs down the hall as his brother slams Katelyn's door open and freezes, his blond-lashed eyes fluttering closed.

That's it. She must have seen. She must be disgusted. He has to do damage control.

With a heavy shove, he pushes past his brother…and is immediately assaulted with the scent of heaven. His head swims in a sudden cloud of perfection that calls to a part hidden deep within him, making him giddy. But before that feeling can take root, his stomach drops a mile as he sees what lies before him. Katelyn is on the floor, dappled with sweat and a small streak of vomit beside her. Little white pills dissolve in the mess as she shudders, folded in on herself, flushed pink everywhere and legs clenched tight.

That's where the scent is coming from.

Elijah staggers. The room is a basket of peaches, and he's never been more starving. He wants to shove his nose right into the apex of her thighs and smell her. Rub all over her. Taste her.

James is a cord on the verge of snapping, but Elijah tries to keep his head. "What's happening?"

Her breath is ragged as she squeezes her eyes closed. "It's a seizure."

She's lying. He can taste it in the air.

Her medicine bottles lay discarded beside her, more pills spilling out from where she likely dropped them. They look like avid threats and smell like poison. He whips up a bottle to look at the label and blanches when he sees the name. These are hormone suppressants…an insane dose. Elijah takes them—all secondary genders do—but this is unreasonable.

There is a delicate container of body cream spilled on the countertop as well, its lid fallen onto the floor. He touches it and his skin immediately stings, and the scent glands on his fingertips dim as he hisses through the pain. Scent blockers so strong, it hurts. Horror threads through his veins. "What are you doing to yourself?"

James looks on the verge of losing control. He breathes the heady word, "Omega" and she lets out a little whimper. Somehow her scent doubles, intoxicating and all too real.

Mine, rings true in Elijah's mind, something so strong it scares him.

"Don't call me that!" She pushes to her hands and knees, swiping at her mouth as she shakes. Her muscles coil, and Elijah knows it's going to happen before it does. She launches herself out of the room, and something vicious in him wants to give chase. Lock her down. Suck the nectar straight from the source.

She needs to go.

Something bad is going to happen if she stays in this house.

But looking at James, it's already too late.

James knows she's his. She's fucking *his* and there's no way to deny it. When she bolts, every instinct says to catch her. Bite her.

Mate her.

His body tenses as he flies after her, his teeth clenched as her scent embeds lacey designs in his pores.

Don't run, Omega. You're mine.

Katelyn is frantic, running circles around the house with Finn hot on her tail. She's as afraid as she is electrified.

Catch me, Alpha.

Be good to me.

Make this pain go away.

Is this what Niles feels? This overwhelming need to play. To challenge. To submit.

She skates around the corner and sees him through the paper screens and heavy rain. He's slowed, watching her, fire in his ice-colored eyes. She could burn up from his attention alone. He wears only thin boxers, the rest of him bare, and she wants to worship every inch of his skin.

Catch me.

Never let me get away.

She's never been more terrified in her life.

He rushes through the courtyard. The living room lies behind her and she dives into it. If she can get behind the couch, she can hide from him. She can fend him off. She can keep his hands off her.

She doesn't make it.

Finn, the Alpha, *her* Alpha, pounces, pinning her belly-down on the floor and diving into her nape, nuzzling her hair aside. She can feel droplets of the rain he carried with him sink into her clothing and slip over the back of her neck, cooling her fever even as it rages higher.

Without warning, he rends her high-necked shirt with his teeth, the ripping sound of the fabric overriding even the beating of her heart. He places a long lick over her exposed mating gland, and she moans a dark sound she's never made before, not even with her hand between her legs late at night. He's breathing against the back of her neck, suckling as he arches into her, his hardened length grinding against her rear. Their clothes do nothing to dull the sensation.

He growls, and she's a puddle, overflowing with slick, soaking her pants, down her inner thighs all the way to her knees.

Taking his weight off her, she feels him fist the shirt just above her bra strap, and he tears the thing in two. Fear kicks in then, stronger than before, and she begins to struggle. This can't happen. She can't give in.

She can never have what she wants.

Elijah pulls at his brother's back, his mind screaming to *Protect*.

He wants her. He wants her so badly, but not like this.

James looks lost, his pupils fully dilated and his lips flushed bright with arousal. Elijah pulls his chin, making James face him. "Other people have feelings," he reminds, holding James's face in his hands until his brother's eyes sweep in his direction, his body trembling with unleashed energy. "You know that. You know we can't do this."

"You don't want to?"

He does. He absolutely fucking does. But Katelyn is rolling over, curling her legs tight and clutching her torn shirt over her shoulders, trying to keep it steady on her small body.

Mine, his inner Alpha demands. She smells so good. So perfect. He'd be so good to her. But she also smells afraid, and that is something he can't tolerate.

Grabbing James by the hair, he tucks his mouth close to his ear. "She's ours?"

James nods against him.

"Then we have to protect her. Even from ourselves."

James is still trembling, but nods again.

Holding his brother, unable to look at his rainbow lest he explode, Elijah asks her, "What do you need?"

If she calls him Alpha, he's going to lose control. If she says she needs him, either of them, he'll devour her whole. Instead, she says, "I can't do this" in a sob so heart wrenching, he can't bear it. "If Thomas finds out…"

Jealousy licks up his spine like he's never felt.

"I'll fucking kill him," James hisses.

"Don't tell," she pleads. "He can't know I'm…I'm…"

Elijah wants to cry. He wants to weep and lay at her feet and do anything. "Do you need space again?" he manages, and it makes James whimper—a sound Elijah has never heard him make.

She says, "Please," and that's all it takes. He half pulls, half drags his brother away, locking them back in their room. James's hands are in his hair and he's rocking again, only further breaking Elijah's heart.

"But she's ours," James says, as lost as he's ever sounded.

Elijah can't do anything but whisper, "I know."

CHAPTER 8
CONNECTIONS

ELIJAH IS DUCKED down on his haunches in the shower, letting the scalding water cascade his raven black hair over his shoulders. The steam fogs his mind and drenches his madness, settling him as he feels the balls of his feet grounded on the bottom of the porcelain tub.

His Alpha has never cried out for anyone before. He's been around hundreds of Omegas across the span of his short life, but nothing has caught him in a snare so utterly, rendering him useless for anything other than obeying her every whim. He loves James, needs James, can't live his life without him, but—other than during his rut—his whole being never begged for him.

But she's in that fucking cult. The Lifestyle. How could she live that lie? With that man?

He grinds his teeth again, jaw sore and a tension headache pounding.

Who gave her that "medicine"?

Did she actually think she could hide it forever?

What a painful thing, and why? The Lifestyle hates secondary genders. They'd string her up like a witch if her secret ever came to light—especially if she's tied to *that man*.

But she mentioned her mother. Elijah knows the trials and tribulations parents can bring to your life. How obedience and filial piety make you chomp at the bit to make them smile. Have them pat you on the head and praise you. And when they look at you with worry, disdain, reprimand, you have exactly two choices. Crumble into obedience or run and hide, like he and James do.

How does Katelyn feel toward her mother? Is it like James's blind loyalty, Elijah's trepidation, or something else? Something healthier? For all he knows, they're best friends. Confidantes.

But something must be wrong if her mother is willing to ship her off to the Bleakers. Or is it possible her mother doesn't know she's an Omega either?

Again, he laments not having the time to research her more before kicking off this entire mess.

With a grunt, he stands and finishes cleaning off, trying to save himself from the memory of her mind-ensnaring scent. When he leaves the bedroom, James is still scrubbing the house down with soaps and sprays, dimming the vestige of peaches into a bland nothingness.

Miss Katelyn Annamarie Jones-Masters is nowhere to be found.

Wordlessly, his brother flicks his eyes in the direction of her room and Elijah takes the hint, tossing a sympathetic glance to the only other person who could understand how he feels.

His steps are sluggish and tentative as he works his way to her door. This time, when he knocks, he waits for permission to enter, dread knotting his chest, thinking that she'll leave him right where he stands.

After much too long, she says, "You can come in."

She's rubbing more of that stinging shit over her neck. He can only imagine how it must burn, like a slap ringing on every sensitive inch of her glands. Other than that first night, her clothes have kept the curves where her shoulders meet her neck hidden, or else he would have noticed. That first night, though… The minute she ran from them in the hallway and landed on her ass, he should have seen. He was too busy dealing with her newness to take in the glossy, thin skin at her wrists and neck. For some reason, it feels unforgivable.

In the nothing-smell of her room, wiped down with more of the bleach James is coating every surface in, he asks, "Can I tell you our names?"

She sniffles, fingers massaging in the scent blocker. "Why would I want to know?"

"Because you can't fall in love with us if you don't know us."

She goes rigid, those jade eyes sparkling with restrained moisture. "I can't love you, regardless."

"I don't believe that. Can't you smell us?"

She nods.

"And don't you want us?"

She closes her eyes and nods again. "But I can't have you."

"Why are you doing this?" he asks, but receives no answer. She caps that horrid skin cream and sets it aside, picking up a cleaning rag from the top of the bureau and tossing it into a pile of laundry. That must be where her slick-stained pants are. She's hiding her scent under the acrid tang of disinfectant, as if she were a mess to be whisked away. He can't stand that.

Going closer, he picks up a pair of her faux glasses from among a pile of them, ones bejeweled with glitter. He slides them on and blinks, still surprised when he meets only glass instead of a blurry world. He earns himself a small smile.

"They look terrible on you," she says.

"Lies. I'm fabulous. Though, trigger warning, I look one hundred percent less jaw dropping when I wear my real glasses. Those make me look like a bookworm."

Her roughed-up voice lets out a breathy, wet chuckle. "Are you?"

"When the mood catches me. I like fantasy novels. Dragons and knights and magic and stuff."

"I like science fiction."

"Hmm… Pseudo-science or technically plausible?"

"Oh God, please don't give me anything requiring brain power. I just like aliens."

He grins at that, removing the glasses and slipping them over her ears instead. When she doesn't flinch away, a part of him relaxes. "My name is Elijah."

Her lips part slightly as she gazes at him, lashes diamond-studded with tears.

"And my brother's name is—"

"James," she says, lowering her chin. "I heard you say it. Before."

A mix of conflicting feelings fight for dominance. Pride that seeing them is likely what put her in such a desperate state, and fear that they might now disgust her.

"He's your real brother?" she asks.

"Stepbrother." He walks to her bed, sitting down with a heavy *fwump* before laying his head on her pillow. Even this smells like nothing. How terribly sad. "When we were fifteen, our parents got married. James wouldn't talk to anyone back then, but I liked to guess what he was feeling. It was like a game. I was obsessed with figuring out what made his mind tick, so I was always hanging around him.

"I was pretty sure he hated me at first. I was constantly up in his personal space, ranting at him, telling him about me and my life even though I was half-convinced he wasn't listening." Elijah's smile is slow and laced with nostalgia. "But he heard every word. And when he finally spoke to me, I was in love. At his very first sentence, he had me wrapped around his little finger. And when he started looking at me, I was lost. No one got the privilege of James's eyes, not even mom, and I can't tell you how honored I felt. How special."

She's facing away from him, playing with her fingers, no doubt tuned into his every lilted tone. That makes him feel special, too. She may not love him, not yet, but she's not dismissing him either.

He continues. "Then James started to seek *me* out. Wouldn't *stop* looking at me. And when we presented," he lets out a rough laugh, "it was all we could do to stay in our separate rooms. James actually tore a hole in the wall between us so we could hold hands during our first rut. It was fucking romantic. Of course, when all was said and done, we had to slide our dressers into the damn corners to hide what he'd done, but we knew. Sometimes, we'd still hold hands at night while I rambled and James kept his heart and ears open.

"When I was eighteen, I got my tattoo." He gestures. "The clock is the exact time we met. James remembered. It was the most pivotal moment of our lives. Not when my mom left, not when his dad died, but the minute I first took up too much space in his life."

Katelyn turns profile and goes cross legged, sitting on the floor while staring at her hands. Pink caresses her cheeks, and her visible glands become rosy alongside them. "How does a rut work with you two?"

He blinks. Not a question he was expecting. He scrubs a hand through his hair. "It's not easy, honestly. Not when we go through it at the same time, at least."

"Why?"

It's his turn to blush a bit. "We have to trade off who tops, but whoever's on the bottom always fights it. Call it Alpha dominance." He smirks, but mostly out of embarrassment. "So, we have to truss the other up. We stagger our ruts when we can because it hurts to be the one all…held back. You can't get what you need. It's worse than having a rut alone because the person you love is right there, teasing you, but you can't have them the way you want. Still, I thought I'd rather do that forever than invite someone between us…until you."

She fidgets, shifting her weight and picking at her clothes.

"Lately, James has wanted to make us a pack, so no one finds out what we're doing together. I want to say I have no idea why he feels that way, but I'm not that stupid. I fought it at first, but who was I kidding, I'll do anything for him. Now, I want to do anything for you, too. That's the thing about being a secondary gender. We know who our soulmates are."

Her breath pulls in quietly.

He risks it all. "Don't you want to do anything for me?"

Slowly, she nods, somber eyes on the floor. "I want to make sure you don't get hurt."

With that, she stands and works her way to her bathroom.

She stays in there a very long time.

Her scent lingers. James tries not to breathe, if only to hide from the aroma of her fear, sorrow, and arousal floating like an airy perfume. He's never lost control like that before. His Alpha has never demanded so forcefully. Elijah is his in every way that matters, but this is new.

This is soul-snatching. This is what it means to know who your mate is.

James keeps firm control on his outbursts. When things don't go his way, he holds it together so much better now than he did when he was young. Things aren't meant to be easy. They don't always have to follow a pattern. People are meant to flow with what life brings their way. Like Sensei Joe says, you need to move your heart the way you move your body: let the current of electricity tingle its way through every nerve and lead you onward. Feel the spark. Feel the static.

Katelyn is electricity.

But she never asked for this. He didn't care before—she was just another of his brother's jobs, a nothing, a nobody—but how did he not realize she was meant to be his from the moment he stood outside the bathroom door, watching the water trickle over her collarbones while the residue of soap disguised the scent that came to her naturally? He'd been moved, but he'd also been stupid not to realize what the new pull to her meant. Even hidden in plain sight, she drew him in.

James shuts his eyes for a brief moment as he wipes down the kitchen table, covering his need for her in the comforting aura of bleach and disinfectant. If he's ever going to calm his racing heart, he needs this. He also needs to face reality. The reality that is Thomas Bleaker…

The thought of her with that man makes his stomach roll.

Elijah is right, though. She acts like she doesn't want him. How could she? She's an Omega. What will happen when the truth comes out? She can't keep it a secret forever. He can smell her heat teasing to the surface of her body, bubbling under the softness of her skin, just waiting to break through. He wonders if she's ever had a heat before. He'd gladly take her first. He'd take her second. He'd take every one of them from now until her last.

The table groans as he scrubs harder, leaving streaks on the wood. He shouldn't use something this caustic on a surface like this, but he can't bring himself to care. The counter comes next. Then the stovetop. That's always worth a good scrub, tiring his arms as he scours every splattered dollop of oil and singed crisp of something that committed *hara-kiri* by leaping over the side of the pan into the blue burner flames.

Rustling grass startles him—though he knows no one could tell by looking—and he turns his eyes toward the garden. The rain has stopped, and the clouded sky has darkened with the dusk, shrouding everything in a gloom that matches his mood.

Katelyn, his mate, something so deep-seated in his biology he can't contain it, has her arms wrapped around herself. She staggers slightly, going to the koi pond and sitting down to watch the fish as they twirl around each other in fin-fluttering waves. It's been hours since he's seen her, which is hours too long. He can't smell her anymore. Not because of the bleach. Not because of what's left of the rain dappling the greenery. It's because of the scent blockers she's poisoning herself with.

Even from behind, he can tell she's exhausted. She wears a different shirt, not the one he'd shredded so mindlessly from her body. It doesn't hide her mating glands, and they sit, pretty and pink on the sides of her neck. His loins stir, but more than that, it's his heart that gets the better of him. Sympathy oozes like molasses. She's trapped. By her biology, by her fanatical fiancée, and even by them.

He wants to bury his face in her neck again, but Elijah was right. Other people have feelings, too. He forgets that sometimes.

Cast in the diffused light from the inner hallways, her skin glows ivory among the blue shadows as she turns to stare at him, eyes red rimmed but unwavering. She looks emotionally wrecked, like the smallest push will send her spiraling into the abyss. James knows what that feels like.

He approaches slowly, trying to be gentle. Unfrightening. Apologies are locked in his mouth as he takes her in—her plush lips, dark lashes, and the perfect curve of her cheeks. If he watches long enough, can he tell what she's thinking the same way he can see it in Elijah?

She seems to shrink as he gets closer, but he can't stop looking at her. She is fascinating.

"What do you need?" He echoes his brother's words from earlier, his voice strangely quiet.

Her lower lip trembles and her gaze drops, tears filling her eyes. Her breath hitches and his heart aches as if he can feel her pain—that sense of being buried in sinking sand. Of overwhelm and hopelessness. Of lack of control. He understands. He knows that feeling intimately.

"Are you broken?" he asks.

A sob rings out, and he wants to hold her. Love her. Save her. She answers with a simple, choked, "Yes," and he knows all his assumptions were right.

Still as stone but shaking inside, James admits, "I'm broken, too."

The garden trees rustle above them, their branches unmoving even as the leaves caress each other. How he wishes he could caress her the same.

"What?" she asks.

Can he tell her? Will he tell her? One thing is for sure, "I don't hate you anymore."

Her eyes go wide for a moment and his shoot to the ground, admiring the alabaster gravel surrounding the koi pond.

"And I think I can save you," he adds.

An unknown emotion creeps into her voice. "From what?"

"Hating yourself."

Afraid to meet her gaze, he steps closer, focused on where the grass seeps rainwater into her soft pajama pants. They're still colorful, even in the darkness of early night, splashed with polka dots of every color. It should be mind-numbing, but instead, he finds it soothing. There is a pattern there. Three, then two, then three. When he finally dares to look at her, her lips are pressed and her eyes shimmer.

"How would you know anything about that?" she asks.

"Before you, I wanted to die."

He knows that expression on her face. It's one that's stuck with him for years. It's shock. Horror. The same face Elijah made when he'd found him lying on the floor swimming in his own blood.

James traces the scar at his wrist, feels the raised skin of it, and without thinking, brandishes it clearly, as if holding out the head of an enemy after a battle has been won. She's up on her knees in moments, and he lets her grab his arm and pull it closer. Her eyes rake over his biggest failure. It slashes over the scent gland at his wrist, and perhaps that will help her. It will put his pheromones on mute and help her withstand this moment.

"Does Elijah know?" Her voice is high, but the sound of his brother's name on her tongue is sinfully good, no matter the circumstances.

He nods.

Her neck tilts fast, finding him as he hovers above her. "Why would you do this?"

"Because I'm dirty." There is no other way to put it. "I want things I'm not supposed to want."

"No," she says, her head shaking back and forth, hard and firm. Those tears still stand there, but so does a certain sort of fire. Is she angry at him or angry at his feelings? "You're in love. You've always been in love. It's not like you chose it, it's a part of you." She erupts from the grass and cups his cheeks, forcing his eyes on her. "You are *not* dirty."

His hand moves slowly, landing on hers with the softest of pressure. He aches. "Say it again."

Firmer this time, she insists, "You're not dirty."

"Again."

"You're not!"

"Now apply that to yourself." He takes her hand and brings her knuckles to his mouth, sweeping over them with the barest of touches and turning her words against her. "You've always been this way. It's not like you chose it. It's a part of you."

Her breath is fast. Her tears spill. Still, he can't stop his words, losing himself in her presence.

"You're not dirty, Katelyn."

It's the first time he's said her name.

It's the first time he's said so much.

He wants to kiss her.

Something *slaps* against his mating glands with a rough, nasty sting, making him drop her hand and lurch back directly into his brother's chest.

"Whoa, boy!" Elijah says, moving to his other gland and massaging in something that feels like fire. What the fuck is he doing to—

"Is that my cream?" Katelyn squeaks.

"Yup!" his brother says. "Figured it's the least we can do."

Elijah's hands are brusque and borderline cruel as they rub in what must be that scent blocking salve. He spins James around and grabs his unscarred wrist next, connecting their gazes and cocking an eyebrow.

"Okay?" he asks.

James keeps the budding grimace off his face. Instead, he holds his hand higher, offering himself to the challenge. His brother grins at him, his eye-teeth showing their delicate points. As the salve is rubbed in, every stroke is painful. His skin ignites, becoming oversensitive and turning red as the white cream sinks in, hiding his scent under a blanket of film.

"I need that!" she cries, trying to reach around James and pull the jar from his brother's hands. He evades her easily.

"Not anymore," he says. "You're going to go off them, and we're going to go on. We have more experience dealing with stuff like this— scents, sexual tension—it's your virgin ass we need to save."

Virgin? She's a *virgin*?

His brother's grin takes on something salacious James would absolutely mirror, if he could.

Okay, he can do this. He'll endure this slow torture. He holds his other wrist up, and Elijah puts a small kiss over his scar before rubbing in more napalm. Katelyn throws up her hands in his periphery, and storms away.

Stupid Alphas. Stupid, *stupid* Alphas.

Katelyn marches down the hallway at a clip, rattling locked door-knobs and looking for a new space to hide. Nothing available, she herds herself into the living room and lands hard on the flat surface of a decorative couch made more for looks than comfort.

She eyes them through the open screen. Finn—no, *James*—is now rubbing her precious, expensive, difficult to get cream all over his brother. Elijah's face is one big wince, exaggerated probably just for the sake of it. It hurts, but not enough to look *like that*. One eye is half closed and twitching, the other bugged wide, and his teeth are bared in something that either looks like a grin or a threat. If you could be a comedian by facial expressions alone, it seems that's what the man is going for. She'd kick him in the shins if this whole gesture wasn't so weirdly sweet. Is that why she's not cowering in her room again? Instead, she's out in the open, plopped on an ornate sofa only steps away from the men who kidnapped her. Keep her captive. Keep her on edge.

And enchanted.

There's something wrong with this picture. This morning's rabid romp should bother her, haunt and terrify her, and perhaps it does, but not for the right reasons. She didn't mind being chased. Pinned. Caught. Breathed in. She was more afraid of the consequences, and all of those lay outside the bubble they've created in this house made of refined Asian beauty.

How is it possible to be drawn to them so quickly? Is it just because they're Alphas? Could it be *any* Alpha?

No. They are special. Like Elijah said, her sixth sense is telling her they belong to her.

She leans back and hides, crossing her arms and slumping down like a sullen child.

If she can't hide her Omega status, what will happen to her? She'll be ousted. Blacklisted. Publicly shamed and ostracized. Without her job and with her only friend alienated by her impending nuptials, she'd truly have nothing.

And without The Lifestyle, neither would her mom.

She misses her. The fussing, the teasing…even all the asinine wedding prep. What is her mother thinking now that she's gone MIA? Has Thomas told her anything? Or is her mother thinking she ran away again, like did when she was a kid? She must be so worried. Maybe even heartbroken. Or even worse, afraid she's been abandoned.

Family is the key, so saith the Lifestyle. *We must teach our children the importance of our stances. Without parents to show them the way, the little ones are lost.*

Katelyn drifts into memory. Long ago and far away, her mother had everything she ever needed to be happy but was lost with grief when Katelyn's father and brother died. Some call must have come in while little-Katelyn was sleeping. Her mother was shouting, but the sound was blurred and dampened by the sturdy walls of their old house. By the time Katelyn padded downstairs, her mother's keens were guttural and horrid, scaring her six-year-old self as she held the trembling adult in her arms. At first her mother wouldn't speak. For days she wouldn't speak. Katelyn didn't even know her family was dead until they just never came back. There was no funeral. As an adult, she realizes that her mother probably couldn't bear it, either emotionally or financially. Little Katelyn hadn't minded—didn't know any better, really—but when her mother stopped eating, her six-year-old self stepped up and started taking on what her father left behind. She was now caretaker. She was responsible. She was going to fix this.

Every day, multiple times a day, she made her mother peanut butter and jelly sandwiches. At first, she was scared of the butter knives. She would spend way too long staring at the silverware drawer with her lips drawn tight between her baby teeth. She wasn't supposed to touch knives—all her food came precut or in nugget form, after all—but she tried her best. With every sandwich, she got better and better about not leaving blobs of sticky, purple jelly everywhere, and she only dropped peanut butter on the floor once.

Days passed, and there was a landmine of abandoned sandwiches outside her mom's room, crusty, hard, and stale. She needed to do something else to ease her mother's suffering but had no idea what.

Thinking of what made her dad feel better when he was out of sorts, she decided to grab his favorite books—spies and mysteries with super-smart private eyes, immune to danger—and read them aloud outside her mother's door. She didn't know half the words, couldn't pronounce even more of them, and at some point, she realized they only made her mother cry harder. It must have been the memories of her father cutting her heart into thin lines. That had been a no-go.

She switched to her favorite books instead, even though they were kid books. Choose your own adventure space stories. At least they were easier to read. She would tell her mom the options to move forward, each time with a hope that her mother would answer. And finally, she did. Katelyn will always remember her first choice. It was between escaping from the green, tentacled alien or confronting it. Her mother, her voice weak and harsh from disuse, chose to escape. It made sense. If something is scary, you run away. Katelyn would have run away, too.

Her brother didn't like those books, but he would read them to her before she knew how to read them for herself. He especially groaned at the ones about unicorns and mermaids but indulged her anyway. Once, her dad tousled his hair with a proud smile. "Atta boy, Brandon. Teach her the difference between 'f' and 'th' while you're at it, will you?" He winked at Katelyn, and she giggled at her own expense. It had just been Father's Day, and she'd hand-made him a silly card. One so ugly, only a parent could love. In big, pink, block letters, she'd put the words "Happy Thather's Day," much to the laughter of her family. Even now, it makes her smile.

What would her father and brother look like if they were alive? Her mother's hair is a deep brown, but her father and brother were both auburn, like her. There are no pictures left, all the albums long thrown away, and she realizes she doesn't remember their faces. They always said that she and Brandon could be twins if they weren't born six years apart. Daddy would joke that he should have wooed mommy sooner so they could have been Irish twins. She didn't know what that meant, but how her mother would laugh…

What is it like to lose your husband? Your lover? Your best friend?

Or your child, for that matter? The baby you cradled in your arms and sang lullabies to. The one you coddled when they got boo-boos. The one you fed vegetables to, even if they acted like you poisoned them.

Katelyn smiles again.

She's surprised by a bang and turns to look over the back of the sofa. Elijah is grappling James, making weird, funny noises as he shoves and pulls at him. James pins him down with a tilt to his lips, the tiniest of smiles, before his brother reverses the position and wrestles him to the ground.

"Every day means every day, Jamsie! I will slap this creamy shit on you every—gah! No! That's my—fuck, don't pull so hard! Argh!"

Katelyn *pffts*, clapping a hand over her mouth as the two men throttle each other playfully. James seems to give up, allowing himself to be pinned, and Elijah grins as if he just caught a nice, juicy dinner after a long day of hunting. Leaning over, he pecks James on the nose, and James's eyes flick to hers for a moment.

"What?" Elijah says. "She already knows. No point in pretending now, don't you think?"

James puts his hand on his brother's face and pushes him back with an "Mm," and nothing more.

Shoved off, Elijah laughs that full belly laugh before jumping up and offering his brother a hand. Once he's out of the way, Elijah raids the fridge.

"What does my rainbow want? We've got more of that leftover pesto pasta, some chicken—though chicken reheats like shit. I've got stuff for hamburgers…"

"It's too late to cook," James says, and his brother snorts.

"Microwaving is fine."

"You can't microwave hamburgers."

Elijah grumbles, never taking his head out of the fridge, his perfectly toned butt sticking out as he bends, the shape still visible in his pajama pants.

James watches him with his hands on his hips. Is that a sign of irritation, or did he just happen to position himself that way? Is it a sign of affection or exasperation? Katelyn wants to understand his every gesture with a deep desire. She can see how Elijah would be so obsessed with him. She's quickly following suit.

"A-ha!" Elijah cries, standing up fast and *BAFF*ing his head off the freezer door. "Shit! Damnit! Fucking cocksucking motherfucker! I've got Chinese food. Good god, that hurt!"

"You ordered out?" Katelyn asks, taken aback and wondering how big of a lump the Alpha must now have on his head.

Her Alpha.

She shoves the thought away.

"*Ow.*" He winces. "James made it. Better than take out, believe me."

She hums, turning fully around with her knees on the sofa. Pointing a comment directly at her stoic statue, she asks, "What did you make, oh culinary genius?"

The tips of his ears turn pink, but nothing else. "Beef with broccoli."

Sounds delicious.

"With sesame oil," he clarifies.

"Does that make a difference?" she asks.

He looks at her but says nothing. Apparently, it does.

"That would be great, thank you."

Elijah is still resting a hand on the crown of his head, tenderly patting at his sore spot and making a face like someone pulled out his bottom lip on a string. He opens a Tupperware box and tosses it into the microwave. "Time?"

"Three," James says.

Elijah's grin returns. "Hours?"

James moves to bop him on his bump and gets batted away.

"Okay! Minutes! I get it! No violence!"

Which is hilarious, given what she just witnessed.

When the food is ready, James plates it in a way that's artful, sesame seeds sprinkled on the top in arcs that look like fallen snow.

Microwaved or not, it's the most delicious thing she's ever had.

Another nightmare.

Heavy, syrupy liquid engulfs her, sucking her down. It tastes sweet in her mouth, sweet enough to make her gag as its scent clogs her nose. Fills it. Travels deep into her lungs.

Katelyn is drowning.

In her own slick.

Thomas stares down from the edge of a small boat. Its silver, metallic sides glisten with her shame as it laps against the surface. In his omnipresent dark blue business suit, he holds a life ring the color of used dishwater braced between his palms, drumming his fingers in rhythmic patterns alongside it as he watches her flail. She struggles to the surface, choking out his name, and he hums in that low voice of his.

"Should I save you?" he asks. "*Can* I save you?"

She doesn't know.

"Do you *want* me to save you?"

She doesn't know that either.

Below the depths of her sin, her two Alphas beckon like sirens, arms stretched up high enough to caress the tips of her toes. If they pull her down, can she become like them, thriving under the flooding tide, breathing it in like air…?

Her mother appears on the side of the boat, her hand thrown out in desperation, her fingertips splayed.

"Come here, Katie!" Her eyes bulge and her hair is disheveled, little wisps framing her face in a hectic halo. "I've got you, baby! Come to Mama!"

Katelyn struggles forward, her fingertips grazing her mother's, but her slick keeps her from getting a firm grasp. Another wave crests, and she chokes, gulping another suck of wetness down her throat. It's as intoxicating as it is disgusting.

The Alphas below have grown sensual mermaid tails, white and black with scales that shimmer like oil slicks, a myriad of colors swirling when you look just right. Their hair cascades in waves as they circle each other like the koi fish in the pond, forever locked in the balance of yin and yang and thrumming with the power of core-deep magic, something derived from the center of the earth and pulling from the arch of the widened sky. Their muscles glisten from the sunlight above as the liquid distorts the star's rays, casting wavering lines over their bodies in whites and blues. They have no words, only allure. Some kind of sorcery that makes her want to give up, give in, and get sucked down into the depths.

But her mother's hand clutches her wrist now, hauling her forward while Thomas watches with a corpse-like expression. His normally emotive face is now dull, blank, and gray. Behind him unfurls a hazy shadow with two glowing dots in its black depths, like the reflection of animal eyes in a poorly developed photo. She knows they're locked on her when they narrow into slits. An aura of danger pierces her as the darkness grows like a thunderhead, billowing until it towers above Thomas, setting him against a sea of darkness.

Corded wire shoots from the void and coils around his extremities, bunching up the fabric of his suit in dark blue cotton twists and knots at his wrists and knees. With a vicious, echoing rip, jagged cracks tear from the corners of his mouth down to his chin, dropping his jaw at the hinges. His expression dulls as he stares at her, eyes now dead and mouth hanging slack and puppet-like. When the strings pull him, he lifts his arms in welcome.

"Come Katie," he says, his voice a gurgle. "My father said I can have you. That I can trap you. That I can put you in a cage." He sags, and the metallic cords hold him up by the hinges of his body. "Can I?"

Her mother pulls her into the boat…

And Katelyn startles awake.

CHAPTER 9
SWORDPLAY

A BUZZ on his night table wakes Elijah, pulling him from the depths of oblivion. He's always been a heavy sleeper and mornings are not his friend. If not for James, he'd sleep until noon. Even so, there is an unspoken rule that waking him up before eight a.m. is not allowed. Too bad whoever's calling never got the memo.

He fumbles with his outstretched arm, eyes still closed as he pats down the tabletop, finding his rectangular vice rattling at an angle uncomfortable for his arm to reach. He groans as he paws at it, grabbing its buzzing surface with groggy hands and peering out of one blurry eye. He needs to hold the phone in that magic sweet spot where his vision is clear without his glasses on before he can read the words "Boss Man" on the screen. Makes sense. Who else would it be, really?

James is already up and out of bed—that early riser—so Elijah rolls to snuggle his brother's pillow for comfort and strength before pressing the little green button.

"Thomas," he says in mock greeting, his voice ragged with sleep. "To what do I owe the pleasure?"

"She told you who I am," the man replies, no surprise in his voice.

"To be fair, we sort of demanded it."

"Not that I'd think any better of you. You Alphas are prone to throwing your weight around. It's what you're good at."

The dick.

"I called because I'm guessing my fiancée had a difficult time yesterday. I wanted to see how she's doing."

Elijah snorts. "Like you care."

"I care very much. If I didn't, she wouldn't be where she is right now."

He says it like he believes it. "That's fucked up."

"Not your place to decide," he says. "How is she?"

Well, first she panicked and ran away. Then she saw me and my brother fucking around and it almost put her into heat. Then she poisoned herself with hormone and heat suppressants, was borderline hunted, got dry humped and sucked on, cried her eyes out, and slept for about twelve hours.

But at least she came out at the end. And ate something. She accepted his overtures for what they were and didn't blame James for what happened. As destined mates, they each took a step towards each other yesterday, something that would only damn her if it came to light.

"She had a rough day."

The man makes a pleased hum that inspires Elijah to put his fist through a wall. Not that he would in this place. James would kill him.

"Does that make you happy, Tom? Go along with your plan? Would you like it best if she cried and hid from us for the next three weeks? Do you even realize how traumatizing that would be?"

"All for the better. I need to get her away from people like you."

"You're a shitty human being, Tommy boy."

"Don't call me that."

"Tom-Tom, then. A name fitting for a child like you."

If Thomas Bleaker were an Alpha, he'd be struggling not to take the bait, but instead he's smooth as silk when he says, "Do you want my money or not?"

He needs it, but he's not sure he gives a shit about that anymore.

"I'm willing to pay extra," the genderist asshole says, "if that's what's needed to keep you quiet."

"This isn't about the money."

"Oh, I see. We're pretending to have principles now, are we? Isn't it a little late for that? Don't tell me you care about her beyond what she can offer you. Things like you don't have feelings."

Elijah's body tenses and he pulls himself to a seated position, wanting to scream. "Neither do you, apparently. And this isn't about my feelings. This is about taking care of the woman you're supposed to marry." Though he hates saying it. Though the very idea puts venom in his belly that soaks into his every cell.

Mine, his heart cries…but only if she wants it, too.

She does want it, he reminds himself. *She's just afraid to give in.*

Too bad he gave in immediately. His doubts crumbled like an avalanche the minute her beautiful scent bloomed.

Mate.

Thomas fucking Bleaker's voice is filled with nothing but smug pride. "Don't you worry. I'm going to have a happy life with my Beta bride, and we'll have beautiful Beta babies."

Bile churning, Elijah bites out, "What happens if one of your babies presents?"

There is no pause. "Then we'll give it away. That's what we do."

His blood runs cold. No wonder Katelyn's been slowly killing herself with those fucking drugs. If she didn't, she'd be abandoned. How young was she when she presented? How long has she been hiding this?

His heart breaks for her.

"What happens when you give them away?"

"They live, and that's all that should matter to you."

The phone goes silent. Elijah pulls it from his ear and sees the dropped call, less than five minutes clocked on the screen. How little time it takes to make murder cross his mind.

He slams his phone down and picks up his glasses, working his hair into a messy knot at the back of his head and looping it securely with the ponytail he keeps around his wrist. He's overwhelmed with the urge to see his mate. To cradle her. To whisper words of solace and peace. To take away her fear and the damage done by people like her soon-to-be husband.

She won't be able to live like that. She won't be able to hide it.

And when it fails, Elijah and James will be there to pick up every piece of her broken heart.

The silent promise calms him somewhat. If this is what she needs to do, no matter how it hurts him, he will wait. He will help James wait. Sad as it is, it will only be a matter of time before she does something The Lifestyle will never forgive her for.

He gets up and goes to the attached bathroom, rushing through his morning necessaries and adding that stinging fucking cream to his regimen. It sits on the countertop, looking harmless and innocent despite its disturbing purpose. The feel of it on his glands makes him have to bite his tongue to avoid letting out a pathetic whimper. He hisses in a deep breath, instead.

He needs to get out of this confined space. He needs the sunlight. He needs nature. He needs ice blue eyes to calm him down and jade green ones to excite him.

When he exits the room and approaches the peace of the garden, an unexpected sight makes him pause. Katelyn is sitting on the white wooden bench...next to James. Her sketchbook is out, but instead of her slender fingers skating a pencil across the page, the tome sits in James's lap as he makes hatched lines in jagged gestures. Despite his expressionless face, Elijah can tell he hates this.

Elijah can only just hear her quiet voice as she whispers instructions on "following the form" of whatever it is she's forcing James to draw, and Elijah chuckles while watching the love of his life indulge someone who isn't him. There is no jealousy like he thought there would be, only a lighthearted joy that wipes away the anger of the morning.

James's hands stop moving, and he stares at his picture for a long moment before hastily ripping it out, crumbling it into a rude ball, and tossing it to the ground with a blank face. Katelyn is pure shock as she watches the crumpled paper roll over the grass, but with the same null expression, James plucks one of the blue flowers from its nest and tucks it into her pages instead.

Her smile is warm, and Elijah's heart has never felt bigger.

He can make this work.

He has to.

And so does James.

Katelyn slides the sketchbook out of the blond Alpha's hands, unable to help her soft giggle. Apparently, illustration isn't his thing.

It wasn't coming out that bad!

Maybe.

Sort of.

By certain standards.

Refusing to keep pencil to paper any longer, he decided to crumple his bastardized landscape and stuff a poor flower into the crease of the book, instead. (And he called *her* a brat!)

At least he picked a pretty one. The gentian's fine, blue and purple petals stick up from the pages in gentle curves, its stamen nestled in the decorative black spots of its silky surface. Maybe she should have had him draw this instead of architecture and koi ponds.

James seems stiff beside her and Katelyn wonders if he's afraid to get scolded. To calm his assumed agitation, she smiles and closes the book on his gift, ready to dry it and keep it as a fragile bookmark to remember this moment. The memories of this place may have to last her a lifetime, after all. A token placed over her eyes as she heads to the funeral pyre, one gold coin from each Alpha.

James smells like nothing now, so all that draws her in is his personality, and that's opening up like one of the garden buds. He's more attentive than she thought. Even when he doesn't look at her, he makes every excuse for their skin to brush against each other. So sneaky. Painfully obvious, but sneaky anyway.

"So, if you're not into drawing, what are you into?" Katelyn asks.

It's like his face takes on life for the first time, and a sly, uncharacteristic smile pulls at the corners of his mouth. Without warning, he jumps up and scrambles to the living room, nearly mowing over his brother who leans against the paper screens. Katelyn hadn't even seen him. His hair is disheveled in a cute, messy bun and he's wearing those glasses he told her about. It gives him an air of intellectualism, if not for the laugh he blatts out.

"HA! Oh boy, now you've got him started!" Elijah's grin is beatific, shining like rays of the sun.

Wielding the stick she'd seen him handle before, James comes dashing back and takes a rigid stance. That smile is still there as his eyes lock on his weapon. He states in no uncertain terms, *"Kenjutsu."*

"I have no idea what that is," she admits.

His smile pulls wider, and he slides his ice blue eyes in her direction. "Swordplay."

James pulls his body into an intentional pose. His legs part and he bends at one knee, holding his—what can only be a "sword"—angled down on his right side. His left shoulder faces forward, as if toward an enemy, and he leans in, poised to receive a blow. It would be the perfect reference picture for a samurai of old. Katelyn's fingers itch to capture it in grays and war-stained reds.

To her surprise, James talks in flowing sentences. "This position is called *Waki no kamae*. It keeps my next move a surprise. From here, I can strike in four different ways."

He swings up and to the left in a distinct swipe that makes a *whooshing* noise. *"Hidari joho giri."*

He moves back to his original stance and brings the "sword" down in an aggressive, diagonal stroke over his head that follows through to the ground, halting just inches away and wafting the short grass in streams. *"Kesa giri."*

He takes his original stance once more before striking a cut parallel to the ground, right to left, causing another breeze to flutter through the courtyard. *"Suihei."*

He resets again. This time the blade comes down from above his head, casting a shadow over his face in a perfect line. *"Kiri oshi."* His grin becomes devilish. "Now combine them."

His sword swoops up and down, left and right in rapid succession as he works his way across the courtyard. He completes two sets before twirling around in a tornado whirlwind and working his way back. Halfway down the courtyard, he halts and throws a kick out, heel first, before moving back into his dance.

In a final takedown move, he growls and thrusts forward as if impaling an enemy samurai. *"Tsuke."*

Standing straight, he rolls his shoulders, holding the pole in front of him. His balance is perfect and his spine is an impeccable, rigid line. "*Kenjutsu* focuses on sword techniques. Katas."

"You can still spar, though," Elijah cuts in. "But if you do it with him, you're bound to come away with something unfortunate broken at a ninety-degree angle."

James pays him no mind, going through the stances again, feet planted and muscles flexing. His strikes are measured, flawless from what Katelyn can tell, and when James finishes his fourth set, he turns towards her, holding his "sword" out in an offering.

"Now you."

Oh, hell no, is Katelyn's first thought, but he looks so fierce, she doesn't dare say it out loud. Instead, she meeps out an "Okay" and sets aside her sketchbook, standing and swiping her hands over her butt as if to dust non-existent dirt off her pinstripe, pink pants.

Already her head is woozy. She didn't take as much medicine this morning, trusting them to make good on their promise to use her scent blockers, but even one pill is enough to pack a punch.

She stabilizes and heads closer, taking the "sword" while James offers a sharp clap and a bow. Following suit, she moves too—but into an old English style curtsey.

Damnit.

Elijah busts into laugher again, and her cheeks flush. James is still bent over, palms pressed flat against each other as he raises his eyebrow. Her throat rasps as she clears it, trying again and bending her waist at a forty-five-degree angle and praying that's enough. It seems to be.

Settling her body into his opening stance, she already feels foolish. Her bright blue high heels sink into the grass, which doesn't do her any favors.

"You've gotta correct her form or she'll get hurt," Elijah calls out.

James seems to do so willingly, platonically grabbing her hips to sink her lower and using his knee to knock hers forward.

She wishes she could concentrate on the moment instead of focusing on where his hands cup her. He works his way behind her and slides his arms around, pushing her left shoulder forward and pulling her right back until she matches the position as best she can.

"Now," he says, "*Hidari joho giri.*"

"Uhh…which one was that?"

Elijah steps closer. "Up and to the left."

James presses against her from behind and grabs her forearms, guiding her upward and turning her body just so, helping it follow through.

"Now by yourself," he murmurs.

He steps back and cool air caresses where he once was, making her feel the void where his aura slid against hers. Breathing a huff through her nose, she resets and tries it on her own, nearly knocking herself over in the process.

"Again," James says.

"You should try this in pin heels," she grumbles, making the bubbly brother chuckle.

"I can see it now, Jamsie. Size sixteens. I'll get you shiny black for that classic secretary look."

James swipes out to bat at his brother, but misses by a mile as he dodges, spinning to Katelyn's front and blowing her a kiss.

"You want me to hit you with this?" She brandishes the stick, but her words come out more giddy than grumpy.

"Only if you kiss it and make it better after." Elijah tosses her a wink this time before skipping out of the way and plopping on the bench to watch them.

Unmoved as always, James just takes a firmer hold on her, the heat from his body radiating through her own. Pinning her ass to his hips, he whispers in her ear. "*Kesa giri.*"

Her arms are brought in a slash down toward the other side. The speed of the movement makes her rock on the balls of her feet, but he keeps her steady. This time he latches onto her biceps and angles her arms upward. "*Kiri oshi.*"

She whips the pole down with all her strength…and embeds it in the ground.

Her face couldn't get any redder as Elijah *PFFFFT*s from his perch.

She flips him off.

There is a huff behind her, and James's breath tickles her ear. She looks over her shoulder and sees that non-expression, but his eyes glint with warmth. There's nothing she wants more than to keep that gentle look on his face, but he turns her around again and settles her in starting position.

"Next is…su…subian?" she tries, her voice airy as he slides his hands down again, resting at her elbows.

"*Suihei*," he corrects, and brings her into a swing to the left, parallel to the ground. She freezes as he nuzzles into her hair, his breath hot and something decidedly firm in his pants as he keeps pressed against her. "Now all of it, Katelyn."

If she could melt, she would. Their lack of scent may be keeping her Omega in check, but she's still a woman with wants and desires, and having someone like James getting hard behind her is enough to make any girl weak.

Elijah's teasing smile isn't helping. It's as if he knows exactly what's going on without having to be told…and he likes it.

Butterflies flutter inside her.

James steps away, his hands lingering for a moment on her rib cage before he's out of reach. She bites her lip and avoids the impulse to step backwards into him again.

"All of it," he says again, low and slow.

Taking a deep breath, she balances herself and tries. One. Two. Three. Four. It's stilted, but she does her best.

"So pretty, my rainbow," Elijah purrs. "I could watch you do this all day."

Those butterflies turn into hummingbirds, their wings beating at maximum speed.

One. Two. Three. Four. It's quicker this time. The makeshift weapon in her hands is heavy and smooth, well worn by the Alpha behind her. She grips it tight and can feel her shoulders burning from the effort, trying out muscles she's sure she's never used before.

Her breath is starting to quicken as she mimics James, taking a step forward on swings three and four. Her head lightens now, and beads of sweat begin to prickle her body. Airy stars sparkle in the corners of her eyes, and that tell-tale feeling of numbness tingles around her lips.

Not now. Please, no.

The weakness in her body gets the best of her, and the pole angles toward the ground as she rocks forward.

She's woozy.

She's going to faint.

"Stop," James commands, scooping her up in his arms. She feels like feathers, a nothing-weight when compared to his strength. She wants to nuzzle in, but instead, her head lolls back and her glasses go askew, riding up above her nose in a purely undignified way. She couldn't care less.

"I'm sorry," she tries, but is summarily cut off by her Alpha.

"Hush."

Alphas are strong, so saith The Lifestyle. *Strong enough to crush you with one hand. Why should we let anyone like that into our society? They are dangerous, no matter how human they look.*

Elijah has his hands out and is waving his brother over, ready to take Katelyn in his arms. With a teasing, exhausted lilt, she reminds him, "No touching," and watches the poor man visibly deflate. She regrets her words immediately, but what else is she going to do? After all, she has to leave them both in the end.

Setting her on the other side of the bench, James kneels in front of her, looking from one eye to the other before setting the back of his hand over her forehead. He looks at Elijah. "Too warm."

Rejected or not, Elijah slides her glasses further up her nose to straighten them. "Is this normal?"

She huffs. "My medicine."

Elijah stiffens and inhales deeply before spitting out a curse. "Can I get you off those, too?"

"Not unless you want me to go into heat right here."

"Yes," James states. "Do that."

A breathy laugh bubbles as she leans James away from her, pressing his shoulders until he gives her some room. "That can't happen."

"It can," he insists.

"It will," Elijah adds. "It's only a matter of time."

Her jaw tightens, and all amusement leaves. "I'll stop it. Forever, if I can. No one knows. No one can ever know. Promise me."

Both Alphas drop their eyes.

Elijah sags. "I won't tell."

James nods subtly.

She leans back on the bench, her head resting over the top edge. "Thank you. Thomas would…" she doesn't complete the thought. That bastard would do a lot of things.

"I hate him," James mutters, and it makes her snort a laugh. He's not alone in that.

"I got a call from him this morning," Elijah says.

"Break your phone," James states, earning a snort from his brother.

Katelyn grimaces. "What did he want?"

Elijah sits back and loops his ankle over his opposite knee, bouncing it and crossing his arms. His voice drips with anger. "To 'make sure you were okay.'"

"What did you tell him?"

"You're not."

He's more right than he knows.

"Fucker was happy to hear it, too."

Of course he was. That's exactly what he wants…to punish her for having an Omega friend. To ensure she won't cause a scandal. He wants her to be afraid.

"I *hate* him," James repeats with an unfamiliar vehemence.

In unison, all three of them let out a collective sigh that would be adorable in other circumstances. That heartache niggles again. This is what Katelyn has always wanted. This closeness. Being in synch with someone.

Who knew it would be two someones…

Elijah slides her sketchbook back onto her lap. When she looks at him, his smile has returned, even if it's dimmed from sunshine to moonlight. "Draw for me. I want to see James's sword forms."

James nods faster than anything she's seen, staring at the book as if it were the holy grail.

Giggling again, a shyness takes over her as she slides her fingers along the cover. "Okay, I guess. He'll have to do those perfect poses for me again, though." James's ears blush pink. "We start with 'wacky karma ji-ji,' right?"

His mouth becomes a flat line and both Elijah and Katelyn chuckle. Still, the Alpha opens her book, tucking the semi-flattened flower behind her ear and smoothing out the blank page. "Draw." He jumps up and goes to where she dropped his faux weapon, snapping it up and leaning back into his opening stance. *"Waki no kamae,"* he corrects, and she gets to work.

Elijah watches her every stroke with a soft smile on his face, leaning his elbow on the back of the bench and propping up his chin. "You know I'm going to keep all these."

"Mm." James nods again, holding his pose. "Look at them every day."

Elijah asks, "You trying to make me practice?"

"No. Just making you look at me."

It's so open, so honest, so sweet, that Katelyn can't help but smile. They love each other so much.

…She wants to love them, too.

CHAPTER 10

FAMILY TIES

Elijah misses his laptop. Doing this on the phone is a pain in the ass.

Miss Katelyn Annamarie has no social media accounts he can find unless she's come up with some obscure username like Hidden-Omega69. Not that he can complain. Neither he nor his brother have anything set up, either. What's the point when all you have is secrets and acquaintances, not a friend in sight.

There are also no announcements on who Thomas Bleaker is marrying, though there are speculative articles surrounding his coming of age. Apparently, people in The Lifestyle must marry before the age of thirty and he's working his way up there. People are fawning over his ideal future, almost planning it for him, and he seems to enjoy sucking up the attention. If his interviewers' body language indicates anything, everyone who talks to him wants to fuck him. He seems to suck that up, too. Both the media and he cite that he's not up for grabs, though. He's been betrothed since youth, as is The Lifestyle's norm, and reporters are up in arms, making ridiculous guesses about who his enigmatic mystery bride could be. Famous Lifestyle actresses and activists. Beta homemakers richer than God who have been trained to be the perfect wife since the time they were five. How disappointed they'll be when they find out it's just a regular woman from a regular family.

Does Katelyn want that kind of heat on her? She doesn't seem the type to hog the spotlight for something like that. She may be attention grabbing, but only for her artistic flare and style, not for the reasons Thomas Bleaker would want her to be.

How long has she been saddled with this pretentious piece of shit?

Elijah stares at a video interview played on silent with closed captioning, able to feel Sir Thomas's smarmy personality ooze from his overly languid facial expressions. It shouldn't be a surprise. Elijah knew he was sleazy. He's seen clips of him before. Who hasn't? The man and his father are all over the news as secondary genders try to rally the government against their ever-growing faction. Mr. Bleaker, good old Tom-Tom's father, is sly, though. Everything above board. "Beta exclusivity is not discrimination any more than Alpha and Omega societies, clubs, and schools are. If we're truly equal, why can't we have the same benefits?"

Maybe because Alphas were physically and emotionally abused to be used as attack dogs in war. Maybe because Omegas were forced into heat to be sex slaves for kings, princes, and politicians.

Not that all Betas are terrible people. They can't be blamed for what their ancestors did. That doesn't mean that the world doesn't need to change into a place where wrongs can be made right.

"I fucking hate you," Elijah mutters to his phone.

Thomas Bleaker is starting a Beta-only college. That must be what he was talking about on the phone when he dropped his personal bomb on his fiancée's life. "Let her have a job," he said. As if it was his gift to grant, not her right as a human being. That asshole.

There are several more articles, but Elijah has had all he can stand of his incompetent rival at the moment. Instead, he digs deeper into the top brass of The Lifestyle. Elders older than God, matrons too young to be married to those bastards, and a woman that catches his attention. She has unfamiliar brown hair and a stocky frame, but jade eyes and a smile so dear it hurts.

Iris Masters.

This must be Katelyn's mother.

She's high up in the organization—a position called an "Acolyte." Clicking in, her profile lists her devotion, successes that can be credited to her, and a story of love and loss, mentioning the birth and death dates of her husband and son.

Katelyn's family had died…? Just like James's dad. No wonder she clings to her mother so hard. They both do. The fear of loss must have been crammed into them since a tender young age. Doing math, she could have been no more than six when it happened. That's the age Elijah was when his mother left. Back then, he'd done everything in his power to take care of his father and ease his broken heart. Had Katelyn done the same? Probably. With only one parent left, one who is grieving no less, what can you do but take the love meant to be split between two people and pump it into the one who didn't leave you.

Iris Masters is listed as "one of the most devout and loyal members of The Lifestyle." She's easily findable online. She has posts of friends he recognizes from the "who's who of our cult" pages. They're at rallies. Events. Fundraisers. Madam Iris is in it to win it.

But is she a good person?

He digs into her public records. No misdemeanors or felonies. No DUIs or car accidents. No home owned, but she does have a consistent apartment in her photos. The address is easy to dig for. It's easy to break into the online records of the housing company, too.

She doesn't own it. And her name might be on the lease, but the guarantor is an account belonging to The Lifestyle.

So…being an acolyte has perks.

Her bank is easily accessible, too. The same company seems to be her only paycheck. She's reliant on these motherfuckers to the nth degree. No wonder Katelyn never let the world know what she is.

Elijah hacks into the financials of other "Acolytes" one after the other but finds no evidence of Lifestyle support. Is it only Madam Iris? If so, why?

Her ties to them run deep. Could she ever let go of The Lifestyle's funding? Bite the hand that feeds her? Switch allegiances? Do something else with her time?

Hm. No previous jobs or online resume. No college records. Dropped out of high school, too. Seems she got pregnant. *Pfft*, and they say Betas are in control of their sexual desires. At that age, no one is.

If The Lifestyle is what picked up the pieces after Madam Iris's life fell apart, it makes sense why she's so devout.

Looking deeper, her parents were members, too. Good old Grandma and Grandpa Masters as well, all the way back as far as free genealogy research will take him. This woman has been born and bred to be exactly what she is. Someone who would despise her own daughter if given the chance. Even that bastard Thomas said that's what The Lifestyle does. If their children present, they "get rid of them."

Iris Masters may be a lost cause.

Katelyn watches the door swing open, a ball of her slick-stained laundry clutched in her arms like a wailing baby, one that screams her leftover pheromones at Elijah as he tries his best to ignore it. She sees what it does to him, though. There's a haziness in his eyes and a tension in his muscles. Will he get closer? Breathe her in? She's not wearing scent blockers right now; how strong is her natural scent?

A few picks of the lock with a tool that looked like a large needle, and Elijah had popped the mechanism and opened the door wide, introducing her to a spacious mudroom complete with a stacked washer and dryer in burgundy red. Very sleek. Stylish, just like the rest of this place. A large window points toward a part of the grounds she hasn't seen yet and…

There's a door.

A door to the outside.

He seems to know the minute she sees it, and places himself in her line of sight, blocking her from the road to salvation. "And this would be why the room is locked." He tries to toss her a smile, but it's tight. "No sneaky ideas, Miss Katelyn Annamarie."

"Where's the Jones-Masters part?"

Now his grin turns cocky. "I'd like to imagine you with a different last name."

"Bleaker?"

"Don't make me retch."

He opens the washing machine's circular door for her but backs away while she stuffs her contents inside. Her shredded shirt is going in too, just to get every molecule of scent off before she stuffs it into the trash.

Giving her space, Elijah leans against the window and watches her layer in cup after cup of detergent. She wishes she could douse the whole thing in bleach. It might ruin her clothes, but it would save her from the constant reminder of her Omega-inflicted humiliation.

It's a blessing the pair of them smell like nothing now. Otherwise, whether she means to or not, when her memory throws pictures of them touching each other at her again, she might repeat yesterday's hormonal outburst. She wouldn't be able to help it. That moment is what dirty dreams are made of.

As she dribbles blue drips of viscous, skin-sensitive soap, the portal to freedom calls. There's no way they could have locked the main door from the outside. If they did, none of them could ever leave this stunning, movie set architecture, and eventually someone will need to get groceries. She secretly wishes to order a pizza. Maybe then she could slink out and hide in the delivery guy's car until she got back to civilization.

What does this place look like from the outside, anyway? Is it a regular roof, or is it that beautiful ceramic tiling that she's seen in history books and foreign movies? How far is she from a neighbor? Is it yards or miles she'll have to tiptoe before she finds respite?

She shuts the washing machine's front with a rubber-padded click and scans the buttons. There are more settings than she knows what to do with, but lands on "Heavy Soil" with an extra rinse. The buttons chime as she tries her best not to look at the outside door, or at Elijah as he guards it. Out of the corner of her eye, he hovers in shadow, backlit by the window behind him.

The smell of fresh pancakes drifts into this hope-instilling space, and her stomach growls, still trying to punish her for days spent barely eating.

"Let's go, rainbow," Elijah says with a chuckle. She only nods.

Before the door shuts behind them, he flicks a lock on the inside of the doorknob and jiggles it to ensure it won't turn. "Don't worry. I'll put them in the drier for you later."

"Ugh. Please don't. Give me something to do. My mind is melting in this place. There's only so many hours I can stare at my wall before admitting defeat and losing interest. What do *you* do all day while I'm avoiding you? Because I'll tell you what I've been doing."

Oh God, here goes her mouth again.

"I ostrich! I stick my head in my pillow and do my best not to suffocate. I have terrible nightmares and these intrusive, obsessive thoughts that twist me into freaking mush while I simultaneously lambaste myself for being stupid enough to get caught in this situation in the first place!"

"You act like it's your fault." He saunters beside her. "I hope you've been using some of your time to mull over what a manipulative dick your genderist fiancée is."

That she has.

"What manipulative people *you* are, you mean?" she says instead. "Willing to take a woman against her will and hold her for an entire month just to try and lure her in with your—" she gestures at...all of him. "What did you think was going to happen?"

"Sex," he states simply.

"Wouldn't James have a problem with that?"

"Nah." Elijah waves it off as they round a corner. "If anything, I thought *I'd* be the jealous type. Turns out, I'm not. It's weird. Seeing you two together feels...right. I can't explain it. James said, if he and I were a puzzle, we were missing a chunk in the center. He was right." Elijah's voice drops to something satin and serious. "You, my darling, are our missing piece."

Her heart throbs.

She wants to bury it in gravel.

"You aren't going to give up, are you?"

"Why should I?" he says. "If I did, it would mean this didn't matter to me." He steps in front of her, walking backwards with his redwood eyes glittering. "But you're worth fighting for. Convincing. Protecting. You're worth learning about, playing with, and teasing, too." He stops short, crowding into her space without touching her, keeping his promise even though she wishes he wouldn't. "I want to know you, Katelyn Annamarie. I want to look into every inch of your backstory and track you down. I want to meet your friends and know what makes you tick. I want to pick you apart and put you back together again. I want to fall in love with you," he says, reaching up as if to run his fingers through her hair, but pulling back at the last moment. "And James does, too."

She can see the Alpha in question now, his broad back and blond head hovering over the stove and fussing with things.

"How do you know?" she asks.

Elijah's smile is like honey. "Because I know everything about him."

He spins on his heels and heads into the kitchen, flitting around his brother. Opening and shutting cabinets, he starts making coffee again, leaving Katelyn to sit at the table and fiddle with her fingers. Her desires are held so close to her chest, hidden away, but he just lays them out on the table. James, too. They know what they want…and it's her.

Omegas are fools if they believe in love, so saith The Lifestyle. *It's all biology. Anything else is a lie they tell themselves so they can sleep at night.*

She looks at her wrist and remembers the purple scar that traces James's vein. It makes a heavy hurt throb within her. If she'd only known him earlier, would she have been able to stop him from feeling so lost? Could she have completed their puzzle and helped their relationship make sense to outsiders? How did Elijah feel, seeing the person he loves so dearly almost end his own life? Their relationship is unconventional, sure, but it's not like they're *real* brothers. Still, she can only imagine what their parents would think. She knows more than her fair share about what it means to put on a show in order to spare their feelings.

You're not dirty, she'd told James. He'd made her say it over and over. Then he'd turned it around on her. *You're not dirty, Katelyn.*

Sitting alone, her eyes well up and she swipes the moisture away with the back of her hand as the coffee starts to percolate. She's so tired of crying.

"You want to drink a mimosa with breakfast, today," Elijah says to his brother, humor lacing his words.

There's no reaction.

"Hm. You want to show off your forms to our pretty little captive some more."

There is a beat of silence as Elijah leans over and rests his chin on his brother's shoulder. "You want me to get the hell out of here so you can cook."

James doesn't change his body language at all, but Elijah clucks his tongue with a grin. "Bingo."

James flops down on the too-hard couch, his knees spreading wide as he settles in. Across the room, Elijah wanders, knocking around this knickknack or that while. To the left, Katelyn perches on the edge of a contemporary plush chair that doesn't match the rest of the décor.

She's farther away than he'd like. Truth be told, his inner Alpha wants her in his lap, his nose in her nape and his tongue on her mating gland, teeth grazing that blushed patch of thin skin. Anything else is an exercise in self-restraint. He's proven himself to be lacking in that.

Oh well. *Nana korobi ya oki.* Fall down seven times, get up eight. In other words: Persevere. No matter your previous mistakes, never stop trying. Said in another way: Don't pin her down and try to claim her without her consent next time.

Why is that so hard?

He tenses his jaw. Every pore and hair follicle stings from her disgusting, scent-blocking salve, tingling as if fire ants were gnawing on his prone flesh. How can she stand it? His head aches from how hard he's grinding his teeth, willing himself not to scour it off under scalding hot water. Elijah, for his part, seems to be taking it in stride, but when has his brother ever liked to show his weaknesses? He has a high tolerance for pain, despite his antics to pretend otherwise.

Elijah opens a secret panel in the decorative cabinet against the wall to reveal a large TV screen. His smirk is devious, and Katelyn's eyes widen like a woodland child seeing a fox spirit for the first time.

"You said there was no TV!"

Elijha waggles his eyebrows. "That was when I wanted your focus to be on me and my junk, but now that I know my rainbow is bored off her ass, I figured a little distraction won't hurt. Besides, wanna know what I have?"

She crosses her arms and leans back. Just looking at her, James doesn't know whether she's curious, sulking, or irritated, but…there's something new he's never experienced before. He can *smell* her emotion. Taste it in the air. She's a stunning mix of all three states of mind, wrapped up in the sweet scent of peaches.

This has never happened, not even with Elijah. How can he possibly read her like this?

…Because she's his mate.

Warmth unfurls in his chest like an orchid in spring.

"What do you have?" Katelyn grumps in his brother's direction.

"Alien movies."

James can't stop staring as she lights up like a star. This expression, he knows. Glee. Her scent backs up his guess, her sweet smell deepening into something succulent and tender, as if he could devour it in beastly bites.

"Really!?" she says.

"Well, I assume," Elijah replies. "We have, like, seven streaming services here."

Eight, actually.

"One of them is bound to have something." Elijiah thumbs on the TV, turns around, and with the air of a temple worshiper, he kneels and offers up the remote, bowing his head in feigned reverence. "My lady."

She bites her lip to hide a smile and takes it, careful that their fingers don't touch. It's a shy and cute gesture. She seems to like Elijah, and it's a relief. Mate or not, that's a requirement.

Between the two of them, it takes a few minutes to figure out how to work the controller. It's like watching a sitcom minus the laugh track. James knows exactly how it works but doesn't bother to interrupt—their muttering, grumbling, and fumbling is far too amusing.

Watching them, they paint the perfect picture. Domestic and

mundane. With them beside him, James can almost pretend this is a real home. That they are his true pack. That there's nothing to be afraid of anymore.

Unfamiliar calm cascades like a bubbling stream from his mind to his belly, cooling the tension that burns him on a daily basis. If he's a desert nomad, this moment is an oasis.

"This one?" Elijah asks.

"Looks too science-y without the fiction part."

Elijah snorts. "This one looks more sci-fi fantasy. It's got green people, does that count?"

She considers, seemingly unaware that his brother is hovering in her space. It must be because of their muted scent. James hates that. She should be as captivated by them as they are by her.

"I could go for some green people."

"We talking tentacle porn or…?"

She gapes and whaps Elijah off the back of the head. Good for her. If she didn't do it, he was about to. "No! We're talking spaceships and *pew pew* battles for alien rights!"

"Do you think the ending will be a happy one?" Elijah teases, unphased by her abuse.

She swipes the remote and shoos him. "Of course. Otherwise, why bother making the movie? Aliens need love, too."

What a heady concept.

James wonders if that's what she thinks she is. An alien. She's separated herself from her body, from her instinct, curling inside herself and trying not to touch the shell of her own reality. He doesn't like that. He wants her to spread into her own skin. To wear it like the tight clothes she's so fond of, the ones that make him hold her in the corner of his eyes so he can admire her every curve.

"Are you in for some *pew pew*, Jamsie?"

Happiness flips a somersault in his chest. "Mm."

Elijah grins that beautiful grin. "Then here we go!"

Katelyn is obsessed. Not because of the movie—though that's also… entertaining—but because Elijah sits on the floor next to her chair like a loyal puppy. He doesn't seem to care about the hard wood, though his thin man-butt must be sore from embedding itself in the dark planks. She can't stop looking at him out of the corner of her eye, feeling the Alpha's heat roll off him. She misses his scent.

Can he smell her? Would he bury his face in her neck like his brother did if she only let go of her self-preservation and asked him to?

She knows the answer is yes.

He gestures at the TV in irritation. "Come on! Doesn't anyone in this stupid battle know how to aim!? Grok has left himself open, like, ten times and not even a flesh wound!"

"Maybe he has a natural shield that deflects the blaster beams?" Katelyn suggests.

"Or the writer didn't feel like giving the Anti-faction at least *one* brain cell to share between them!"

"B-movie," James says.

"C-movie!" Elijah corrects.

"But Grok is kind of endearing," Katelyn says, immediately drawing the slitted eyes of the two Alphas in the room. Are they jealous? Their feathers are definitely ruffled.

Elijah pouts, hiking up his knees and resting his chin on them. "I don't see how. He's been blasé for the past hour and a half."

"It's all in the voice," Katelyn says, tapping her throat. "It's gravelly when he talks to others, but sweet when he talks to his creche. It makes you want to give him a hug for being so melty soft on the inside."

"I'm melty," James states.

Elijah juts a thumb over his shoulder toward his brother. "Truer words have never been spoken."

The movie ends with a cheesy walk into the sunset. It could be an old time western, except for the three suns of different sizes, all in neon colors. That planet must be boiling. Maybe that's why Grok's species is crimson red. Ultra-violet rays are a bitch. Why this movie was almost three hours, Katelyn has no idea.

During the scrolling credits, most of which have last names ending in "vanovich," she says, "I want a do over. Let's actually look at the star ratings this time."

Elijah *tsks*. "Nope! It's lunch, then it's Jamsie's turn." He looks over his shoulder. "You in the mood? That new one came out."

James doesn't smile, but he tilts his head ever so slightly down. It's the most subtle nod she's ever seen.

Reactions aside, he must be excited. Enough to get the meal over quickly, at least. Lunch was the least elaborate thing he's made during her time in this locked-up purgatory. It's a simple set up of peanut butter and jelly sandwiches, with Elijah's crust cut off.

"Are you a child?" she asks.

"Hey, he's been doing this for me since we were fifteen. Who am I to switch up the program?"

James makes a subtle nod again.

There are choices of marshmallow fluff, grape jelly, strawberry jam, or bananas. Bananas! Who puts bananas on peanut butter!?

James apparently.

Well, better not to knock it 'till you've tried it, but she'll stick with strawberry jam. Elijah's smile curls soft and slow, a daub of peanut butter dotted along his lower lip. Why is that sexy? He looks at her with that sly expression he gets, his eyes half-lidded and his eyebrows up.

"What?" Katelyn asks.

"Just wondering."

"Wondering what?"

"How sweet that will make you taste."

She shoves her sandwich in her mouth, taking a choking-hazard size bite to avoid a response.

Elijah takes full advantage. He leans closer, speaking just outside the shell of her ear. "If I were to kiss you, run my tongue along yours, you'd taste intoxicating. Though, I'm sure you'd bewitch me any day. Do you think I could come from just from feeling your lips on mine?"

She sputters and snarfs, breadcrumbs lodging themselves in the back half of her nose.

Having sympathy, he pats her hard on the back a few times while James hands her a glass of milk.

"Not allowed!" she chokes out.

"All's fair in ruts and heats," Elijah says, still smiling at her. She has half a mind to smash his lunch in his face. Thumping her on the back a few more times, he helps her clear her throat. "Do I count as endearing, too?"

"Annoying," James corrects, but that doesn't stop him from leaning across the table and swiping the smear of peanut butter off Elijah's lower lip. Elijah closes his eyes and feels the slow drag before trying to nip his brother. For his part, James ignores him, but suckles his thumb to taste what his brother almost wasted.

She's going to choke again, but for different reasons. "S-so, what's the next movie?"

"*Martial Law Four*," Elijah says through another bite. "I guarantee it will be better than the trash we just watched."

"Not a high bar," James monotones, shoving the last bite in his mouth and dusting his hands.

Katelyn frowns at both of them. She should have checked the star rating.

In the end, they watched two more movies. *Martial Law* was exciting. It had excellent fight scene choreography and witty banter that reminded her of both Niles and Elijah. Her dark haired Alpha sat across the room this time, leaning back on his hands with his legs stretched wide. His laughter at the jokes was infectious, and Katelyn found herself smiling along with him.

She'd wanted to pick the next movie, but James simply "No"ed her, grabbing the remote control and putting on a sweeping fantasy with dragons, willowy elves, and a banner-hoisting medieval flare. Elijah "Huzzah"ed with glee and settled himself between his brother's knees this time.

Somehow, it made her happy that they weren't just giving in to every one of her whims. This was more reciprocal. Less fake and forced, the Alphas dropping their roles as seducers. This is more about give and take. Something for each of them. Everyone belongs.

During the movie, Katelyn glanced over to see that James had taken out Elijah's messy man-bun and was running his fingers through his hair, scratching his scalp absently. For his part, Elijah looked more content than Katelyn had ever seen. No sexy sleight of hand, no mischievous playing, no reassuring chats to bring her out of her shell. He just looked relaxed. At home. He didn't really live here, but she had the feeling that, wherever James was, was home.

Home. She feels like she's never had one. Places to live, surely. Places to leave her laundry laying on the floor and decorate with every blinding color and pattern she can find, but never a place to feel like Elijah looks right now.

What would it be like to have a home with them? Be a part of this dynamic? Even if she wasn't an Omega, she might want this. Was this the kind of behavior she missed while she was hiding away in her room? This obvious love between them?

James catches her staring a few times but says nothing, though the corner of his mouth does tick up into a smile.

Watching them has her spellbound.

Which is why she needs to escape tonight.

CHAPTER 11
LETTERS AND GOODBYES

Dear Thomas,

Or should I say: "Fuck you, Thomas."

KATELYN PRESSES her pencil down so hard on the paper, it digs into the pages stacked behind, leaving lumps and bumps that will destroy any drawings future-her might want to make.

I was never happy about my life with you, but I was resigned to it. I thought you were kind — to me, at least — but I never understood why you or The Lifestyle hated people you've never even met just because of something twirled into their DNA. It doesn't make them the evil you want them to be.

Why are you like this? I know you were groomed from a young age but come on! When your teenage pimples popped, you should have had some goddamn ideas of your own!

But he did. Katelyn remembers the "conversion program" he'd shared with her the last time they'd been face-to-face. How, if Alphas and Omegas could just prove they were fighting against their nature, he'd try to show them leniency. Allow them into The Lifestyle, as long as they were self-loathing monsters and not those who reveled in the joy of existing.

Will she be the first to join his pitiable ranks?

You don't know me. No one does. Not my mother, not even my only friend, which you took away from me.

How could you trap me here? How could you let me taste this life and expect me to give it up?

Because he didn't know she was an Omega. This was supposed to be an exercise in building up her disgust, proving her commitment, ensuring she was pure, demure, and ready to marry the future leader of the biggest cult in the country. It *wasn't* supposed to be an exercise in self-control, rejecting your instincts, and scathing self-recrimination. But that's what it is.

What kind of person does this to someone else? I knew you had warped values, but this is criminal. When I go back to you, what am I supposed to say? What am I supposed to do? Our wedding is scheduled for, what, the day I get out? You'll take me from this place and whisk me off to hair and makeup, stuffing me into a white dress and pretending the tears in my eyes are from joy?

Her bleak future stands before her.

If she'd never met her Alphas, could she have kept in her secret her whole life? What would happen when her body couldn't take it anymore and forced her into a heat? Would Thomas pity her as she begged him for sex, slicking up their fine rugs and causing a scene with his maids?

I hate you.

She writes it because she can never say it.

Fury sizzles her sensibilities as she writes, *I hate you, I hate you, I hate you* all over the page, stabbing her words in as if tattooing the paper. It's ugly and scrawling, like a teenager gouging dirty words in a bathroom stall. "For a good time, bomb Thomas Bleaker's house. His address is 555..."

Her jaw sets as she rips the sheet out, covered in gray graphite curses and vitriol. She can't shred the paper small enough. The moon laughs at her as she dices the page like a witch preparing ingredients to hex a wicked puritan, one that pretends to be holy as he hangs her coven sisters by the throat with nothing but the love of God on his mind. She wants to make it snow with all the little pieces, but instead tosses them into a trash barrel containing the hair wrenched from her hairbrush and the shirt she can never wear again because her Alpha wanted her so bad, he lost his mind.

Her hands cover her face as she tries to breathe. She didn't realize her lungs were frozen in place until they began to burn. Her head throbs as she sinks back onto the bed and grabs her sketchbook once more, flipping to an unmarred page.

Dear Mom,

I wish I could be honest with you. You've tried your best to take care of me, even after dad died and you were alone. I know you struggled. I know the only people you felt you could rely on were the elders, but don't forget about me, too.

I made you dinner when you couldn't stop crying. I

drew you pictures to try to make you smile. I loved you with my whole heart then, just like I love you today.

I know I'm not the best daughter. I'm whiny and stubborn. You don't like taking me out because of my clothes. I'm not good at picking out wedding flowers or pretty veils. But we're in this together, no matter what happens.

I won't leave Thomas. I know what will happen to you if I do, and I won't put you through that, but can I ask you a favor? Just like I protected you, can you protect me, too?

Her lower lip trembles.

Things are about to get really hard for me. Harder than they've ever been. I hurt all the time. My doctor never told me how long I can be on this medicine, but surely not forever. If I go into heat, will you hide me? Will you forgive me? Will you please still love me?

If I have children, what will we do then? The doctors will surely know what I am. And even if they don't tell Thomas, Omegas are supposed to be really protective. Will I give myself away? Will it be obvious when my body tells me to rub my scent all over my little one to make sure everyone knows they're mine?

Thomas isn't who you think he is, Mom. He's done something horrible. He's trapped me with the world's most perfect Alphas.

I'd rather he had thrown me in a cellar. Not because

I'm afraid of these men, because I'm not anymore. I'm afraid of myself. Of how much I want them.

I'm not going to talk to you about sex, I promise, but this is more than that. All my life, I've never fit. I'm weird. I'm an outsider. But they want to let me in.

Fate chose me for them, and they're making sure I know it. They're not wrong. I can feel it all the way down to my atoms and quarks. This is meant to be. They're mine. I'm theirs.

But, for you, I will walk away.

I miss you, Mommy. If my secret comes out, please keep loving me, because it's not my fault. I would change it if I could. I promise.

I'm so sorry.

There's never been a more repeating phrase in her mind. No matter how her mouth has a habit of running on its own, there are things she can never say out loud. This pathetic "Please love me" is one of them. "Please forgive me" is another. But "I'm sorry…" that one she says even when she did nothing wrong. She'll make any excuse to apologize to her mother. She'll cough on purpose just to let the words fly from her lips when a heat cramp throttles her belly. It's not her fault, but it's her fault anyway.

You're not dirty, James had said. Maybe that's true. And maybe it doesn't matter.

This letter is torn out much more carefully, not leaving behind any shreds along the interior edge. Instead of slashing it to pieces, she folds it into a paper crane, line after crisp line. Origami cranes are folded in order to help someone make wishes, and they belong in a beautiful space such as this. She'd need a hundred of them to have her dreams come true, but she's not a child anymore. She knows that wishes are nothing but words thrown into the air.

One last letter, and then she'll go to the door of escape. She's stayed up so late now, her Alphas must be asleep. Red rimmed, her eyes squint with exhaustion, but even so, threads of tension weave into her bones.

When she gets out, she's going to have to run. To where? Who knows. The only thing she's taking is her medicine. Goodbye, wardrobe. Goodbye, sketchbook. Goodbye, sweet dreams.

Dear Elijah and James, or should I say "Zeb" and "Finn."

You've made me feel more in two weeks than I've felt in a lifetime. Shock and horror among them. Lust and fascination, too. More than that, you made me feel like there is a future that's different than the one laid out for me. The sad part is that I don't believe in that future. Or rather, I can't let myself.

You kidnapped me. Funny enough, I forgive you for that. Just goes to show how stupid I am. I'm not afraid of you anymore, either. Elijah, you helped me with that. You were gentle when I needed you to be. You also played with me. Even when I was young, other than my brother, no one else did. You made me smile, even when you weren't looking.

James, you absolved me. You made me feel like I didn't have to be lost. That I wasn't alone. We may be broken, but we were broken together. I wish we could have found the glue to put ourselves back together again. If I had my way, I'd erase all your scars, even the ones I can't see.

I'm sorry for running away. I know this means you might not get your money, but maybe Thomas will be proud that I found a way to escape. I think it's obvious what my feelings about him are, but you have to trust that I'm doing this for a reason. And maybe, just maybe, I can convince him over time that Alphas and Omegas aren't bad.

I'm sorry, but I have to beg you again to keep my secret. Keep this letter, burn this letter, do what you need to do, but make sure no one finds it.

If I were a different woman, I'd rub it all over me to remind you of what I smell like, but that's too cruel. I'll remember your scents, though. How could I ever forget? Together, you're like a forest I'd like to build a cabin in. Light a fire in the hearth, settle down, and stay.

Life is funny, isn't it? And terrible, too.

Be safe, be happy, and find yourself an Omega who will love you for everything you are. You both deserve the world.

Katelyn

She stares at her signature…

It looks incomplete.

What is their last name? She wants to imagine it sewn onto the end of hers with the finest embroidery. She wants to write it in cursive on blank notebook pages, imagining life by their side. Fantasies of them might just be what keep her alive over the next fifty years, or maybe they'll only cause her anguish. She'll be left envisioning the contentment of having her hair stroked. She'll ruminate on fighting James for control of the kitchen. She'll get lost in the idea of giving in to all of Elijah's dirty talk.

No. It's better to forget.

If only she could.

This letter will actually find its way to its owners. It's taken out gingerly, just like her mother's, but she doesn't fold it. She reads it two, three, ten times before laying it on her bedspread, resting halfway against her pillow.

She can do this. She can run.

She has to.

The hallway is silent. Even her toes feathering on the floor make no sound. The only echo is the nighttime crickets in the courtyard, but even that is dimmed to a shallow hum with the paper screens shut.

She counts the doors. One of them is the bathroom, one is the unnecessary gym, one is filled with hidden art she's sad she'll never get a chance to see, and the last one is the door to freedom.

She slips her palm around the door handle and turns it slowly, not daring to make a creak.

There's no movement.

Not that she expected there to be.

Getting down to her knees, she looks for the pinhole in the center of the doorknob. Elijah had poked something in there to pop the lock, which seemed simple enough. Thank God James had snagged her makeup bag.

She works a bobby pin out of her pocket and bites into the top, wrenching off the plastic bulb that prevents her from stabbing her own head whenever she pins up her hair. Using her teeth, she unbends the metal to an obtuse angle just wide enough for her to be able to insert the tip of the pin. The tiny clicking and clacking sounds of metal on metal make her wince, and her jaw tenses in the silent night, knowing that as soon as she finds the inner mechanism, the *pop* it makes may as well be like throwing a pan on a tile floor.

She's not wrong.

Her shoulders hike up to her ears when she hears the sound, but there is no time to hold back. Twisting the knob, she throws open the door, letting it bang against the wall behind her as she scrambles to the outer door.

The deadbolt is thrown—which shouldn't be an issue other than that it wastes precious seconds—but it sticks like a motherfucker. Turning it makes her grunt with effort, as if the bolt is made of nothing but red rust. She's almost got it. Almost—

But a hand loops around her stomach and pulls her back.

"No!" she yelps. The scent blockers have worn off in the night, and she can smell Elijah behind her. She struggles as he tries to shush her, but his grip is iron. Not cinched tight around her, but immovable, nonetheless.

"Shh! Shh! I told you, if we let you go, he might get someone else to take you. How can we protect you then?"

"How can you protect me now?" she cries, kicking out her legs and trying her best to make her weight drag him down. It doesn't work. He's too strong.

"I thought we were having a good day!" he tries. "We hid our scents and didn't touch you. We weren't going to put you into heat, I promise!"

"That's not it!"

"Then what is it?"

"I can't!" she wails.

"Can't *what*?"

"Fall in love with you!"

The admission makes her sag, her breathing ragged and heavy.

He keeps her from collapsing to the floor, his forearm locked tight under her breasts and the other around her belly. Words caress her mating gland, and she shivers.

"Listen. Whatever happens here is a good thing. There's nothing to blame yourself for. This is natural. It's supposed to happen."

"Natural for you, maybe!"

His words are quiet, but loud as a gong. "You're an Omega, sweetheart. No matter how much you try to fight it, you can't cut it out of yourself. You can't pretend forever."

"You don't know that!"

"I do."

Those words, those two little words lance her, a picket spiking from her spine to her lungs.

"Omega, listen to me. It's going to be okay. If you fall, I'll catch you. If anything goes wrong, if you have no one else to turn to, you're not alone. You're mine, do you understand? *Mine.* And I'll move heaven and earth to keep you safe. To keep you with me."

"With us," a deep voice rumbles. Katelyn casts her eyes over, and it's James. He looks hulking in the low light as he works his way over. Not fast, not slow, but as if he owns this space. And her.

"Why are you doing this?" James asks.

Katelyn swallows hard as he stands in front of her, blocking her view of the front door. Who was she kidding? She was never going to make it. She's a fool. "Because I need to get out of here."

"Not that." James ticks his chin toward the door, expressionless as always. "This." He reaches forward and caresses the curve of her neck. The edge of his thumb slides over her mating gland, making her cry out and buck.

"No touching!"

"I never made that promise," he reminds, swirling patterns over her sensitive skin. "Why are you hiding yourself?"

Honesty pours from her, her body singing from his touch. "My mother. She doesn't know. She's in The Lifestyle and if—God, James—if they find out I'm an Omega, they'll—"

A rough moan tears from her throat as he continues to caress her. Slick is starting to gather in her panties, and his nostrils flare. He knows. He knows and he likes it.

Elijah groans behind her, his grip tightening as he rests his brow against the crown of her head. She can feel his lungs balloon and clenches her teeth.

"They'll kick my mother out. It's all she…she knows and…it's her…her entire life and I…"

"So, she sold you to Thomas Bleaker," Elijah rasps.

She tries to pull away, but she's pinned between them both. She's lost in the trees of their scent, petrichor and cedar, and she thinks she might die. "It's not like that."

"Then what's it like?" James asks, his fingers caressing down the column of her throat this time, marking her as his.

"I'm saving her!"

"From what?"

"Her loneliness! My b-brother and father died, and she's been all alone, except f-for The Lifestyle."

"She's not alone," Elijah whispers, his breath coming fast as she gets wetter and wetter. Cramps are starting in her lower belly, and she aches so badly. She's empty. She's never put anything inside herself, but she knows what this feeling is.

"She has you," James intones, lips nearly touching hers.

"I'm not enough." Her voice breaks as she repeats her mother's words. Both males tense.

Elijah's thumbs caress the bottom of her breasts, making the soft flesh ache. "Then she doesn't deserve you."

Katelyn whines, but she's not sure if it's their touches or their words. "But I love her."

James tilts her chin up, whispering, "You deserve to be accepted as you are."

Her eyes flutter shut, but her brain scrambles for a response. "Is that what your parents do? Accept you? Do they know who you are? Or do you hide, just like me?"

James winces, and it breaks her heart.

Panting as he breathes her in, Elijah murmurs, "But if you make us a pack, we won't have to hide anymore. Where's your 'out,' Katelyn? When can you be honest about who and what you are?"

James crowds in, and his chest presses against hers. He starts lining kisses over her forehead, each touch of his lips lighting a flame in her heart.

Slick runs down her leg under her pajama bottoms and both Alphas let out hushed sounds of wanting.

"Stay with us," Elijah breathes, his erection lengthening and pressing against her rear. "Be who you are. Let us love you."

It's when he licks her mating gland that her body ignites. Pain squeezes her womb in a way that begs for attention. She needs to be filled, and she needs it now.

Her flesh breaks into goosebumps as a layer of sweat paints her. "Let me go," she groans, her legs trembling.

"We can help you." The heel of Elijah's hand presses hard on her lower belly, relieving the pain and making her cry out. "Omega, please."

"Please," James echoes before ducking down, putting his mouth on her other mating gland, and *sucking*.

Her gasp is earsplitting and the Omega inside her roars, binding her in sensation.

It's everything.

It's too much.

It's not fucking allowed.

"No!" she screams once more, throwing herself to the side and out of Elijah's vice grip. This time, he lets her go, and she stumbles into a run. Her gait is stuttering as she clenches her abs, trying to stave off what she knows is coming.

One hand plunges into her pocket and snags a pill bottle, opening it and pouring tablets into her hand. She can barely swallow them all as she tries to get to the bathroom. She needs cold water. She needs to freeze these feelings away.

The next pill bottle pops open and she takes them dry again, praying for salvation that's not coming. She knows it. It's too late to stop this.

Her stomach rejects the medicine like always but she works her gullet to hold it down. Hormone suppressants, heat suppressants, but none of it's going to work now, is it?

She twists the shower's knob with shaking hands. Frigid rain falls down as she gags, crawling on her hands and knees into the tub, praying this will work. It has to work.

Her gut clenches and she loses her battle, throwing up everything she just swallowed. Little pills swirl in the water, breaking down into white spirals that trickle down the drain.

She's going to burn up.

She's going to faint.

She's going to beg to take everything her Alphas have to give her.

Elijah rushes in and turns her over, pushing her soaking hair out of her eyes.

"Alpha, make it stop," she whines.

His eyes are wide as he touches her all over, her shoulders, her cheeks, her forehead, swiping tears from under her eyes. "Tell me what you mean."

What does she mean? Does she want him to hold her closer? Give her to his brother? Keep her forever? Make love to her until the sun comes up and the pain stops?

"I want to go home," she says instead, bursting into sobs. They flare from the depths of her and explode to the surface, twisting her face as she curls into a ball in his arms.

He looks like she broke his heart. He pauses, brows knit as he caresses her before calling for his brother and asking for something Katelyn can't hear over the pounding of blood in her ears and the rushing fall of water. Her lips are numb as she hyperventilates in this confined space, the porcelain bath and the Alpha pinning her without space to breathe.

This is it. She's dying. She's finally going to let it kill her.

Mama, she thinks, her brain spiraling. *Help me.*

And that's where she is when the world goes dark.

ANOTHER NIGHTMARE.

No…a dream. Something sweet. It floats in her mind like cotton candy, begging to be tasted.

A rogue and a warrior stand side by side atop a mountain covered in blue gentians and lush, verdant greenery. The flowers look like glowing Neptunes nestled among sage and olive blades of grass which sway with a barely-there, whispering breeze. Sparse brushstrokes of cloud-cover sink low and their white wisps decorate the two men's heads like airy crowns.

There they are.

Her Alphas.

Elijah is dressed in an earthen, rawhide vest wrapped snugly around a cream linen shirt. It laces from his mid chest to his collarbone, and the eyelets stretch with the breadth of this chest. His forearms and wrists are wrapped in leather and pressed-metal gauntlets with those same gentian flowers carved into the surface, giving a delicate look to the pieces meant for protection and defense. His boots are all buckles at the ankles and he has the air of someone who would rob you just as fast as he would save you.

Suave, graceful, and in control, he reaches a hand toward her.

So does James.

James is clad in plated iron, dented and dinged with deep scrapes that mar the metallic sheen. A broadsword is clutched in his other hand, looking heavy and dangerous, like it could crush your skull with a single overhead swing. The heartline of the piece glows in ice white, imbued with a magic that draws characters in the air she doesn't recognize. They swoop in intersecting lines, making squares and slashes, and she wonders what spell they're weaving. Probably one meant just for her.

A rainbow draws itself in a line across the sky, a representation of what she could be. The arc curves around the Alphas, as if holding them in a cocoon of color. A nest made of refracted light.

Both Alphas stretch their hands in her direction, firm and strong.

"Omega," Elijah purrs, his voice a throb in the ether. "Stay."

She's naked on her knees before them, her skin raw along the knuckles and bruises leaving wide circles on the thick tops of her thighs. She was in a fight. Judging by the pain in her body, she did not get away unscathed. But did she lose or did she win? Does it matter?

"Please," James says. He leans in, one hand still on his blade as if to defend her from enemies looming behind. Elijah follows suit, tipping his head against his brother's shoulder, but reaching ever closer.

Wrist limp with exhaustion, her hand lifts. It trembles, her fingertips soiled and stained with blood. Hers? Her enemy's?

She doesn't want to get this filth on them. They are pristine. They are like paintings. They stand on the mountaintop, kissed by clouds, and who is she to stand by their side?

"Even if we're a pack," her voice drifts like fading music notes, "we're too small. Packs are five, six, seven people. Betas won't accept us. Pairs won't accept us. Packs won't accept us. Where will we belong?"

Elijah's smile is as thrilling now as it's always been. "With each other."

How simple. He makes it sound so easy. Effortless.

Her return smile is watery. "And you'll love me?"

"Always," James states. His white lashes close over his crystal blue eyes in the most solemn of vows.

"I believe you," she says. "But I'm afraid."

Both Alphas nod.

Reverence on his face, Elijah says, "Bravery isn't about fearlessness, you know. It's about feeling the fear, and still moving forward in spite of it. You can do this, Katelyn Annamarie. Be brave."

"Be our queen," James adds, falling to his knees before her.

Their scent is heady as it takes her over. It's comfort. It's solace. It's hope and promise.

She wishes, oh how she wishes she could take their hands.

But instead, they fade away, leaving her with nothing but the pain of loss…and she wakes up.

Katelyn's body is lava. The thin sheet over her is sticky with sweat and she wants nothing more than to tear it off, but it's been tucked in tight around the sides of the bed, trapping her in a soft, familiar space.

She's in her room.

Her room at *home*.

The popcorn ceiling is jarring after so much time spent with that smooth surface she was tempted to splash with color.

Or…no…it wasn't that long at all. Seven days? Ten days? How long did it take for her body to give in?

The shame comes, and with it a sense of loss. Her Alphas brought her home, like she'd asked. But what happens now?

Her heart beats like the wings of the devil, pounding the inside of her ribcage and forcing the blood to rush through her ears. She is both lightheaded and heavy in her own body, unable to drift away no matter how much easier it would be. She's awake now, and things are wrong. Her skin is made of crawling spiders, her belly a fist, and her thighs glide over each other, slick wetting them all the way to the mattress, her underwear doing nothing to hold it back.

She needs to get into that cold shower again.

She needs her medicine.

A wave of pain rolls through her lower belly, a cramp that clenches on nothing. Her eyes squeeze shut as she rides through it, cresting the whitecaps before fumbling atop the rest of the undulating ocean that makes up her first heat.

Because that's what this is.

And there's no stopping it now.

"What have you done?"

It comes out as a whispered sigh. A mournful sound that hurts Katelyn in new, unfamiliar ways.

Trembling from her scalp to the tips of her toes, Katelyn's eyes drift down her bed to find her mother sitting on a chair by her feet. Her mouth is a grim, straight line and her eyes bore holes in the floor.

"They…those *creatures*…brought you to a hospital." She huffs a sound through her nose. "They seemed surprised to see me. As if the doctor wouldn't call your only emergency contact." Her sudden glare is scathing, pinning Katelyn to the spot. She asks again, words staccato and dark, "What have you done?"

Katelyn flinches. This is exactly what she was afraid of.

Locking her eyes on her wringing hands, her mother continues, "Can you imagine my terror when I saw those beasts sitting in your room, watching you lay there defenseless? Why would they do that?"

Katelyn's mind whirls. She doesn't know. They should have just dropped her like a rock, but the fact that they didn't both hurts and heals her. Hurts because now there is no avoiding this confrontation. Heals because this means they brought her somewhere to make sure she was safe. They didn't leave. They were afraid for her.

Her mother has never seemed more far away. "The nurses said the hospital was understaffed, so they couldn't spare an orderly, and I knew I couldn't lift something as bulky as you on my own,"—her mother skids her eyes in her direction—"so they made those things bring you to my car.

"They realized before I did that I couldn't get you into the apartment, so I had to *ride* with those demons. Can you believe it? *Me!* If the elders found out, they would have my head for that alone.

"As if that wasn't enough, one of those…disgusting monsters put your head in his lap and pet your hair the whole way. *Pet you*, Katelyn. He had no expression, like a statue, but he held you like…like he *knew* you. Like he *cared* about you!"

Unbidden, Katelyn's heart throbs.

"What have you done? I've missed you for *days*, and the first word I hear is that you're unconscious! I wanted to burst into tears. Seeing you lying in that hospital bed was terrifying enough, even without those vulgarians. You looked like you'd been killed." She scoffs softly. "Imagine my surprise when the doctor told me something went wrong with your suppressant doses. I had no idea what that meant. I was too embarrassed to ask, so I just sat there with my mouth open. I must have looked as stupid as I felt, because he explained you were taking medicine that was 'holding back your heat.'"

The world grinds to a stop.

"A *heat*, Katelyn. Is that what this is?"

Katelyn can't speak. All words catch in her throat. There are no excuses to make now. No fevered sickness she can feign. No lies to beg her mind to dream up and force her through her mouth.

"Thomas told me he sent you on a special retreat, no expense spared for his bride, and *this* is how you repay him? Playing around with those"—her face twists—"*Alphas* until they, what? Converted you? *Altered* you?"

Katelyn's brain hitches. This is total Lifestyle propaganda. She's seen it in pamphlets and heard it in sermons, but who in their right mind would believe such a thing? You can't catch a secondary gender like a cold, and there are no mad scientist Alphas in labs drafting up schemes to irradiate all the women of the world and turn them into willing, compliant, knees-spread Omegas.

"What did they do?" her mother hisses. "What did they give you? I need to report this to the elders!"

"They…" Katelyn pants, curled up and on fire. "They didn't do anything. They couldn't. That's not how this works, Mama."

"So what? You're going to tell me that *you, my daughter*, are an OMEGA?!" She spits the word like filth. Ripping her body from the chair, her mother starts pacing, running her hands through her frazzled hair. The lines around her mouth have never been so deeply chiseled, and Katelyn's heart sinks.

Despite her pain, Katelyn pushes down the covers with effort, trying to pull herself into a sitting position. The mother from her dreams evaporates in the winds of truth. The one who called for Katelyn as she was drowning doesn't exist. The one she could beg to save her was a fantasy. There is no salvation here.

All she can do is admit it. "I...I presented when I was younger. You r-remember when I ran away? I..." Another squeeze ruins her lower belly, and she bites back a cry. "I found a doctor... a Lifestyle doctor."

Her mother's head snaps up. "There are others who *know about this?*"

"It's..." All Katelyn wants to do is disappear. Her fear claws at her. "It's not what you think. He helps kids suppress it. He gives m-medicine...but it hurts, mama. I think it's killing me."

"Then you should die!"

The words pierce the air, smothering the heat in Katelyn's body and lining it with frost. Everything stops as Katelyn watches a look take over her mother's face. One she's never seen before.

It's hate.

"What...?"

Her mother refuses to look at her again, picking up her pacing. Her beige stockinged legs slice through the air and her demurely heeled shoes pound in dull *thuds* that go nowhere in the carpeted space.

She laughs darkly, as if someone's played the world's cruelest joke on her. "Don't you know what parents in The Lifestyle do if their children present?" She throws daggers at Katelyn with her sudden stare. "They abandon them."

The words are like death by a thousand cuts, the way they slice and rip. Something in Katelyn breaks. "But you wouldn't abandon me, right?"

Her mother's back straightens, bone by bone of her spinal column stacking on itself. "Why not?" That hate turns into a sick scowl. "I did it to your brother."

Katelyn's jaw falls slack as the room spins, everything tilting in carnival funhouse shapes, warping reality into something sinister. Sound elongates as those words repeat into infinity, and Katelyn's heat is forgotten in a rush of panic.

"But your father was weak. He claimed to be committed to The

Lifestyle, but when he had a chance to prove it, he decided to take that monster and run away instead!"

"Dad's alive?" Pieces start snapping together in Katelyn's mind. "And Brandon? He wasn't sick?"

"No! He went into a filthy rut and broke my heart! And now *you*! How *dare* you? What's wrong with me? Is my stupid body so broken that all I can make is creatures like *you*?"

The words, "I'm sorry," drag from her throat by habit. "I'll stay on the medicine, just… please, Mama…"

"Please what? What is it you expect me to do?!"

Hide me, Katelyn's heart screams. But then reality sinks in.

Her brother.

"He was so young…" Katelyn says, mourning his loss in new ways.

Her mother sneers. "That was my one blessing. I was able to get rid of him before he was paired with a bridal match. I'd never have lived that down if I wasted someone's time on a *defect* like him!" She jabs a finger toward Katelyn's chest with a manic smile. "But The Lifestyle saw my sacrifice. They took care of me." That smile pulls down into an unknown darkness. "And now they're going to say I hid you on purpose. Tried to give you to The Lifestyle's *heir* to ruin their reputation. Can you imagine the scandal?! *What have you done to me!?*"

"All I did was exist! I've been hiding it *for you*! I've been hurting myself *FOR YOU!*"

She remembers her brother's cries ringing out, and the sorrow for her mother as the woman laid in tears all alone, praying for sympathy when everything she did was her own fault. She discarded her own family.

All desire to comfort her mother wisps away.

Katelyn's hands ball into fists, whirling the sheet into spiraling roses. She growls, the first time she's given in to such a sound.

"Get out."

Her mother locks in place for a moment, eyes wide in disbelief. "How dare—"

"Get. Out." The words come through clenched teeth.

Her mother's chin juts forward. "You think you can scare me?"

Viciousness hidden deep inside Katelyn bubbles to the surface, and all love for her mother dies. "No. But my truth can destroy you. Without me, you have no skills to manage your own life, no one to care if you're left behind. Especially not me.

"Enjoy your solitude, Mom. You've earned it."

Recoiling, her mother acts the victim, looking as if her heart will give out from grief. Katelyn remembers all her brother was—kind, caring, and indulgent; all her father was—jokes, teasing, and laughter —and absorbs the knowledge that they didn't die. They were taken from her. And all that was left behind was the broken glass of a woman Katelyn tried to glue back together, no matter how she cut herself on the shards in the process.

Spinning around, her mother snags her purse hanging on the back of the chair and storms into the living room.

Katelyn still winces when the door slams shut, but she's never felt such anger in her entire life. Such betrayal. She was too little; how could she have seen it for what it was? But now that she knows, it makes perfect sense.

Why didn't her father take her away, too?

Katelyn covers her eyes and collapses back down on the bed. Crisis over, her body kicks up again, that burn starting low in her groin and creeping up into all her special spots.

Fine. Enough is enough.

Throwing off the covers, Katelyn stalks into her living room and locks the door, keeping the world far away. Turning quick, she sees her pill bottles laying on the kitchen table, a bare few tablets still laying placidly at the bottom.

Another cramp hits her, but it doesn't matter. She grabs the bottles, staring at their orange bodies and white labels. These have spent their lifetime saving her. Or have they?

Stomping into the bathroom, she lifts open the toilet lid, staring at the still water inside…and flushes them all away.

If she's to be an Omega, let her be an Omega.

CHAPTER 13
LONGING

THIS PICTURESQUE HOUSE is empty without her. The feel of this place, though still dreamlike and captivating, is now sterile.

James wishes he didn't understand Katelyn's feelings—that urge to hide. The world should be as simple as this: if you want each other, you should have each other. More than that, you should be able to be who you are without fear. James has never felt that way. His mother hid him from the world for all his faults, protecting him from threats that never appeared, making him afraid of the judgment of every set of eyes.

He can hear her soft words, faded with time, but no less rooted within him. *"James, you're not like everybody else. You're special. Sometimes that's a good thing, but sometimes it can get you into trouble. People look at you, you know, and not in a good way. They wonder why this grumpy boy doesn't talk to anyone. Make eye contact with anyone. Acknowledge anyone. They think you're stupid, but I know better. I see behind those eyes. I see your fire, baby. You're excellence. If you can't come out of your shell, it's alright. I'll take care of you. You can stay with Mama forever."*

He thought he would. He would take a deep breath and let his mother trap him in her love, further isolating himself from the world, shrinking into the safe shelter of her arms…until he met Elijah. Until he dreamed of meeting *her*. And when he finally saw her for what she was, his raw tornado of feelings exceeded his expectations. She and

Elijah, the way they look at him is magical. Beyond imagination. Beyond the best of dreams. It's proof that they are meant for him. They make him feel beautiful. Precious. Singular and irreplaceable.

Katelyn is so different from his stepbrother. She's *koi no yokan*. Love at second sight. It didn't happen at a glance, but there was a feeling of inevitability. It was why he hated her. He was taken completely and utterly off course. It makes sense now. She was his fated future. He felt that transcendence, if only for a moment. If only for a breath.

"*Umarekawattara, anata o motto hayaku mitsukeru darō,*" James whispers.

"If I were to live again, I would find you sooner," Elijah replies, translating for him perfectly.

In the orange glow of the evening, James dips his hand into the cool water of the courtyard pond, skimming his fingertips over the white koi fish. Its scales slip along his skin, and it makes no effort to swim away, instead mouthing at the food James brought. He forgot to feed them this morning. How unlike him.

The fish aren't hovering around each other today. The black one is in the far corner of the pond where Elijah sits now, pants rolled to his knees and feet in the water as he broods. Can fish be empathetic, feeling his distress?

"Do you want to get out of here?" Elijah asks. After looking at James for a brief moment, he adjusts his statement. "No. You want to sit here and remember."

James breathes deeply, acknowledging the truth of the statement. She was in this space. They were in this space. It belongs to the three of them, even if she never gets to see it again.

"We promised we'd keep her secret," Elijah murmurs, guilt raining sorrow down on his features.

A pitter patter disturbs the surface of the water as James sprinkles more food, his fingers pinching and crushing the pellets. "How could we know her mother would come?"

"How couldn't we?" Elijah's head dives into his hands and clenches his own hair, his dark locks splaying over his shoulders. "Panic made us stupid. This is exactly what she didn't want."

The bits of fish food bob, and ripples echo around his brother's shins, pulsing in time with his heartbeat. James imagines he can hear it throbbing in his chest like an aching drum.

Elijah laughs, but it's a terrible sound. "I thought we could pick up the pieces, you know? She's stubborn and scared, a terrible combination, but her body is going to do what it has to at this point, whether she likes it or not. I thought she might go through it, move past it, and handle that…that fucking *Thomas* on her own. She could have kept her secret but still told him to go pound sand. Tell him what he did to her was unforgivable and used that as an excuse to get away. We could have stepped in then. Been there for her. With us by her side, she could have learned to relax into it, come to terms and come out by herself when the time was right. I had this all planned. I lived a year in a minute of my mind. But now, it doesn't matter. Everything's fucked."

"The only one who knows is her mother. She won't say anything. She may hate us, but she loves her daughter."

"She might have, until she heard the word *'heat'*. You don't know what I do about Madam Iris Masters. She's more than indoctrinated, she's high up in the ranks. She lives her life sucking on the fucking *tit* of The Lifestyle. You think she's going to give up her entire existence for her daughter?"

James can only hope.

"I know what you're thinking," Elijah continues, "but her family is just like ours. If mom and dad found out the truth about us, there's no turning back. You think they want us the way we are, all tangled up in each other? No. They'd peace right the fuck out. Treat us like the plague. Trash our baby pictures and pretend like we died."

For that, James has no words. Pulling his hand from the pond, he rests it on his knee and lets the water trickle down his bare leg. He looks at his scar again. Traces his finger over it. Even now, it's a gaudy, purple line. If Katelyn leaves them, truly never comes back, he'll lose everything, won't he? Her. Elijah. His family. Himself.

Suddenly, Elijah is on him like a jacket, arms wrapped around James's stomach as he leans his heavy chest along the expanse of James's back. Elijah cradles him, lining up his legs on either side and resting his cheek against James's shoulder, offering all the comfort he can. His brother's touch is welcome. The only feeling he wants. Other than the someday caress of their Omega.

"I didn't mean it," Elijah says. "Don't listen to me. I'm all…on edge right now. Who knows what mom and dad would do. Maybe they'd still love us. Maybe it would help them understand why you and I are so close. Why we never see them, no matter how much mom calls…"

"We love each other," James says, hanging his head. "It's not normal."

"Fuck normal," Elijah says. "I haven't been normal a day in my goddamned life."

James's lips tick up for the briefest of moments. That's probably very true.

"I need a drink," Elijah says. "And we need to get out of here. It smells like her and I just…I need to walk away for a bit."

"Mm," James allows.

"Besides, it's only a matter of time before our asshole benefactor comes to call when he realizes we let his quarry go."

"Don't call her that."

"Then what am I supposed to call her?"

James threads his fingers through his brother's. "Ours."

Elijah buries his head between James's shoulder blades and squeezes him tighter. His voice is raspy and lost when he says, "I don't know what to do."

Unfortunately, neither does James.

Death and pleasure blur into a spiral Katelyn can't pick apart. She writhes on the wide expanse of her gray bedroom carpet, distantly thinking it will need a deep clean after this is over.

She's covered in sweat and slick, above and below, her hand trying its best to alleviate her need. It works at a speed she could never fathom before, strumming and begging to be enough, but no matter how often she comes, she's not satisfied. Toys don't exist in her home —penetration of any kind is not allowed—but, oh, how she's tempted to make do with what she has. Though, what could her slender fingers do? Could they fill her? Stroke that sweet spot she's supposed to have inside?

No.

No, it's too embarrassing, even now.

Her sheets and blankets lay all around her. Towels, cushions, and anything she could think of. She's made a nest, and the inclination, the *instinct*, would be amusing if not for the fevered state she's in. Her creation is bigger than her, spacious and round. It's built for three. Still, her legs wrap around a corner of bedding looking for friction as she soaks through the fabric.

"Elijah," she pants into the soft light of her room, a single lamp lit on the far side night table. His filthy words taunt her. His flirting that bordered on bedroom talk. The way he'd eaten her food, basically licking it from her fingers. The way he'd dived into her neck and put his tongue on her, drawing a soft line from the top of her sweater to the back of her ear. His breath had hitched. Even muted, he had smelled her scent, and it pleased him.

"James," she breathes this time, tasting his name. Her smell had done more than please him. It drove him mad. If she'd let him go a little bit further, what would have happened? Would he have licked her back? Grinded between her legs? Touched her breasts?

She skates her hands up to do so now, pinching at her rosy nipples, flushed from her heat. The glands at her wrists are pink as well, and she can only imagine the flush of her mating glands as they beg to be bitten.

Giving into her lust fueled fantasies is like ambrosia. She wants them to bite her. Mark her. Make her theirs.

Who is she kidding? She's already theirs.

She whispers their names again, running her hands up and down her abdomen. Are their hands calloused? James with his practice, Elijah with his penchant for taking down criminals…would that have roughed them up? Maybe their fingertips would stroke her like the finest of sand, just enough to draw her attention and make it special. More rugged. More real.

What would it be like to be in between them? They could

completely control her. Dominate her. They could bend her in half, one thrusting into her folds from behind while the other slides into her wet mouth, groaning before he comes down her throat.

She cries out at the thought, her hand moving between her legs again. Her sinful thoughts are bringing her toward another precipice, and she chases it like a rabid dog with bared teeth.

Her body is on sensory overload. The carpet feels like millions of tiny fingers caressing her and the air is a mouth breathing heat on her already hot skin. The silence fills with her ballooning lungs and little mewls, sounds that turn her on even as they embarrass her. Masturbation is supposed to be a means to an end. Silent. A release like a sneeze, strong for a moment with no aftermath…but *this*. This is a train made of millions of cars running over her, not giving her a moment to breathe. Her actions do nothing to quench the emptiness inside. The place where her Alphas belong.

She begs the faraway men to find her. Their knots will fill her until she screams. Their seed will ease this pain. They will please her again and again, one then the other, until her mind whites out and this experience ends.

There is no future. There is only now.

And now hurts as much as it feels good.

—

Elijah has a headache. A shitty, idiot headache.

Maybe it's because he cried like a baby before they left their idyllic garden.

No. That's wrong. Not like a baby at all. Like a restrained Alpha with silent tears burning his eyes as he held back his emotions in a manic-tight grip, just like all men are trained to do. Alphas especially. According to Thomas fucking Bleaker, he's not even supposed to *have* feelings…but he does. They won't stop choking him today. Maybe that's why he has this fucking headache.

God this is depressing.

James sits to his left, his standard glass of water—no ice—leaving dribbles of moisture on the surface of the hideaway pub's weary bar top. It's the kind of place where one-night stands are born, libidos meeting in a flurry of murmured praise, hurtling hormones, and luscious, batting eyelashes. Bar fights might not be too far out of character either if the scuffed-up wood tells any tales.

These kinds of places tend to be so steeped in back-alley stories, their bartenders are immune. The resident mixologist-wannabe hovering in front of them is seemingly no different. His rail thin, barely legal frame seems resigned to his role as secret keeper over the panties (and pounded out teeth) shed in his liquor-addled office. It's the perfect place to mope and nurse your sorrows. To forget a long day's work after the sweat has dried from your brow.

Isn't that what they're doing? Isn't their work over now?

His stepbrother stares into the circle of his water glass as if it held the solution to life, the universe, and everything. Elijah, for his part, takes in the glint of the neon signs that hang edge-to-edge along the paneled walls, their loops and electric squiggles promising the hard hit of straight liquor when all they're really serving you is watered down sugar mixed with nail polish remover. He'll stick to predictable beer, thank you.

Beer isn't the answer, he knows. Or if it is, it's a crappy, temporary one. What he needs, *they* need, is their mate. He hadn't believed in it— thought he and James's relationship to be above that primal need, maybe—but like always, James had a knack for knowing.

But is it just hormones? Can this feeling of longing be chalked up to something as simple as that? Or was there something tangible there? A future. A love to put the universe to shame.

Elijah categorizes all the things he likes about their little rainbow, beyond scent. Beyond chemistry. Beyond his Alpha's pull to every inch of her.

Knocking back his glass, he counts her plusses out loud, his buzz removing what reservation he has. With a harsh bang of his mug on the table, he declares, "I like that she was feisty. When she chucked her dish against the wall, all I wanted to do was get in her face and wag my imaginary tail for attention. She never put up with our crap and stuck to her guns. That's worthy of respect, don't you think?"

Silent as stone, James drags a finger through the droplets left by his sweating glass, drawing nonsensical words across the bar top.

"But when I pushed just the tiniest bit, she got soft," Elijah continues. "Or she listened to my ranting, anyway. Let me tease her without cutting my balls off. The true sign of a saint. She got sweeter the farther along we got, too. We had her laughing. Smiling. Yeah, I liked that smile."

The bartender comes over, offering to refill his beer, but Elijah declines. Their meager budget will only take them so far.

"She was sexy. She had a great ass. I liked her hair, weird clothes, and her freakin' hoarder's collection of glasses."

"Fake glasses," James reminds, but it only serves to further warm the lump of coal in Elijah's chest.

"That was the cutest part. It was her 'aesthetic.'" Fiddling with his glass and rolling it between his palms, he sighs. "I loved how she drew. That kind of talent is special, you know? Think of how many hours she must have invested to be able to draw you like that. It was perfect. Like a photograph. Better looking than the real you, honestly. Who needs to bother with your actual face when they can just stare at that picture all day instea—*fuck*, James! Seriously?"

James withdraws his hand from the sharp pinch he'd just given his brother.

Grumbling, Elijah drinks the dregs of his beer, letting the foam bubble him up and sucking it from his top lip. At least it's making his headache better.

"I liked the way she drew you, too," James says.

"Little, duplicitous, cartoon me."

"She captured both sides of you."

"You mean my sexy side and my stupid side?"

"Mm."

That clenches his chest again. "She captured you, too. That's why she could make you so beautiful. You know, whatever you said to her that night in the garden meant something. I could see her change a bit after that."

"I told her I was dirty," James says, running his fingers over the glass with a faraway look. "She told me I was wrong."

Elijah blinks at his brother. Vulnerability is hard to come by with James.

"I told her she wasn't dirty either," James monotones. "But I don't think she believed me."

That, she didn't. She couldn't have. Or else, she would have stayed.

Elijah leans in, resting his forehead on the bar top. "I also liked that she was kind of at our mercy. Reliant on us. Sorta pining for us and unable to get away. Does that make me an asshole?"

"Mm."

There is a harsh sound as Elijah claps a hand on James's back, squeezing his shoulder. "Your turn. What did you like about her?"

"Before or after I went crazy?"

Elijah has to chuckle at that. "I think you liked her even before that fateful encounter."

When James starts doodling in the water again, Elijah knows he's got him pegged.

"Bingo, Jamsie. You just didn't want to admit it. Let's see…you liked that she challenged you. She was a 'brat,' I believe you called her?"

James makes the hint of a grimace. "She *was* a brat."

"But you didn't say you didn't like it." Elijah winks at him. "I'm a brat, too, after all."

James dips his fingertips in his water and flicks droplets in Elijah's face. Swiping it away, he grabs those messy blond curls and brings James's head over for a kiss to the temple. At least here, like this, they look like just any other couple. But there's something missing…and now that he knows what it is, Elijah is empty without it.

Rubbing his eyes, he throws out a twenty, hoping that's enough, because he doesn't have much more. Thankfully, the heavily pierced bartender gives him change, which Elijah happily slips into the tip jar. The man let him nurse two beers over the course of an hour, after all. Good Samaritan and all that.

The bar fills with new arrivals, the night growing later. They're dressed as if "Blue Collar" is their middle name, playing darts and queueing up the old school jukebox with heavy metal of all things. James immediately sinks into his chair. He's not, what you would call, a music guy. Especially not a "loud music in a crowded bar" guy.

"Need to get out of here?" Elijah asks.

James's silence says all it needs to.

Grabbing his hand, he leads his brother out into the warm, city night air and immediately feels that sting again. That incredible feeling that she's supposed to be with them. Maybe on his side, wrapped around his arm, maybe on James's, tucked into him. Maybe between them, their hands linked as she tosses one of those rare smiles in their directions, letting out one of those belly laughs that puts his to shame. He only heard it once, and it was a perfect match for him. He'd wanted to make her laugh more. Forever.

Why did she have to leave them? Reject them. Why couldn't she accept herself? Why did he let her mother shoo them away like that? Like dirt. Like disease. How could he leave her apartment when she smelled like *his*? Like she needed him. Them. Is she really going to live like this? Hurt herself like this? Is she really going to be with *that man*?

Shit, here he goes again.

He forces himself to stand straight, no matter how much he wants to curl over and tug his shirt to his nose, burrowing into whatever sweet scent she left on him. He wants to dive into his old clothes to try and find her there. Read her curlicue cursive goodbye letter twenty thousand more times.

She's theirs, and she knows it.

And she's gone.

"Maybe we can find another Omega," he says, the words like sour dirt on his tongue.

James snaps his hand away, refusing Elijah's touch. It's the last straw.

He raises his voice. "Look, I miss her, too! I want her, too! I want her so bad, I can taste it, but we can't have her!"

James looks away, treating him like every other person he "nothing"s, and it hurts like a needle under his nails.

"You think I'm stupid," Elijah says, earning no reply as cars sweep by. "You think I'm a coward." Somewhere, a horn beeps, but James still says nothing. Swallowing thickly, Elijah says, "You think we'll die without her."

James's mouth thins. With a harsh gesture, he grabs Elijah's arm and leads him on.

"Where are we going?"

Ice blue eyes focused and determined, James states, "Home."

The idea is laughable. "We don't have a *home*."

Rushing them down the street with a set to his jaw, James says in no uncertain terms, "Yes, we do."

CHAPTER 14
LOVE

O*MEGA IS in full heat now.*

There's no denying it. This is so much more intense. Her scent permeates everything, even stronger than it was when they'd left her earlier today. How can he smell her so easily?

It's because her windows are open above, a foolish, rookie mistake for a floor so low to the ground, but Elijah will take every mote of her sweetened air and drink it like wine.

His preternatural hearing opens wide to take in the faint sound of her. No Beta could ever hear her far away stifled cries, but he is enraptured by every one. Looking at James, he is too. He's practically vibrating, his muscles tight from holding back. Elijah understands. He's doing the same.

His skin itches. Why isn't he beside her yet? Why isn't he soothing her pain?

From above, he hears his whispered name, followed by his brother's, and salivates, all blood shooting downward.

Omega needs us.

Now.

Elijah holds out his hand, and James takes it, squeezing to the point of pain. Neither says anything. They just follow their noses, follow their Alphas, and go home.

James's heart is a sledgehammer as he watches Elijah pick locks around the building. The outer glass door. The inner glass door. Once inside, they fly up the apartment stairs, eagles soaring until they reach the last barrier between them and their mate.

Elijah fumbles his lockpicks like an inept child trying to catch a ball, and they clatter to the floor with a metallic chime. He grunts in frustration as he tries to pick them up, but his hands are shaking so hard, his fingers can barely grab hold.

James doesn't mean it, but his impatience skyrockets and he lets out a dark growl, one that only makes his brother huff a wisp of a laugh before hanging his head, taking a deep breath, and trying again.

When the lock pops, James is already inside, nearly ripping the door off its frame. The familiar space only takes five strides to leap across before he's at her open bedroom, only to find her curled in on herself, naked and glistening in the soaked cradle of a nest.

Their nest.

She's beautiful. Stunning. Looking at him as if he were her savior, her jade eyes swim with unshed tears of need. Her hair splays in a halo of shimmering auburn, and he wishes he could adorn it with flowers. Jewels. She's perfect, and his heart aches as badly as his loins do.

On his knees faster than a whip crack, he spreads her legs and revels in her sharp cry.

Other people have feelings, too, Elijah had told him, so he grits his teeth and grinds out, "Tell me you want this."

Her voice is pure seduction when she moans, "Alpha, please."

James dives down to put his mouth on her sweet center. That scent of hers is overwhelmingly erotic. It screams of her yearning in a silent, desperate, unending cry. She tastes like heaven and he wraps his arms around her thighs, pulling her closer and tilting her just right to give him full access. This is a meal...and he is starving.

Elijah is on her next, lifting her chin and pulling her into a deep kiss, drawing another sweet sound from her pretty throat. James locks his eyes on them together and a sense of rightness sweeps over him.

This is how it should be. How it needs to be. They are a pack, and together, they'll love her until the end of time.

He doesn't know what he's doing, but lust drives him on as he laps from her tiny entrance to a nub at the top, one that makes itself obvious just before her downy hair drapes around her sex. She lets out a nasal squeak when James's tongue flicks there, loud and clear despite his brother's debauching ministrations. When James flicks again, her legs twitch.

That's it. That must be the spot.

He takes the training hard-earned from catering to his brother's desire and focuses where he knows she needs him, swirling his tongue around that fleshy spot as it hardens into a pearl under his lightly scraping teeth.

Elijah has moved to kissing down to just under her ear, groaning sounds that she echoes. His fingers trail a line between her breasts down to her belly before latching onto James's hair and pulling him harder against her. He sucks, and her cries become a harsh, beautiful, breathy shout.

"James," she gasps, trembling with pleasure, and God, how he needs her.

"That's right, gorgeous," Elijah purrs. "Say his name." He angles himself to ride her hip, pressing his tight jeans against the jut of her and stuttering a breath. She ekes out his name next, and somehow, that turns James on just as much as hearing his own.

"I need…" she tries. "Please…"

Elijah's voice is pure sugar. "What do you need, Omega?"

James sucks again, and she bucks against his mouth.

"More," she says in a whimper that sounds like a plea.

Her slick is leaking like slow maple syrup, and James can imagine how empty she must feel. He's felt the same when his body begged for attention. Working his hand between her legs, he runs his finger through her soaking wetness and softly growls against her. Its resonance is deep, rumbling, and familiar, yet new all at once. He's on sensory overload, but in the best way. In the way that makes him want to use every word in his vocabulary to praise her—both her and the man who belongs to him—but he refuses to move an inch from where he laps at her center, feeling her thighs shake as they narrow in around him.

He swirls one finger around her entrance, and her panting doubles.

"Yes, Omega," Elijah intones. "Let him love you."

James slips his finger inside, just barely, captivated by her fire-hot skin. She's tight, so ridiculously tight, and his memory floats the fact that she's a virgin back into his mind.

Perfect Omega.

Mine.

…Ours.

He presses deeper within her, and something gives way with a sharp breath from above him, one Elijah swallows as his fingertips skim her breasts, finding her peaked nipples and tracing them in circles.

James's eyes slip closed, leaving his brother to his prostration at her altar as he focuses on pumping his finger in and flattening his tongue as he bears down on her flesh. That trembling in her legs works its way up to her belly, and he knows—whatever he's doing—he's doing it right.

As she loosens up, her slick making her soft as satin, he presses another finger in and uses them to probe and search. If he has a spot inside that drives him crazy, maybe she does, too.

He tests in press after press as she quivers and moans in high-pitched squeaks. There is something. Something where the texture is different. Keeping his touch to the pads of his fingers, he strokes it, and watches her pull away from his brother's mouth to let out a decadent sob of pleasure.

Chuckling softly above him, Elijah murmurs, "Bingo. There we are, Jamsie. Do it again."

He suckles once more, flicking his tongue in fast swipes as he strokes her special spot, pulling out and pushing in, curling his fingers, and repeating the process.

"Alpha," she squeals on a harsh breath, legs clamping together as tight as they can with him between them, spreading her apart. Her muscles flutter around him, both inside and out, and he keeps his rhythm unshakable. This is it. He's milking pleasure from her, stroke by slow stroke.

She wetter than ever before, and James hears Elijah's encouragement above him. "That's right. Good Omega. Sweet Omega. Do you know how wanted you are? How adored? You're so sexy like this, all spread out and waiting for us to find you."

She's rocking her hips now, riding his fingers and matching his rhythm. Her breathing is reaching a fever pitch, each one a gasp that hovers on the edge of a cliff, ready to hurtle over and into the depths of bliss.

"Do you know what you do to me?" Elijah says, setting the heel of his hand over her fluttering belly and bearing down. James can feel the pressure on his fingers from inside her. He can only imagine what this feels like but, in this moment, seeing her face cinch and her cries double, he wishes he was her.

"You set my nerves on fire," Elijah continues. "You taste like sweetness. You sound like a forbidden fantasy."

Katelyn is thrashing, her hands fisting the sheets and blankets that cocoon them in this moment. Fabric pulls and bunches, the edges of her nest unraveling and exposing the bare carpet, but James shifts his focus away. Let her pleasure tear this nest down. It doesn't matter. When she tries to make another one, he'll happily let her destroy that, too. He won't let her escape this anymore. She's never going to do this alone again. He forbids it.

"Close," she whines. "I'm so close."

"That's right, Omega," Elijah purrs. "I like that. Let go. Be a good girl for your Alphas. Make us so proud. Do what you were made to do. Show me. I want to see. I want to watch your pretty head rock and your back arch. I want you to scream for your Alphas. I want stars to explode behind those gorgeous eyes. Now…come for me."

On those last words, she breaks, like the perfect mate she is. Submissive. Giving. And, God, how James takes.

As she tries to pull away, he kisses the insides of her pale thighs while one hand pulls her hips toward him and his fingers continue to work their magic, extending her cresting wave until she begins to beg. She needs reprieve. She needs a moment.

Too bad he doesn't want to give it to her.

Elijah thinks she's going to die for as hard as she's coming. Her screams fill the air, and he knows even the deaf could hear her now. Like sonar, her cries make ripples that paint his body in desire. He needs to shut that window to the outside world, blocking any other Alphas from hearing her decadent cries, but walking away from her now would be torture.

"Jamsie," Elijah says, "clothes off."

Swiping his glistening fingers into his mouth, his stepbrother has never moved faster.

What does she taste like? Peaches and cream on a summer day?

He wants to suck her dry.

Katelyn Annamarie, their irreplaceable rainbow, has become clear sky, and he can see every bare inch of skin from her toes to her crown. She's presented herself like a sip of sin, and he's never been more grateful as she comes down from her high and puts her shaking palm on his cheek, pulling him into another kiss.

Omega wants me.

His heart throbs as he kisses her, soft caresses of his lips and tongue, as sweet as he can make himself when all he wants to do is devour her. Eat her alive. Bite her everywhere, until she's covered in his marks, utterly possessed. Owned.

"You, too," she whispers against his mouth, and he realizes he's just as eager to obey. His Alpha rages needy words he lets fall from his lips like drops of honey.

James's perfect body is on full display as he runs his meaty hands over their Omega's knees, waiting for her next command with a tight jaw, holding his instinct to *take* at bay.

Good boy.

Looping his fingers under the hem of his shirt, Elijah tears it off and makes it part of her now-messy nest, big enough for all of them and proof that she wants them both. They are a pack, just like James said. They were meant for each other. Her skills, sass, and scars have nestled into theirs, making her part of them.

This is right. And he'll never let it go.

His pants are off next, his erection so hard it hurts as he turns to rub against her again. Sweat dapples her, making her scent as bright as sunshine as he kisses her shoulder. The crook of her neck. The crest of her collarbone. Anywhere he can reach, he lavishes with attention he wishes he could have given the moment he met her.

"First or last, Jamsie?" he asks.

There is a delighted purr that hums from his brother's chest, sending another spike of lust into his body.

"First, but there is no last."

Elijah lets out a breathy chuckle, but it's his Omega that answers.

"Because we're doing this over and over again." Her legs spread wide as she sweeps her eyes back and forth from Elijah to James, awe on her every feature. "Alphas, please."

"Please what?" James asks, so precious, so pure.

"Please stay. Not just now. Stay forever."

A mist of held back tears burn Elijah's eyes as he wraps one arm around her.

James goes to his hands and knees and crawls up her body until his cock lines up against her core, the plush, purple head visible just above her downy thatch of hair. "You want us?"

She nods.

"Both of us?" James demands.

She nods again.

Surprising Elijah, James leans in and uses firm fingers to tilt his chin up, kissing him long and hard, nipping at his lips as he hisses in sharp breaths through his nose. When James pulls away, he stares at Elijah, his blond lashes half-lidded over pupils so wide, they've become a sea of black. "Even though we're like this?"

Katelyn rocks her torso to the side until she's nestled against Elijah's shoulder, cheeks flushed and lips red as rouge. "*Because* you're like this." She turns to face James, trailing caresses over his cheeks until his eyes flutter closed. "Alphas, please be mine."

That seems to be the only cue James needs as his hips tip back and he grabs himself, angling, positioning, and rocking into her. Katelyn's eyes pinch shut as Elijah watches his brother enter her, slow and gentle, until he's seated flush against her skin.

"I want to watch you knot her," Elijah says, ignoring his own need. Turning, he runs his tongue over her earlobe and catches it lightly between his teeth, the points of his canines sharp. "Would you like that, Omega? To have him locked inside you?"

She lets out a harsh gasp, whether at his words or the feeling of James inside her, he can't be sure, but it doesn't matter either way. As long as Omega is satisfied. As long as they're giving her what she needs.

"You," James says, shaking his head before lifting his eyes to look at Elijah. "Need it to be you."

Elijah's heart pounds so hard, he can feel his pulse in the veins of his neck, wrists, and the thick shaft of his cock. His glands tingle, wanting to be claimed. Bitten. He wants his mates to tear into him and taste his blood.

He's going to lose his mind in about three seconds.

"Would you like that, Omega?" he asks. "Can I take you? Knot you? Can I fucking mate you, sweetheart?"

James leans forward to kiss her, shifting his hips slightly back and forth and pulling a low moan out of their precious girl. As soon as he pulls away, she turns to kiss Elijah next, a hand drifting across his chest and down to caress his erection.

"Yes, Alpha. Both of you, make me yours. Before this is all over, I want your teeth on me."

Sudden and sweet, James comes on a silent breath. He'd barely even started, but Elijah knows that face better than he knows his own. That look of ecstasy. That rare expression he loves so very much. The thought of claiming their Omega must have been the last straw after pleasing her for so long. Elijah would laugh if it wasn't so fucking endearing. Instead, he kisses her one more time before leaning up to take the mouth of the man he'd die for.

"Good boy," he praises, holding James's face between his palms.

He presses his lips everywhere. His mouth, his chin, the crest of his cheeks, his forehead, his temples. Why is he so perfect?

"Elijah," she says, her back arched as she takes James's seed. "Please Alpha. Now you. I need you."

And who is he to refuse?

James pulls back, his knot blown just outside of her, and she lets out a small cry at the loss. It's only moments before Elijah replaces him, his imagination running wild. How wet is she going to be? How hot is her flesh? Will she be like a vise, clamped around him so tight it's almost too much?

God, he's going to enjoy this.

They're not in rut, so they'll definitely have to take turns with her. Their stamina will only take them so far. Still, she's going to need them. For days, she's going to be needy, greedy, and begging to be showered with affection.

With that thought locked in his mind, he rams himself inside.

Katelyn's eyes roll back as Elijah splits her in two. Where James took his time, her other Alpha does not, dominating her from above and bending her legs until her knees hover over her shoulders. Their bodies make lewd, wet slapping sounds as they connect, and it's hotter than anything she's ever heard. Having Alphas inside her, sliding home again and again, forcing her open and taking what's theirs, is something she never knew she could have in real life—especially when the Alphas are these men, who teased her, touched her, and made her crave.

The heat-pains that wracked her have melted into rapture, and her heart plunges into the well of truth like an arrow hitting bullseye.

Omega.

I'm an Omega.

And I want my Alphas.

Accepting it is a maelstrom of relief, swelling her breast with emotions so blended, she can't pick them apart. This is beyond sex.

This is a force of nature. They gave her the foundation her new future will be built on, one where she is accepted for who and what she is. Where she can let go and just be. Where she has permission to feel things she'd forbidden. These Alphas took on her suffering alongside her, just like good mates should. They care. They need. They love.

Her heart opens wide.

Elijah is like a piston, and her body can barely keep up. Her mouth, that too honest mouth, the one that threatens to get her into trouble, is babbling words like, "Yes" and "Please" and "Alpha" and "More."

James's hands are all over her as he lays at her side, spooning her with his forehead pressed against her shoulder. Dark as night, he growls, "*Motto fukaku.*"

And Elijah drives deeper.

She's going to dissolve beneath him. Her soul is crying for theirs as she feels her inner walls clamping against the girth inside her. Her undeniable, newfound heat makes her want it so bad, she can barely keep from locking her legs around Elijah and swallowing him down. No matter how hard he rams in, there will never be enough of him. Either of them.

Her eyes zero in on her lover's mating glands, flushed pink on his pale skin. She only gets peeks as his long black hair rocks back and forth with his efforts, but she wants to see them. She wants to lick them. Suck them.

She wraps her hands around his forearms and pulls. "Closer. Please, Alpha."

He obliges, but he can only lean down far enough to kiss her. Even bent in half as she is, she can't reach where she wants to be. Instead, she swirls her thumbs over that thin skin, feeling every pore, and Elijah muffles a cry into her mouth.

James picks up her cue and lifts his brother's hand, sliding the hair tie off his wrist and sitting up to pull Elijah's tresses into a messy knot, freeing the curve of his neck for attention. Elijah's movement stutters and freezes as James leans in and licks a stripe up his neck, catering to the skin that needs to be broken. That needs to bleed for the sake of their pack.

Elijah pulses inside, his muscles clenching as he tips his head to the side and gives in completely to her other Alpha's attention. His eyes are squeezed shut as he pants, his broad, half-tattooed shoulders tensing as he struggles to hold his own weight. He looks like he's about to collapse on top of her, and she would gladly accept him into her embrace.

The tips of her fingers, graced with short nails, run circles over his other mating gland, and he pulses inside her again. He's somehow growing bigger, hardening, lengthening. It's like he's going to fill every inch she has. She wants him to move, but she also wants him to stay exactly where he is, trembling above her as she gives back just a tiny bit of the pleasure he's given her.

"Where are all your dirty words now, Alpha?" she asks, and she's never felt more in control when he whimpers. Even James's lips tick up at the corners, and she feels like howling to the sky that they're *hers*. A possessive streak she didn't know she had tears into her. "Neither of you will ever touch another Omega."

"Never," Elijah agrees on a heavy breath as James follows suit, nodding in the crook of his brother's neck. "And if any other Alpha touches you…"

"I'll rip their throat out," James picks up, his teeth bared.

"Because I'm yours," Katelyn says.

Elijah's redwood eyes snap open to pin her down. "Fucking right you are."

And his pace picks up again. Moans pull from the bottom of her lungs as James moves to her breasts, his teeth grazing as his hand works down to where his brother enters her. She watches as he spreads his index and middle fingers and clamps them at the base of his brother's erection. That must be at the root, where he'll knot.

Elijah's pace stutters again. "Jesus fucking Christ, James."

But the other Alpha only hums over Katelyn's flesh, the rumble vibrating her nipples as he sucks and swipes at them the same way he did with his mouth on her center. "Don't stop."

"You're going to kill me. Both of you are a fucking wet dream. Omega, can I make you come again? Can I knot you? I want to be inside you and fucking stay forever. Want to wrap around you and tie my arms together so you can never get away. Please. Oh God, I need it. Please."

James presses his hand down, and she can feel it on her clit. With every grind of Elijah's hips, it presses James's hand harder, making a decadent throb of pressure against her bundle of nerves.

"Yes, Alpha," she groans, barely able to stand the onslaught of sensation. "I'm close again."

Elijah's strokes are shorter now, but the length of him still nudges against the top of her. Stars sparkle in shimmers behind her eyes as her heart beats in manic throbs, James's palm moving in slow circles as she and Elijah grunt in tandem.

"So fucking close," Elijah hisses in agreement.

And it happens. He thrusts as deep as possible, and something at his base flares inside her, sending a burst of pleasure up her body. It's the last straw. Her head rocks to the side as she screams out her orgasm, clenching around his length as he fills her, his knot keeping every drop inside.

James is just as unrelenting as before, keeping his circular motion going until she's begging him to stop. That little smile is all he gives for a few seconds, still suckling against her, until he finally gives mercy and Elijah collapses on top of her.

Their skin sticks together as if it never wants them to part. James kisses the top of Elijah's head, then kisses the top of hers. Over and over again he kisses hers.

"*Arashi no nochi ni watashi no niji ni natte kurete arigatō,*" he murmurs.

Before she has a chance to ask, Elijah translates, breathy and spent. "It means, 'thank you for being my rainbow after the storm.'"

A smile spreads on her face, her Alpha's weight atop her and her legs wrapped tight around him. "I like that."

"I like that, too," Elijah agrees.

"Mm."

James watches as Elijah slips her legs down and rolls on his back, their Omega top of him. Both of his loves are covered in sweat, smelling like a grove of sweetness, and it's enough to get him half hard again.

"We belong," he says, and he means it.

His Omega's smile is radiant as she rests her cheek on his brother's chest. James nestles into Elijah's shoulder, so he and Katelyn are face to beautiful face. That smile becomes shy and her cheeks flush deeper, like an angel painted in blush pinks. He wants to keep that expression. He wishes he could draw too, if only to capture this moment forever.

"Do you still hurt?" Elijah murmurs in his spent, after-sex voice.

"No," she says, her grin wider. "But is it stupid that I still want you both so bad?"

"It's natural," Elijah says, cupping the back of her head and stretching beneath her with an indulgent smile. "And the feeling is very mutual."

James runs a hand down the curve of her spine, mischief on his mind. "You need to take both of us." He sweeps his hand down and presses just above her stuffed-full entrance to the pucker of her backside. She jumps and Elijah gasps with her motion. "Next time, one of us will be in here."

Face red as flame, she buries her nose against Elijah's breastbone…

…and nods.

Grapes. The interwebs said their Omega needs grapes when she's in heat. The sugars, the water content, the shape, everything is supposed to go along with an Omega's current needs, which is why Elijah finds himself with his Omega draped over his lap, parting her pretty lips so he can bestow a gift that doesn't consist of one of his body parts for a change.

James had placed an online order for grocery delivery so they wouldn't have to leave her, and the delivery guy—a Beta, thank God—did his best to ignore the wails of pleasure coming from the other room. Guys like him are used to heat and rut runs, and no doubt he'd seen and heard worse. Still, Elijah wanted to puff up his chest and rip the man in two for daring to flick his eyes in the direction of their mate's sensual cries. Good thing he learned how to keep his Alpha in check years ago. Mostly.

"Ah, ah," he chides. "Please swallow before I shove more in your mouth."

Katelyn's grin is devilish at his unintended innuendo. He loves seeing it. She's smiled more in two days than he'd seen her smile in two weeks.

James is passed out in her nest, totally drained—quite literally. Elijah can't wait until they time their ruts to flow along with her heat. Then they'll give her a run for her money. But for now, his stepbrother's slightly curled hair is mussed against a pillow dampened with every droplet of moisture they're capable of making. Cum. Sweat. Tears. It all blends into something purely them. To Elijah, it smells like love.

Katelyn makes that little, raspy noise she gets when she's getting another wave of heat fluttering through her belly.

He chuckles. "Ready to go again?"

She tucks her face into his naked abdomen, still a bit shy despite everything they've done. "Talk to me more, first."

"About what?"

"Tell me about little Elijah." She smiles against his skin, eyes closed and content. "What did you do when you were a kid?"

"Don't make fun of me."

She scoffs. "I never."

"You would."

Her smile grows bigger, and she nips along the side of his belly button. At that, he happily stuffs another grape in her mouth.

"I liked to draw," he admits.

She glances up at him with her cheek half full of fruit, one eyebrow cocked.

"Ah, ah. You promised not to make fun."

"I didn't!"

"Your eyebrow did."

She rolls her eyes and swallows, opening up for more sweet treats.

Elijah continues. "It was kid stuff. Dragons and bubble letters and, weirdly, dolphins. They went along with my middle name." Before she can ask, he pops in another grape. "It's Finnigan. James was teasing me when he called himself Finn. Dol*phin*. *Finn*igan. I almost died when he said it."

"What's your last name?" she asks.

"Are you wondering what your last name will be, rainbow?"

She gets shy again and stuffs her face into his belly.

"It's O'Reilly."

She eyes him, disbelief written on her face. "You don't look like an O'Reilly."

"Mom was dark and exotic. Guess that's the side that stuck. Bone structure, eye color, hair color. Ever heard of a red-headed step child? Well I was the black-headed version. Copper colored dad with a blonde stepmom and stepbrother. I fit in about as well as a freakin' toucan in a half-built skyscraper.

"James last name is the same as mine, though. His mom switched them both over when she married my dad. I think she wanted to forget about his real father. He died really slow, and it sort of traumatized her. That's why she clings to James so hard, I think. Afraid to lose him, too."

"Is that why he wants a pack so badly? To keep his relationship with her?"

He bops her nose. "That's definitely part of it. I've learned that his instincts tend to be straight on, though. Maybe rationality led him to it, but he never would have been so stubborn about an Omega if it didn't feel right to him."

She falls silent for a moment, her brain ticking away with thoughts he wishes he had a window into. "What was his last name before?"

"Goosefeathers."

She snorts and whaps him on the chest.

"Meh. It was something blasé and benign. James Richard Ross. My life changed the day I met that alluring, awkward as fuck teenager, and he took my last name before I even knew I loved him. Now I'll give it to you."

Her adorable face turns the color of cherry blossoms while a slow smile curves her lips. It doesn't last long. It falls into a look of insecurity as she nuzzles in. "Will your parents like me? The way I've lived my life is…"

"*Pfft.* The Lifestyle? Why do they have to know?" He runs his fingers through the messy waves of her hair, knotted in the back from rolling her head around for days. "James and I are used to keeping secrets."

"Like you kept *my* secret?" she snarks.

He takes a deep breath and leans back on his hands. "I didn't mean for that to happen. I'm sorry." Tipping his head to face the recessed lights in her ceiling, he braces himself on his arms, a simple fact sinking into his chest. "She'll never accept us, will she?"

Katelyn's face becomes a storm, one he hasn't seen since they were locked inside their idyllic palace and she was chucking plates against walls. "Why should I care what she thinks?"

Elijah ticks his head to the side.

She turns fully into him, curling her knees around his hip and cradling her arms close. "She's always told me…something. But she's a liar. I can't forgive her for this. For what she did. She took everything away from me, and I never even knew. I never even guessed. I was just too little…"

Alarm bells ring, and his scent must change, because he sees James's eyes blink open behind her.

"What happened?" Elijah asks.

So, she tells him. And tells him and tells him until his blood runs cold, then terribly hot. James's face is blank, but he smells like pure horror.

"I wish my dad had taken me, too," she says, soft and quiet, like a child's whisper-wish upon a star. "I don't know why he didn't."

"Ask him," James states, making her turn on her back in Elijah's lap to see her other Alpha.

"How?"

"I'll find him." Elijah nods, firm and unshakeable. "And your brother. It's what I'm good at. I'll get their records and track them down. Simple as syrup. Anything you need, we're here for you. Anything you want, we'll give it to you. Just tell us, sweetheart, and we'll move the fucking moon."

He'd have it no other way. If this is what he can do for her, he'll do it in a heartbeat. This is his mate after all.

And she deserves the world.

Romantic thoughts coat Katelyn in adoration. How can he say these things so easily? It makes her believe they're true.

Her elbows hinge as she lifts up, propping herself on Elijah's thighs with her lips parted. "You could do that?"

"Mm," James answers on behalf of his brother. Like a panther, he prowls over to kiss her shoulder and the idea falls over her like an airy curtain. It seems unreal. Could she really meet her long-dead family again? See her brother alive and breathing? Ask her far-away father why she was left with a woman who could never truly love her?

Katelyn has wanted to fall into Elijah's arms from the moment she met him, and her heat has given her every excuse to do so, but for the first time, despite the tension in her belly and the next budding wave of her heat, she wants to be in his arms for new, undeniable reasons. Beyond sexual tension, beyond hidden desire to give in to her nature, this is special. This is sacred.

This is when she falls in love.

I'm broken, too, her beautiful James had said, echoing her own heart...but maybe they don't have to be broken anymore. She is that puzzle piece Elijah talked about, there's no question anymore. She fits snugly into their open spaces, ones left by the universe just for her. They are her mates. Not just because they smell like heaven, but because, like James said, they belong. *She* belongs. That intimacy she's always wanted, that honesty she never thought she could have, that absolution she thought she never deserved, they give it all, like she's worth it. Her mother said she wasn't enough—but to these men, these Alphas, she is.

"Can I mate you?" she asks Elijah, soft but without a whisper of fear.

His eyes glimmer and a look of reverence graces his face. "Please."

Instinct leads her on, and she lets it. She nestles her knees on either side of his lap, her sex grazing his. He's hardening now as she feels her slick make him glide through her folds, and knows she's wanted here. She's safe. Like them, she's come home.

With the slowest of gestures, she caresses the curve of his neck, sweeping his dark hair aside and nuzzling into his warm skin. He trembles and she can almost taste the overwhelming scent of his emotions ramping up. She doesn't know what they mean, but they must be good, because he is a summer forest of scent wrapping around her, no trace of frost or snow.

James's rainfall scent falls over her now as he comes at Elijah from behind, freeing the other side of his neck and putting his mouth over his mating gland. Elijah's tremble becomes an earthquake beneath her fingertips, and she's never wanted him more.

She presses her tongue on that soft, paper-thin skin, and swipes across, tasting it. Tasting him. He's an aphrodisiac, hazing her mind until all that exists is this.

James's hand finds its way into her hair, tangling within the messy strands. Cupping the back of her head, he pulls her down harder against his brother's most sensitive spot, making Elijah whine. She imagines his inner Alpha begging for everything they have to give him, and she's not going to hold back anymore.

Voice calm as a still pond, James says, "Now…"

And Katelyn bares her teeth. The burst of blood on her tongue is immediate and intoxicating, filling her head with a euphoric bolt of ecstasy that travels all the way to her toes. Elijah grunts, harsh and low, only to cry out again in just moments. James must have done the same on the other side.

Mate.

Their mate.

"Don't let go," Elijah says. That baritone vibrates within her as she keeps her jaw locked tight. Feelings seep in, and they're not her own. Feelings of elation. Of desire. Of utter joy and bliss. They compound her own thoughts, laying on top like butter on bread, melting until they swirl within her, beyond decadence.

These layering emotions aren't hers…

Their Elijah's.

She can feel him.

James has wanted this for a decade.

His. Elijah is finally *his*. But it's not enough.

Releasing with a sweet suck, the saliva in his mouth seals his brother's wounds as he leaves a ring of teeth marks that prove Elijah is mated, owned, and adored. Slipping a hand around Elijah's jaw, he turns his face to kiss him, blood still tracing his tongue. Elijah must taste himself, because he lets out a growl that turns James molten from his heart down.

It's still not enough.

Sweeping in front of him, James also straddles the edge of his brother's lap, laying his erection along Katelyn's backside. His Omega. Their rainbow. She tenses for a moment when he slides his hands over her the curve of her back, letting out a groan as she releases the man they've claimed. He reaches around and cups the swell of her soft breasts, pulling her back until she's flush against his bare chest. Her arms lift, and her hands latch around the back of his head, nails scraping against his scalp as Elijah follows in and locks his lips on hers.

Tethered. The three of them.

Exactly as it should be.

He dives forward with a vampiric speed, clamping down and breaking Katelyn's skin in one swift plunge. Her cry only makes him bite harder, tasting the red wine that flows into his mouth, drunk on her. On both of his mates. He can feel them in his head like a whirl-wind now, pulsing, pulling, and pushing.

That means they're soulmated. Not just fated, not just paired.

Karera no ai wa hoshi ni kaka rete imashita. Their love was written in the stars.

Katelyn bucks against him as Elijah takes her other side, conse-crating their union. Leaving their marks behind.

James can feel his Omega's pleasure and pride course through him. He can feel the surge of satisfaction that runs electric through his brother's veins.

Mine.

…Ours.

"Now me," James manages, releasing her and lapping at what he left behind. He needs them to feel him in the same way, soul deep and endless. Elijah always knows what he's thinking, but not the depth of his heart. The intensity of it. The dark pool he hides away like a dragon with cursed treasure. Elijah only ever sees the blue glacier tip of James's iceberg, and that's something he can no longer stand.

Throwing Katelyn down into her soft nest, he lands on top of her, shoving his mating gland against her lips. Like his perfect Omega, she licks and sucks, excitement building inside her. Their new connection is a live wire. She wants this. He can feel it in his bones.

More than that, Elijah wants it, too.

Nante kanpekina nda.

How perfect.

Elijah listens to James's soft grunt when she breaks the skin. Her glory in the conquest strikes him like the brightest of light, burning him in its rays. Sanctifying him.

He folds his body over James's, careful with his weight, and places open mouthed kisses on his shoulder blades as his brother's muscles flutter. Through his connection with Katelyn, he can feel ripples of James's emotion as soft whispers, but that's not what he wants. He wants to drown in both of them until he doesn't know who he is anymore.

Still, he waits. He waits until she pulls off his brother. He waits until she's lapping at the wound she left behind. He waits until she tips her head back and her jade eyes fall onto his, urging him forward and giving him a silent command. Then, he grabs his brother by the throat, lifting him and tipping his head back. He's not going to mark the other side this time. No. He's going to draw the symbol for infinity into his brother's skin.

Clamped tight on James's throat, he can feel him swallow as Elijah places a long lick over Katelyn's marks. He can taste her spit and the leftover remnants of James's blood, and it makes the Alpha in him run his tongue over the inside of his own pointed eye teeth like a wolf poised for the kill. Because that's what he is. A predator.

Nuzzling down, he positions his mouth just right, feeling her teeth marks against his mouth, and James submits completely. It's heady. It's enthralling.

And it's all his.

Unable to hold on for even one more breath, his teeth sink in…and it's like finding God.

CHAPTER 15
DETERMINATION

THEIR UTTER DEVOTION makes her glow.

Katelyn's never felt like this before. This is mind blowing. She can't hear their thoughts, it doesn't quite go that far, but every emotion, good or bad, flows through her like a river.

Their soft heartthrobs when she smiles.

Their spikes of lust when she begs for them.

And, funny enough, their relief when they got to sleep at the end of her five-day heat. It amused her to no end—until she passed out herself, completely spent.

Now Elijah is full of adoration as he scrubs her hair. They're in a bath way too small for them, stretching their flexibility to the limits as both sling one leg over the side of the tub to make the tiny space work. James doesn't like to touch others' soapy skin, so he's brushing his teeth nearby instead, humming agreements every now and then as they chat, his face blank as ever but his heart a kaleidoscope of happiness.

Bubbles cascade down Katelyn's back as Elijah froths her hair up. His skrich-scratching on her scalp feels better than any Swedish massage her mother dragged her to. She sits between his legs, one knee crammed to her chest, but she couldn't be more content. The real world is a distant dream, one she can't be bothered with, still living in the newness of being mated. *Soul*mated.

"I love you two," she says, and feels their immediate floods of tenderness.

"I'll raise you one," Elijah says, pouring a cup of warm water over her head. "How about I love you both to the edge of the universe."

She giggles. "The universe is ever-expanding."

Elijah curls his arms around her, nuzzling in. "Exactly."

Her Alphas' feelings have dipped from elation to trepidation as they travel the city. How far can they go before her ability to feel them ebbs?

Katelyn sent them to see their parents. They wanted her to come, James insisted actually, then Elijah muttered that he'd use his Alpha command—something she knows from The Lifestyle's preaching would override her ability to do anything but obey—but James had quickly slapped a hand over Elijah's mouth, and both gave in when she swore she'd feel better if the awkwardness of their family conversation had passed before she met her new step-parents. She didn't want her introduction to their family to be when conflict might rear its ugly head. Never mind a possessive streak, the urge to defend her Alphas is stronger, and she's not sure she could have kept her mouth shut if push came to shove.

"Damnit," she grumbles, scratching at her neck like a dog. Her shirt itches. Almost everything she owns has a high neck that covers her mating glands, but she'd never really felt their coarseness before. Her creams kept her focused on the sting. Now it's unbearable. She vows to go shopping at that Bohemian store she likes as soon as possible. Paisleys and prints, please and thank you, and wide open at the neck to show off her new bites. She'll run like an alley cat to that store...

...once she gets out of her job interview.

"Eeeeee!" she squeals out loud, still giddy.

"..." her childhood teddy bear says, sitting atop a bookshelf.

"…" she replies, eyeing it from its threadbare bottom to its missing ear.

She feels her Alphas' amusement to match her own as it bubbles up inside her. She can picture Elijah laughing for no reason other than he felt her burst of emotion, and chuckles to herself, wondering if he'll look borderline insane if he blatts out laughter on the subway train car. James might smack him off the back of the head and they may get into one of their brotherly mini slap fights. She almost wishes she was there to see it, but she's got a task to do.

"This is just a formality, you know," she tells her teddy bear. "My old boss said so. The contractor they brought on to fill my space doesn't seem to jive with the office culture." She snorts. "The man must hate communal coffee time, and that's how real people bond."

She tugs on her panties, bright red and lacy for no reason. Her bra doesn't match. It has a childish series of hearts in all colors. It, too, is her aesthetic.

"I get to see Niles again!" she says before souring. "Do you think he'll forgive me?"

Maybe she'll show him her mating bites and let them tell the story without her saying a word.

Who is she kidding? She's going to gush. Now that she finally can, she's going to let her truth fall out and her mouth run wild.

There is a click, and she turns toward her closed bedroom door. Beyond it, the main door to her apartment opens unexpectedly, and her brow knits in confusion. She was tired of getting her locks picked so she left all the brass twirly buttons untwirled, but there's no way Elijah and James would be back yet.

She fumbles into a skirt, too tight to not have to wriggle, and hears a voice that sends prickles up her spine.

"Katie?"

Her adrenaline spikes.

Confusion and concern come from the other side of their bond as the terrible scent of coconut fills her nose, stronger than ever before. All her senses are heightened now that her medicine has gone swirling down the toilet bowl like a dead goldfish.

She never wanted to breathe this man in again.

Thomas.

Her Alphas' panic screams over their connection as her stomach drops to her knees. They're going to come home for her, she knows, but they've been gone a good half hour. They can't save her from this. She can't escape.

What's she going to do?

—————

James's sudden grip on his brother's hand makes his bones ache.

"What just happened?" Elijah asks. He seems to lose all focus, his gaze hovering on the middle distance, as if wishing to see through her eyes. "What could make her so scared?"

"Her mother," James says.

"Or her fiancée."

A tornado of his own jealousy mixed with Elijah's deep worry stacks like stones in James's heart. "I'll kill him."

"No," Elijah warns. "Because then you'll prove him right about people like us." He squeezes James's hand tight. "Not to be rude or anything, but fuck mom and dad right now. We have to go back."

Not quite the sentiment he'd use. Still, James answers, "Mm."

The tension makes James sweat as her emotions waterfall through him. Panic. Worry. Fear. Disgust. He wants to send back something soothing, something reassuring, but his feelings can't lie. He can't push out something fake, can he? If so, he doesn't know how.

Elijah's jaw clenches as he bites the inside of his cheek. His emotions are raw anger now. "We shouldn't have left."

But how could they have known?

When the piercing screech of the train car brakes claws at James's ears, for the first time it doesn't make him want to curl into a ball. It's a relief. It means *out*.

Rude and abrupt, they force themselves through the afternoon crowd and across the brick tiled platform. The whole station is dark and grimy with decades of commuter patina and parasites floating on every surface. Luck gifts them a fairly well-kept Green Line train going in the opposite direction with blocky electric letters glowing on its side panels, promising to take them home. Her home. *Their* home. There's no way they'll leave her now. James will lay flat on the floor and dare her to move him. Elijah will give all that's left of their money to pay for the cost of two huge men in her space, eating her food and breathing her air. They'll take turns sleeping in her bed, the other begrudgingly exiled to the couch, and if they have to, they'll snuggle on the carpeted floor when they give in to their need for just each other.

It would be worth it.

There are no seats left, so James is left grabbing onto the dull metallic rung hanging overhead. No doubt millions of germs are working their way into his skin, but he will endure. Women eye them, some men too, warily watching one dark Alpha on the verge of snapping and giving seductive smiles to another pale beast who looks calm as clouds. Omegas or not, people like them both, regardless of sex, but if one dares touch him right now, he'll throw them down the aisle.

This is why he hates crowds.

His body rocks as the train moves forward, and a burst of determination fills Elijah.

"We'll get to her," he reassures.

James doesn't deny it out loud, but a sinking feeling tells his truth for him. Elijah turns to face him with a gentle wave of sympathy. This is what James wanted. To be felt so endlessly. It's a comfort that blankets the roiling inside him.

"We will," Elijah insists.

And James lets himself believe.

"Katie?" rings out again, the front door shutting behind the man who had her kidnapped. The man who tested her until she failed spectacularly. The man who will inherit the core of The Lifestyle and all the political and social tentacles that go with it.

There is a knock on her bedroom door, and she bristles, her follicles pulling taut until every hair on her arms stands at attention.

"Katie, are you in there?"

She stumbles back on the bed, still stripped of all its sheets, and it makes a *fwump*ing noise while the springs squawk their displeasure at her sudden weight.

She curses under her breath. There's no pretending she's not here.

There is a huff of breath from behind her door and a groaning creak, as if he's leaned his whole weight on the wood and managed to stretch the metallic hinges. She hopes they let go completely so he can fall on his perfect face.

"Katie, don't hide from me. I'm sorry. I went too far."

"No shit," she spits, only to cringe at her own filthy mouth. She never cursed in front of him before, always focused on being what her mother wanted her to be, but if anyone deserves her vitriol, it's him.

There is a dull *thunk*. This time she imagines he's bopped his forehead off the door. His sigh is deep, and she can hear his remorse. He's always been so good at that. So suave. As sweet as pie when he wants to be, as strong as iron when something gets in his way, and as fiery as dragon's breath when he thinks it will gain him even an inch. Now he sounds pathetic and contrite...but she's tired of being manipulated.

He speaks, distant and muffled. "When those damn Alphas stopped answering their phone, I gave it a few days. Then a few more, but I got worried. I went to that weird house to look for you, but the whole place was empty. You don't know how scared I was. I didn't know what happened to you."

His voice sounds strained.

She doesn't care.

"Leave," she says. "I don't want you here. I don't want to see you, I don't want to talk to you, and I definitely don't want to marry you."

There's that sigh again.

Ignoring her completely, he says, "I'm proud of you, Katie. If you're here, that means you escaped, right? You must be so smart to get away from those monsters. I would have thought they'd sniff you out and hunt you down." He lets out a soft laugh. "At least this means I don't have to pay them."

Katelyn sees red. Her Omega wants to rip his eyes out for sloughing off her Alphas like they didn't matter. Like they didn't have plans. Like they didn't need a place to live, clothes, and food.

"What if I told you they let me go?" she says. "That they were so worried about me, they opened the door and carried me out, themselves."

He scoffs. "Then I would call you a liar."

There is a creak from the doorknob, and it starts to twist. Her Omega says to run, but she doesn't need pills to put it in its place. Her Alphas are on high alert, but she tucks their feelings into the corner of her heart so she can focus on the now.

The door opens, and he looks disheveled. Dark circles mar the sunken-in spaces under his eyes. He seems exhausted. His hair is separated into wiry clumps, as if he's been raking his fingers through it nonstop. His business suit—that omnipresent outfit—is wrinkled and shabby. His tie is nowhere to be found, and the buttons at his throat are opened below his collarbone. His normally straight back is stooped in contrition, and his eyes don't rise above the floor. Until they do. Until they land on her and immediately warm despite her clenched teeth and tense limbs.

"There you are, pretty girl." The corner of his mouth lifts into a half smile. That charming, oh so swoon worthy expression that makes other Lifestyle ladies fall to their knees.

But that's not who she is.

She lets her honesty out of its cage. "You make me sick."

His eyes fall to the floor again. "I don't blame you for being angry. I really don't. But I was under so much pressure from my father. He had people ask around your office and," his voice dips, "that unapologetic Omega seemed to be your only friend. You don't have any Lifestyle friends, Katie. Just him. And he flaunts his secondary gender. Not to mention his perverse sexuality. My father kept saying…" he trails off and swallows hard. "But I finally told him off. I'll never do this again. Not to you, or to anyone else. I want to make changes, not go backward. I realize what this must have done to you."

"You don't know the half of it," she says through her teeth.

Wait.

It dawns on her then that she's feeding into his narrative. He thinks she was afraid—and she was. But not of them. It was of what they made her feel.

She clenches her fists. "They're not what you think they are. They're kind."

His smile is sardonic. "Says the woman who screamed she was terrified they would hurt her."

"I would have said anything I could to get you to let me go! Do you think they'd really do that?"

"They're Alphas. You know what they're capable of."

She jumps to her feet. "Don't talk like you know them."

His expression falls and his brows cinch together, becoming a furrowed line of black. There is a heavy silence, one with the weight of a thousand bricks. "You *are* a sympathizer, aren't you?"

Rage builds up, and a lifetime of secrets refuse to be kept anymore. "I'm an *Omega!*" It rips from her throat with all the pain of the years being trapped there. "And I've *ALWAYS* been an Omega! You people made me fight it so hard, I was killing myself, but not anymore!" She points at nowhere. "You have a Lifestyle doctor who 'helps' kids like me. He puts us on so many suppressants and scent blockers that it hurts. My skin was always on fire. I wanted to throw up every day. I was weak and almost fainted every time I shoved those pills down my throat! You don't know what I've been through!"

Against all odds, his eyes soften, a fondness growing there. "You did that for me?"

She loathes the hope in his voice. "I did it for my mother, I did it for you, I did it out of—"

"Oh, Katie," he cuts her off. "This makes you even more perfect."

Her face falls, steam out of her sails. He steps into her space, and she steps back to keep her distance. The bastard doesn't even seem to notice.

"Remember my conversion program? This is our opportunity. If you hid it for so long, you must know that these instincts of yours aren't right! You wanted to be like a Beta!"

"I just told you it was *killing* me! The secondary genders shouldn't be made to suffer just to fit into *your rules!*"

"But I can get research behind it now! If it doesn't happen with unknown doctors in secret alleys with scared kids, I can get people who can find the right mix of what you need to keep it all in check. It doesn't have to hurt. There can be studies. You could be my first. You could be cared for by the best of the best!"

She gapes, stepping further away.

"Katie, listen to me. What better way to prove that I believe in this program than for me, *ME*, to marry an Omega? One who wants to be like us!"

"I don't! Not anymore! We're just people! Who is The Lifestyle to judge who's good and who's bad? Betas aren't all bad, but Alphas and Omegas aren't all bad, either! *The Lifestyle* is bad! *YOU* are bad!"

That iron will shows itself as his demeanor changes. He straightens and his fists clench at his sides. "What do you think will happen if I tell your mother?"

"She knows," Katelyn hisses. "After this whole ordeal, I went into h—"

"If you leave me, I'll make sure she has nothing. She gave up everything for you. Are you really willing to destroy her?"

She stands tall, her chin up. The words fall from her heart instead of her brain, the sentiment ringing true, even to her own ears. "Sometimes, pieces of people need to be destroyed so they can become something better."

Narrowing his eyes, something in him flips like a switch. A dangerous, venomous switch.

He lunges, wrapping his arms around her waist and driving her to the floor. Buzzing fills her ears as she hits her head so hard, she bites her tongue and tastes the copper tang of blood. Rough and fast, his leg pushes hers apart, her skirt rucking up in the process. Worse, he reaches down and tugs the fabric up so high, he rips it. His fingers trail along the edge of her red panties as his other hand pins her by the throat, one of her arms tacked painfully beneath his knee while the other one scrabbles, but gets nowhere, unable to work her nails through the thick fabric of his jacket.

"This is what you need to fall in love, right? All Omegas just want to be fucked into submission."

She bucks with her legs, but it doesn't matter. He's just too heavy.

"That's not what it's like!"

"How would you know, my little virgin? How about this: I'll pretend to be an Alpha for you. Call you my Omega. Call you my *mate*."

Her stomach turns over. How strange that these words from another man's mouth could make her bile rise.

He leans in to kiss her, but she thrusts her head forward, clocking him in the nose in a heavy *thwack*. The cry he makes is pitchy as he stumbles back, and Katelyn scrambles to her feet.

What happens now? What can she do?

Against the wall is her curtain rod, still no fabric adorning its metal length. The last she'd seen it, she was wielding it against kidnappers.

Now she's going to wield it against a rapist.

She snatches it and wraps it in both hands, bending her knees and pointing it in his direction. He's rubbing his nose, a red trail smeared across his face as he wipes the blood away. Cold as a winter frost, he laughs.

"What are you going to do with that, Katie? Beat me to death?"

A twist pulls her lips into a scowl...then it comes. A lightbulb flashes in her mind's eye. A courtyard with blue flowers. A shallow pond filled with koi.

She knows what to do.

"*Kiri oshi*." James's words fall from her lips as she swipes the pole over her head and down onto his shoulder. Not too hard, but hard enough to get her point across. His flinch and yawp is so satisfying, she feels a trill of pride.

"*Suihei*," she says this time, doing a sideways swipe that clips his arm. He fumbles to a stand, holding his palms out in front of him and waving them, peppering "Wait," "No," and "Stop" into the room around them.

"Really? I've got two more moves in my repertoire. Sure you don't want to see them? James taught me. My Alpha."

He blanches, hands lowering. "Your what?"

"You heard me. James. Elijah. Those Alphas you treat like trash. My *pack*."

His mouth opens and closes, as if he doesn't know what to say.

"And while they are wonderful people, I imagine they won't really like what you just tried to do to me. And, you know what, according to the law, it would be within their rights to tear you apart. Do you feel like losing an arm, Thomas? A leg?" She points the pole downward and channels her best Elijah. "Or how about your skinny dick?"

That seems to get him moving.

He doesn't toss a threat over his shoulder, he doesn't leave on a parting word, he just whips around and stumbles out of the room, one hand clamped on the arm she's most likely bruised to high hell.

She takes a shaky breath before nodding in a rough bob and dropping the curtain rod with a dull clatter on the slick-stained carpet.

Good fucking riddance.

Elijah's Alpha is raging at him to *Protect*. Save his Omega. Save his *mate*.

When he tears into her apartment, James right behind him, she's laying on the living room floor, colorful patchwork pillows stuffed all around her head and an ice pack over her eyes. Her skirt has a tear up the side, showing what's meant to be hidden.

He wants to kill something.

A growl sinks his words to an acid threat. "Who did this to you?"

She chuckles softly. "It doesn't matter. I scared him away."

"Him?" James asks, a sandstorm of feelings inside.

"Thomas," Elijah says. It's no longer a question. "Did he hurt you?"

James leans down and slowly lifts the ice pack. Elijah expects bruising. Swelling. He expects to go rip a genderist's throat out, and God damn the consequences.

But there's nothing. Just those jade eyes. Her smile is honest, and she opens up wide, sending him love and relief. It's overwhelming, filling in the gaps between his cells with nothing but *her*.

He lets out an airy, breathless laugh, and runs an adrenaline-fueled hand through his hair. "What happened?"

Smug, she says, "I have achieved ex-fiancée status."

"Let's rectify that immediately," James says, pressing a kiss onto her forehead. Her eyes sink shut with a dragonfly-flit of happiness traveling from her heart to theirs.

"Is that an official proposal this time?"

Elijah *tsk*s. "I think we can do better."

His brother grunts some sort of approval, more focused on playing with her collar, lifting it as if checking to make sure their bites are still there and unharmed.

Elijah plops down beside her, resting the ice pack back over her eyes and leaning his temple on James's shoulder. Like this, his Alpha recedes, giving him space to act on more than just survival mode. *Protect* mode. Who knew it could be so strong? Taking a deep breath, he forces himself to let go of the coiled knot in his chest and slow his racing heart.

He still scowls, though.

"I'm going to mess up dear old Tom-Tom's sexy face someday."

Katelyn snorts. "I'll help."

"I refuse," he says, bopping her nose.

"Well, then you can't do it either. I'd rather not have my Alphas in the spotlight for mauling Thomas Bleaker."

"Looks like he mauled you first, rainbow." He doubts she ripped her skirt by herself. He hopes that asshole did it while begging on his knees opposed to any alternative.

He bristles again.

Lifting that ice pack once more, she looks up and pats his face. "Don't worry. Seems Sensei Joe's tips and tricks have served our little pack well."

James beams like he's two seconds shy of getting raptured. "Really?"

"You taught me exactly what I needed to know," she tells him. "So, I sort of, kind of, might have almost broken his arm."

Instantly, James ducks down to claim her in an upside-down kiss, her nose slightly smashed by his chin, making Elijah laugh for real.

"Come on, Finn, be nice to our captive," he teases, only to receive a muffled "Shut up, Zeb" from both his mates in response.

Oh yeah. He's going to like this life.

Mom was…silent. For a long time, she was silent.

Again, James wishes Katelyn would have come. He'd love to have shown her off instead of letting Elijah flash (one of) his mating bites to their family. James wouldn't show his. He knows Elijah doesn't regret biting him in the same spot Katelyn did, but they'll ease their family into the idea of a pack before bombarding them with "pseudo-incest."

Elijah's father seems to know anyway, but that disconnect Elijah and his father have had for years didn't seem to grow any wider at their news. Instead, his father smiled. "We'd love to welcome her into the family." Then he shook his head. "At least I finally understand why you two have always been so…close."

Yes. He definitely knows.

Now, he and Elijah are both coming home to their Omega. They stand outside her apartment, *their* apartment, just staring at the window she always leaves open, no matter how many stray cats work their way in.

His stepbrother grins. "Happy? Now we can be close to them again. You can stand with pride and love them as much as you want."

James feels a mixed bag of emotions, and Elijah cocks an eyebrow.

"You don't want to love them anymore?" Elijah asks, then shakes his head. "No, that's not it."

This soul connection is going to make his brother's mind-reading act so much easier.

Elijah sighs through his nose and kicks a rock at his feet. "I bet it's that you've always loved them, but as big as that feeling was, your fear has always been bigger."

James says nothing, but a sense of rightness fills him. Elijah slings an arm over his shoulders in solidarity. In understanding. Acceptance.

"Are you still afraid now?"

James lets a rare smile bloom as he tips his face to the summer sun.

"No."

And it's the absolute truth. There's nothing to punish himself for anymore. He's not dirty, just fated. He may be *other*, but he's loved for exactly who he is.

Maybe it's time for the broken pieces inside him to finally heal.

What a relief that would be.

He rubs his fingers over his scar, the scar where he tried to end his life, and just lets it become part of his story instead of a scarlet letter. It's time to move forward. There's a whole new future ahead, and its time to live it without fear. Without shame.

After all, he's exactly who he needs to be.

"I'm home!" Katelyn calls, rattling her keys in the doorknob. Keys that now *everyone* has and must *use*.

She kicks the bottom of the door with one high-heeled shoe, yellow patent leather so shiny she can see the reflection of her red feather earrings when she bends down.

Collapsed cardboard boxes, plain as the brown paper they're made of, lay stacked against the outer hallway, and she drags in a few more. They smell like overripe bananas, but she'll take that over coconut any day.

"Yo!" Elijah says, jogging over a few steps with his hands out, swiping her glasses with one and taking the boxes with the other. He rests her owl-eyed frames over his thin, oval ones, blinking through his own prescription and her thin pane of glass. He snorts and says, "Aesthetic" under his breath.

James sits on the floor, filled boxes all around him, labeled in a neat, blocky hand. How she ended up with a full box of just utensils, she'll never know, but here we are. Clumped in his lap are clothes for all three of them, some of the last things to go before they leave tomorrow, and he's folding them in military-crisp piles and tucking them into a box with dull pictures of oranges along the side.

"Niles says hi," she tells them, dropping her keys on the kitchen counter. "He told me that you were both very handsome."

"From him, I'll take it," Elijah says. "If you can ever pull him away from his boy toy and his bestie, we should go out for dinner again."

"Not pizza," James states, fluffing out something before folding it. It's small and white and…is that a handkerchief?

IT'S HER UNDERWEAR! Her slick-stained. granny. panty. *underwear*!

"James!" she squawks, lunging over and nearly plummeting into his lap, snatching them like a frog catches flies. Her Alpha gives no reaction, but her insides swim with his question marks. "Do you have to touch them?" she whines.

"I've had them in my mouth," he states.

Her aggrieved cry makes her freshly tattooed Alpha laugh so hard he slaps his knee, the new ice blue and jade green dragon contorting to follow the shapes of his muscle.

Coiling into a ball amidst all the perfectly folded laundry, she begins to roll, ruining everything. "But what if they're dirty? What if they're old or ripped or…?!"

James grapples them away with his blond lashes blinking over eyes that could never comprehend the disaster a woman's underwear can be. Stubborn, Katelyn pounces on him, reaching up to grab at her unmentionables and knocking him on his back. She flails a hand in grasping waves, but his arms are longer as they vie for power in a decidedly one-sided battle. His expression is slack, but his insides are howling laughter, and a tiny tick of a smile finally curves his lips.

It only makes her fight harder, despite the grin on her face.

In the midst of their tangle, Elijah decides to get in on the action, crying out a fake roar and plunging into the fray. He smooshes James's face to the side, and when the poor man says, "Why?" his brother responds with a playful bite to the blond's meaty shoulder.

Katelyn's not immune to his onslaught either. His fingers dance on her ribcage, tickling her while his brother pulls him into a headlock.

"If you keep it up," she wails in high pitched shrieks of laughter, "I'm gonna pee!"

"Well, we have to wash these carpets anyw—Good godamnit, James, I said don't pull my hai—fuck, fuck, alright! Arghh!"

The tables have turned! Katelyn jumps atop Elijah, straddling him as he wriggles in James's grip with a grumpy growl in his throat. It's her turn to work her fingers into him now, and James eggs her on, grabbing a firm fist around one of Elijah's wrists and lifting it high, giving her perfect access to his armpit—that most sensitive of tickle spots.

Before she can get there, he rolls, dragging Katelyn beneath him with James on top, like a thick Elijah-sandwich. They pause for a moment, looking at their predicament with heaving breaths.

Elijah's grin is sly. "Well, look where we ended up." His hair is utterly mussed and strands poke into his eyes. He puffs his cheeks and tries to blow them out a few times before giving up and just exuding the most charm he can while wearing two pairs of glasses and being squashed under their shared pale Alpha.

"I'll bite you again," James says.

"By all means."

Elijah pivots his hips between her legs, pressing against her core before he retracts, and she knows from the flare of interest on James's side that Elijah just rubbed against his crotch as well.

"We haven't done this position yet," Elijah murmurs, leaning in to kiss her…

…only for her to raspberry his lips and slip out from under him, waving her panties in the air like a flag.

"Got 'em!" she calls, doing a small victory dance…that is, until she notices the rest of the pile of her undies spattered beneath her two Alphas.

Elijah puffs at the black strands in his eyes once more, his grin like the devil, and he picks up another pair. He doesn't say words. His emotions are beating in her chest with the silent sentiment: I WIN.

James flops down his full weight and pins his brother with an "*Oomph.*"

"Enough," James says. "Fold or bubble wrap. You pick."

Elijah's eyes sparkle. "Bubble wrap."

As expected, really.

James lets his brother up and, after he places one set of glasses back on Katelyn's face with a kiss to her nose, he straightens his own and throws his hair into a messy bun.

Katelyn stands silent for a moment, looking at her happy home. James has piled her underwear elsewhere for her to deal with on her own while he's focused on the rest of the rumpled closet-mess. Elijah stands in the kitchen, wrapping plates with a serious look of concentration, only to bite his lip, pop a bubble, and let a ripple of joy tingle through her chest.

She marvels. How did she get here?

However it happened, she will be forever grateful.

But first thing's first.

She pries her feet out of those pretty-but-sadistic yellow heels and tosses them across the room into a wide box labeled "Shoes." It's a bit mountainous, everything from hooker-high to flip flops, but she admittedly might have a bit of an obsession with good footwear. Grabbing a roll of bubble wrap, she sits by the pile of knick-knacks and gets to work. A bird plastered with loud stickers calls to her first, and she begins rolling it up when a little thrill of happiness hits her again followed by a tiny *pop* ringing out in the kitchen.

Her smile makes her cheeks hurt in the best way. How can she love so hard, so fast?

"Are you sure you're really okay with moving?" Elijah asks, bringing in a box folded shut. "This place really seems like a home, not just some replaceable apartment."

She picks up a mini piggy bank this time. It's only big enough for a quarter, but it's the map of Europe painted on it that matters. She's always wanted to go to the belly button. And by that, she means Greece.

"We need a bigger place." She shrugs. "Especially a bigger bedroom."

"With a bed for three," James says with no room for argument.

Elijah sits beside him and picks up more clothes to fold. "I'll turn the whole room into a bed, if you want. That way, we can all cuddle and roll around as much as we want."

James seems to contemplate for a second, then nods firmly. Possibly eight times. Ten. And Elijah laughs so hard, James puts a hand over his mouth again.

This is how it should be. Maybe how it always should have been. Alphas, Omega, it wouldn't have mattered. As long as she met them, she knows she would have loved them. And as long as they're together, wherever they are is home.

CHAPTER 16
EPILOGUE

THE SKY IS a vast azure stripe hovering over the horizon. From this angle, Katelyn can see the curve of the earth, cities and blocks condensing down into unrecognizable shapes, just dips and bumps on the valley of a living map. Wisps of moisture draw sugar floss clouds across the blue heavens as her wings spread wide. Up high like this, the crisp temperature frosts the dew drops on her every feather. Scarlet, emerald, and amber, they're all streaked with the wind as her muscles pump, bringing her ever higher.

Elijah flies above, dark like a raven, a daredevil lilt to his voice when he yells, "Watch me!"

His wings fold in tight against his body, and he plummets like a stone.

Black feathers are left seesawing in his wake as he rides gravity toward the rocky ground, so far away, but getting nearer as his body shrinks with the distance.

Katelyn's hand flies to her mouth, but there's no need. James darts after him, his golden wings held straight back to heighten his speed as he plunges after his brother, Elijah giggling wildly from meters down. He knows exactly what he's doing.

It's like a golden parachute when James spreads his wings wide, his body the shape of a cross in mid-flight. From where she hovers, Katelyn can see him wrapped around Elijah's waist and tugging him upward, flawless in his grace despite carrying the weight of another full-grown Alpha. Elijah's wings hang limply as his weight tugs him straight toward the earth from the hips down. Still, he turns his face towards the sunlight, toward Katelyn, and she can feel the triumph in him. He did it. He was brave enough to fall from heaven.

It's her turn.

She folds her hands over her heart and takes a breath so deep it threatens to split her at the seams. Can she do this?

She can.

She will.

Closing her eyes to the sky, she flexes, and her wings wrap around her like an embrace. A sense of weightlessness holds her for the briefest of moments. A moment where her hair flutters up around her and she seems to hover in her own body. Then the wind takes her.

She'd always thought falling would be like riding a rollercoaster, that her stomach would find its way into her throat and threaten to let go. This is not that. This is being caressed by the sky.

The world calls to her from below, a never-ending threat of danger, death, and defeat—somewhere she never wants to be, not even in nightmares. She's struggled so hard, year after year, all by herself, tangled in weighted secrets with no one to keep her safe where she belongs…

But she's not alone anymore.

Elijah's arm wraps around her waist while James positions himself below, as if he would take the pain of the earth first, before ever allowing her body to touch it. All six of their wings unfurl in a single burst, golden, black, and jewel bright, and they rocket back to where the air is cleaner, away from the poisons of a dying world. Up to where V-shaped flocks fly. Up to where the stars burn bright. Up to where she'll never be alone again.

And a kiss caresses her forehead.

Katelyn blinks, her troposphere wisping away into a dreamy fog. Her eyelashes are still a bit clumpy from the makeup she didn't wash off the night before. She and her Alphas had spent the night reading books out loud to each other, and Katelyn's had her ugly crying when she got to the mother part.

"Rise and shine, rainbow," Elijah says before laying another kiss on the crown of her head.

"*Mlurf*" seems to be the only sound she's capable of until he rests a café specialty on the night table, the plastic cup sweating over caramel colored, creamy goodness. "S'dat coffee?" she manages.

"Yep."

"From Sam's?"

James rolls onto his side next to her, spooning in and stuffing his nose in the crook of her neck. "It's not six."

"Yes, it's from Sam's and no, it's not six. It's 5:45, but if we don't get up, we won't make the plane in time."

James nips Katelyn's shoulder before shoving himself up and out of their enormous bed. The man is a wonder. Dead asleep one second, bursting with energy the next. He has to scoot over three times to make his way off the left edge of the bed, but Katelyn just rolls over to the right, and right onto the floor.

Elijah snorts his amusement, but only repositions the coffee cup under her face until her wandering lips find the straw and she becomes human again. "You ready?"

Katelyn blows bubbles into her sweet, caffeinated delicacy. "No."

She feels his wave of affection as he starts to tug off her sleep socks. "What do you think is gonna happen? We're going to fly across the country and they'll just put you back on the plane and say, 'Nope! Return to sender!'"

James comes over to place a lick up Elijah's mating bite before nipping him, too.

"Get some pants on!" he says, waving his brother away. "Why am I the only one with pants on?"

A wave of amusement braided with naughtiness comes from James's side of the bond when he pointedly leaves his clothes off, modeling his bare butt on the way to his morning routine. Elijah watches him go with one eyebrow up and a smile on his face. "There is no way I'm getting him on the plane like that."

"I'll confuse the guard while you sneak him on," Katelyn says. The straw is at her mercy while she sucks down coffee fast enough to get a brain freeze, but Elijah doesn't give her time to drain her drink dry.

With James in the ensuite, he scoots her in her mismatched undies to the guest bathroom and shuts her in.

"Showers are optional, peeing is not."

"That could be considered a Golden Shower," she calls through the door.

She can physically feel James's "ew," and Katelyn laughs as she swipes sleep from her eyes. From the bedroom, she can hear Elijah fussing with suitcases and zippers. Almost everything was packed last night, they just need toiletries and last minute "Oops" items. Like tampons. Yes, she should bring tampons.

"So, what else do you want to do when we're there?" Elijah asks loudly.

"Sensei Joe," James calls back, audible between the two bathroom walls.

"Do you one better, Jamsie. I saved up my dollars and cents. You're getting a one-on-one lesson…with a real katana."

Something clatters to the floor in the other bathroom and Katelyn pops her head out of her door, toothbrush crammed into her cheek. James wanders out, still naked as the day he was born, with his hands clapped over his face.

"Really?" he asks. For the first time, his voice is dipped in something childlike, as if someone offered to give him the world's best bicycle for no reason other than the fact that he looked like he wanted one. Katelyn's heart swims with James's wonder and an excitement so hardcore, she can barely keep it in.

Elijah's grin is unending. "Yeah."

And Katelyn spits out her toothbrush with laughter when James tackles his brother to the ground, glommed on like chocolate on a dipped strawberry. After what sounds like a sharp head crack and a groan from Elijah, she watches the two hold each other with nothing but joy in her heart. After eight or nine kisses, Elijah smacks James's bare butt and pushes him off, shooing him to go do what he's told. Katelyn's happy to do the same.

After all, they do have a plane to catch.

Without her medicine, the world smells new, everything amped up and carrying its own special flavor. She'd never understood when people meant when they drank wine and said they could "taste notes of cinnamon," but now she gets it.

Other Alpha/Omega pairings have a special bonded scent. She and her Alphas smell like an orchard, for instance. The woman and her mate over there smell like what meditation would be. Lavender, patchouli, and a hint of rosemary. Those Beta friends walking down the sidewalk smell softer, like their scents haven't really bloomed, but they're still there under the layering scents of the rest of the world. Air fresheners, antiseptics, cough drops, cologne, gasoline, body odor, new leather, grass, ozone, burnt pancakes—the world is now a prismatic symphony for her nose.

But something is familiar.

Katelyn stops dead in her tracks, clutching her hands together. "I can't do this."

James is on her left, placing his palm on the small of her back. "You can."

"What do I even say?"

Elijah chuckles and takes her hand. "I'll give you three words. 'The Lifestyle sucks.'"

She can't help but laugh at that.

Just in front of them is a doorway laced with ivy. Inside, fairy lights trail the walls to keep the atmosphere cozy while fake candles flicker in the center of wider tables. It smells like garlic, basil, mozzarella cheese, and tomatoes. It smells like marsala, mushrooms, and well braised meat. Her mouth and stomach have ganged up against her, begging to go into the restaurant, but her feet refuse to move. Inside, a hostess looks at them from behind her podium with a confused half-smile, as if to say, "Are you coming in or do you just want to look at me for a minute?"

Katelyn will happily look at her for a minute.

"Don't be afraid," James tells her, getting a firmer grip about her waist.

Elijah laces their fingers together. "Come on, rainbow. Let me show you what a good job I did."

The door opens and the scents brighten. All of them are well known and well-loved, but still there is that pull. That tug.

Her eyes flit over every face, touching them like a tap on the shoulder and testing them for validity. Is it you? No? You, maybe? Maybe you?

Finally, her gaze comes to rest.

She's looking at a male version of herself.

Auburn hair, jade eyes, and a look of shock, because he sees her, too. Beside him is a man from the haze of long ago. He has shades of gray threaded through his hair at the temples and deep lines bracketing his mouth, but it's still him. Both stand, jaws slack as they look at her, father and son, missing from her life for so long.

"You can do this," Elijah whispers, urging her forward. James gives her the tiniest of smiles, and she returns it tenfold, a mist of tears clouding her eyes. She is afraid, but she's also filled with an ocean of nostalgia. And happiness. And hope.

Turning to face those familiar scents, those distant memories, Katelyn opens her mouth, takes a deep breath…

And says hello to her lost family for the first time in over twenty years.

AUTHOR'S NOTES & ACKNOWLEDGEMENTS

To my beautiful reader,

Thank you so much for taking this journey with me. It's been a doozy! This book is my love letter to a Chinese Danmei (boys love romance) called *Mo Dao Zu Shi*, or *The Grandmaster of Demonic Cultivation* by Mo Xiang Tong Xiu. In it, we have a dark-clad, good-to-morally-gray guy who does everything from martyrdom to murder, all while laughing. Meanwhile his white-clad counterpart is the epitome of stoicism and righteousness. Of course, they fall in love, as they should. These character dynamics inspired Elijah and James. Mr. Happy-go-lucky in spite of everything meets Mr. Silent, broody, deep-well-of-emotion man. Truly, a match made in heaven, and a standard trope in so much of the BL I've read!

Still, they took on a life of their own, making them completely separate from their source of inspiration. Elijah's blind protectiveness of his brother, for one thing, and James's neurodivergence for another. I'd not yet read a love interest whose brain worked like that—obsessed with time, cleanliness, and over-focused on certain hobbies. Difficulty expressing themselves, sure, I've read that, but to James's degree? That was new (for me at least). I continually work not to rehash the same male leads in every romance I write, so I wanted Elijah and James to stand out as their own people. I really hope I achieved that.

In many ways, this was the hardest book I'd ever written. A trope I love is "star-crossed lovers"—and so that taboo of true love between siblings was very appealing to me. I almost made them twins, tied to each other since the moment of conception! But going that far made me afraid I'd get cancelled, so I was too scared to make it, lol. As it is, if my very religious mother happens on this story, I'll have to hide under a rock.

There's another reason this story is special to me, though, and it's the touched-upon relationship of James and his mother. It really tapped into my fears of what I could become someday. See, my elementary-age son has high functioning Autism, and I find myself protecting him from things he's not good at or that might trigger him. In my mind, I'm trying to save him from stress and the pains of this world, but there was a situation that made me realize I was going too far.

He had a swim test so he could go to without a life jacket during summer camp. I knew he could doggy paddle, so I figured we were all set. Then we got to the testing pool and these kids had to put their faces under water (something he can't stand), do the overhead stroke all the way to the other side of an Olympic pool, do the breaststroke coming back, and then tread water for a full minute. I panicked. I was like, "NOPE! He doesn't know how to do any of this!" So, I asked him if we should leave. Nonchalantly, he said, "No, that's okay," so I figured he didn't understand. I made sure he watched those other kids and realized that this is what he *had to do*, and not just what they were deciding to do on their own. Still, he waved me off and stayed in line to take his test.

When I tell you I was anxiety personified, it wouldn't be a lie. It completely took me over. I thought he'd get frustrated, sink, need to be rescued, and be embarrassed in front of all of his peers. Knowing him, that would have stuck with him for the rest of his life. Still, he just kept moving up in line while I chewed my lips off.

When he jumped into the water, he surprised me by trying the right strokes. He even willingly put his face in the water. Now, he did give up on that quickly and turn to the doggy paddle, and in the middle of the pool, he did panic. I ran up to the water like mama bear, telling him it was okay to come out. Just swim over to the side to me, and I'd pull him out. He ignored me and, red faced, bullied on. He got to the end, turned around, and struggle-doggy-paddled his way back to the life-guard. The Lifeguard told him to go ahead and get out, but my son said, "No. I need to tread water for a minute now." And that's what he did.

When he got out, the lifeguard was apologetic, but let him know he'd have to fail him. I was waiting for the meltdown. It never came. My son just returned to me and the towel I had waiting, and I asked, "Why did you do all that?" He looked down at the floor, and firm as flint, said, "If I'm going to fail, it's not going to be for lack of trying." Whether he heard that from me, his social worker, or freaking YouTube, I have no idea—but he said it.

I'd never been more in awe of my son. It was a big lightbulb moment for me. As much as I was trying to "save him", what I was really doing was holding him back from challenging himself, just like James's mom tried to do to him. He needed Elijah to believe in him in order to escape that toxic love.

Silently, I promised that I would give my son permission to fail. If that means meltdowns, I'll help him manage through it, but I won't hold him back from life. I need to encourage, but not pressure. It's a delicate balance, but one I'm determined to try.

I hope you enjoyed my story. I hope it was about more than just the romance for you. Everyone deserves to be themselves and be loved for exactly who they are. That means us, too.

Shout-out to my biggest cheerleader throughout writing this book —Mari. Without you, my dear, I would have never had the strength to keep going. Your enthusiasm, love of, and belief in this book is what kept my head in the game. I couldn't have done it without you.

To Dawn, my editor, you walking me through my own traumas and reservations over this book is what got it over the finish line. Thank you for that gentle, patient, considerate kick in the ass.

And to my readers, thank you again for enjoying this series. Don't forget to leave a review, tell your online friends, and I'll see you next time.

With all my love,
Nix

ALSO BY NICHOL GOLDSTEIN

ALL'S FAIR IN RUTS AND HEATS

Omegaverse, Dark Romance - Heat level: 4/4

After defense attorney Caleb Reed is trounced in court by a rookie lawyer - an Omega no less - he knows one thing and one thing only. Ari Jacobson was meant to be his mate...whether she wants to be or not.

With everything he's done, can Caleb go from enemy to lover, or will his blind obsession destroy them both?

ALSO BY NICHOL GOLDSTEIN

FATE KNOCKS ON NILES'S DOOR IN THE SHAPE OF JASON, A SWEET BETA. HE FALLS HEAD OVER HEELS FOR NILES AT FIRST SIGHT, WILLING TO "JUST BE FRIENDS" WHILE HOLDING HIS BREATH FOR SOMETHING MORE.

BUT HE'S NOT THE ONLY ONE.

ENTER TRISTAN, NILES'S VOLATILE FIRST LOVE FROM HIGH SCHOOL. THE SCINTILATINGLY SEXY ALPHA RETURNS JUST IN TIME TO BEG FOR A SECOND CHANCE.

IT'S SAFETY VERSUS SULTRY. WHICH WILL NILES CHOOSE? AND WHICH HAS A SECRET THAT GOES WAY BEYOND SIN?

ABOUT THE AUTHOR

From the Boston area, Nichol is a fan of all things art. Known for her weirdness and general snarkasm, Nichol works to engage her audience in several mediums. Many stick to one favorite genre, but she can't seem to make up her mind. You will see her dipping into everything from graphic horror, graphic novels, to graphic romance. Trust the descriptions, mind the tags and just know that, if you like her writing, you're in for a good ride.

Visit her at nixcomix.com to read exclusive short stories, see more about what books are coming out next, watch author interviews and more.

Find her on social media:

Twitter / TiKTok / YouTube / Facebook / Threads
   Nixcomix

Tumblr / Instagram
   Nixcomix1